THE BONE RELIC

WILLIAM MESUSAN

William Mesusan, Publisher

Dwell not upon thy weariness, they strength shall be according to the measure of thy desire.

ARAB PROVERB

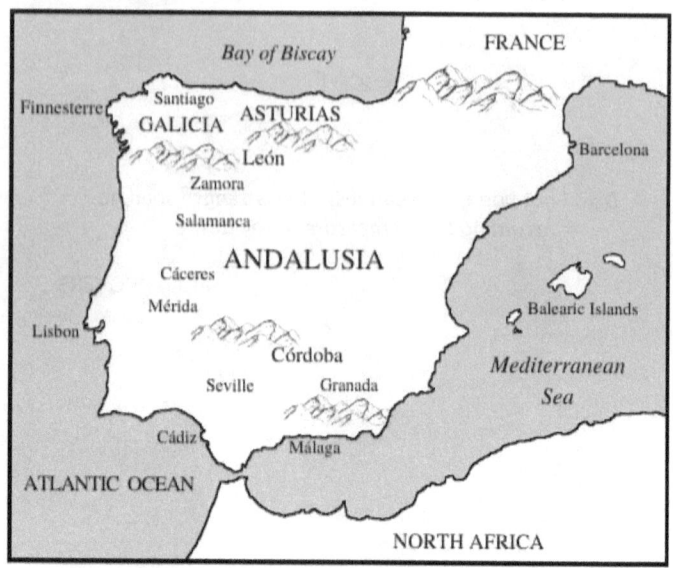

Tenth Century Islamic Spain

CHAPTER 1

How swiftly the fortunes of Solomon Levy changed.

The wealthy poet no longer earned his living as a translator. He was free to do as he pleased. Yet he still worked in the predawn hours of the morning to bring to completion a translation of the writings of Aristotle from Arabic into Latin.

The poet worked quietly, dipping his quill into a small bowl of oak gall and withdrawing it to place the tip on a piece of paper illuminated by a softly burning candle. He loved the black iron color of the liquid and the flow of letters dancing along the page to describe the discoveries of the Greek philosopher and natural historian.

Solomon didn't have to awaken during those early morning hours, yet he did so willingly as he eased his way into his new life. A life based on the largess of Caliph Abd al-Rahman III and the financial rewards given him for his investigation into the disappearance of a Galician singer who also happened to be a murder suspect. One whose actions might have brought the kingdom of Andalusia to a premature and unwelcomed end.

He now had time and money, so he might have passed his translation of Aristotle off to others in his field. But he felt determined to see the continuity of his interpretations through to the end. The field of translation was considered a creative vocation in 10th Century Andalusia as that society attempted to fashion a unique understanding of the legacy of Greece, one that it could apply to its own world view. A decidedly Arabic viewpoint.

The poet simply didn't want his hard work to be muddied by a translator who sought foremost to put their own stamp on the work. He had developed a fascination, and an appreciation, for Aristotle's desire to experience the world through the use of the five senses. A way of being in the world that Solomon Levy was attempting to carry over into his poetry. For this he was rewarded with a lifelong perspective as he took to heart the philosopher's words, "In all nature there is something of the marvelous."

In the course of his work, Solomon had learned that Aristotle was a teacher to Alexander the Great, and that many considered him the world's first scientist. To the poet's mind, the philosopher's importance could not be overestimated. He saw the Greek as the first and greatest teacher in everything. Shells, fish, plants, animals, man; there was nothing that didn't interest him.

Observe the world using the senses is what he taught. Before Aristotle, all things under heaven and earth were attributed to the gods. Solomon's love of nature and culture made the philosopher an endearing figure, and he was certain that Aristotle's works would've been lost to history if not for the interest Arabs in Baghdad who, in their thirst for knowledge, were determined to preserve Greek texts.

The soon to be retired translator worked hard, quill to ink to paper, as the candle slowly burned down. He'd pause to contemplate one of Aristotle's ideas written in Arabic, a language that held the disparate cultures of Andalusia together like a strong, thick glue.

The multi-lingual poet would then interpret the

thoughts into his third language, Latin, which he'd studied at the University of Córdoba, knowing that he and his fellow poets, both men and women, would have to earn a living while working on their avocation in their spare time. They received scant support from a community of Arabized Jews who wished to maintain the status quo. Only understanding patrons like his older cousin Hasdai Shaprut, the kingdom's Foreign Minister and personal physician to Caliph Abd al-Rahman III, made their continued efforts possible.

He'd complete his translation, but Solomon's greatest desire was to be out in the world experiencing life and sharing his perceptions of the world with others. Especially his fellow poets who, like himself, were attempting to take the Hebrew language out of the synagogue as they strove to create a revolutionary, secular tongue. A language able to convey the joys they experienced in everyday prosaic life, one using words and cadence to express their thoughts, feelings, sensations, and intuitions.

These Jewish poets tired of seeing their Muslim counterparts using Arabic to write poetry, and to describe the secular and scientific world of their times, while Hebrew remained almost exclusively used for religious purposes. Their efforts would eventually bear fruit. They were the precursors, fashioning an evolving language that would soon create a new world. One called "The Golden Age of Judaism."

Later that morning, Solomon hoped to find time to review his impressions of the Roman occupation of Mérida, centuries earlier, for a poem he was working to perfect. A poem that explored the almost palpable physical and spiritual presence of the conquerors in that Iberian city. At least this is how he hoped his day would evolve. No reason to believe otherwise.

But there soon came an interruption. A knock at the door. An unusual occurrence for the poet.

Solomon put down the quill and went to see who was causing this disturbance. He opened the door and smiled as he found himself looking into the luminous eyes of his cousin, Hasdai Shaprut.

"Hasdai!" Solomon exclaimed in surprise. "What are you doing here?"

"May I come inside?"

"Of course."

Nobody refused the requests of the Foreign Minister of Andalusia's Umayyad Caliphate, the most powerful empire in Europe. He wouldn't refuse in any event since he considered Hasdai his favorite cousin.

Solomon closed the door behind them.

"Please sit," said the poet as he motioned to a small couch. He grabbed the chair from his writing desk, sat down nearby, and waited for his older cousin to begin

"I wasn't going to insult you by summoning you to al-Zahra once again," Hasdai explained. "Not after all you've done for me."

Such a reversal. Solomon's first two missions had been arranged inside Hasdai's vast if not opulent office in al-Zahra, the new administrative capital of the Caliphate, located seven miles to the west. Now they were here in Solomon's tiny apartment, in the old Juderia. Now it was Hasdai who seemed reluctant. Like he couldn't find words adequate to the situation. Is there a new mission? Hasdai wouldn't. He couldn't. He'd promised.

He observed his cousin closely. He wasn't wearing his silk tunic, the one he accentuated with a brocade vest. Maybe this wasn't official business. Hasdai only wore cotton in Córdoba's Juderia. As *Nasi*, the spiritual leader of all Jews living in the Iberian Peninsula, he wouldn't take on airs. He simply couldn't afford to distance himself from his people through ostentatious display. Anyway, this would be impossible given his humble attitude of service to his community.

Something felt wrong.

What's going on, Solomon wondered. He had been summoned twice before and pressed into assignments that insured the survival of the Umayyad Caliphate which also meant the survival of his people. He'd been resistant on both occasions.

"Why have you come to see me?" asked the poet.

"I'm afraid there's a new assignment for you," Hasdai apologized. "I'm so sorry."

"Not again," Solomon protested.

"If it were up to me, I wouldn't be here," came the earnest reply.

"I thought we had an agreement."

"We do, but I'm under orders from the Caliph to intercede in this matter."

"The Caliph?" questioned Solomon. "Why in heavens does he want me?"

"The Imam of the Great Mosque made a personal request for your services," Hasdai responded. "He holds much influence with the Caliph."

"The Imam?" Solomon wondered out loud.

"He obviously thinks highly of you."

Solomon reflected for a moment. He'd only met the holy man on one occasion. That was during the last mission Hasdai had given him. Forced upon him was a more accurate description. He and the Imam had gotten along well. They seemed to share a mutual admiration in spite of their different ethnic and religious backgrounds.

"There's been a theft. It may call into question the legitimacy of the Umayyad Caliphate."

Solomon sensed the urgency in Hasdai's voice and appreciated his hesitation to involve him so soon after his recent ordeal. He knew that the position of the Foreign Minister required compromises, especially when decisions impacted the continued success of Europe's most enlightened culture. A society where Jews not only survived, but actually thrived.

Solomon moved his chair in closer as he took a good look at his cousin. Hasdai appeared healthier than during their last assignment. The sandy colored beard looked fuller, and he'd put on some weight and the light had returned to his eyes. Gone was the look of sadness, but Solomon still sensed a deep apprehension. No doubt caused by the current predicament involving the Imam of the Great Mosque.

"What's happened?"

"The Great Mosque has been desecrated and the Empire's most sacred relic, the arm bone of the Prophet Muhammad, has been stolen."

Of course the Imam would ask for him. Solomon had recovered the Lost Manuscript and tracked down the Galician Woman. The Imam knew this. Almost everyone in al-Zahra and Córdoba knew of this. It made perfect sense. Sometimes he laughed at the absurdity of it. The idea that he somehow possessed magic powers and that no one else could have succeeded in those missions.

He might have tried to decline this mission if anybody other than the Imam had requested his services, but he knew he couldn't refuse an old man whose eyes were infused with the light of wisdom and serenity. A man he held in high esteem.

It was all beginning to make sense. Hasdai's clothing and the feeling of concern that he'd conveyed. He'd probably been summoned while at home by a dispatch from the Caliph himself. One displaying the royal seal. Told that the Imam of the Great Mosque needed his help immediately. No time to waste. No time to go to al-Zahra as part of his official duties.

Solomon couldn't say no to this assignment. That much he knew for certain. Time to find out more about the robbery at the Mosque.

"Are you telling me they post no guards at the Mosque to protect the relic?" inquired Solomon. "Hard to believe."

"The guard stationed at the treasury room, where the relic is kept, was badly beaten," Hasdai informed him. "Others patrolling the grounds of the Mosque heard a commotion. They intervened and gave chase, but they were unsuccessful in their attempts to apprehend the criminals."

"I'm still surprised they weren't more prepared for such an occurrence."

"Who could imagine such a blasphemy in Andalusia? There's writing on the wall," added Hasdai. "And it's written in blood."

"Animal blood?"

"Probably, but the Imam also says that the message disturbs him." Hasdai folded his hands, and they fell to his lap as he trained his eyes on Solomon. "He needs to talk with you about it. And, one of the thieves left behind a sandal while trying to make his escape. The Imam is holding it for you. I'm sorry, but that's all we have to go on."

"Who would perpetrate such a despicable act?" asked

Solomon. "And why?"

"That's what we need for you to find out," declared Hasdai, gazing directly into the eyes of his cousin. He waited patiently for Solomon's answer. Waited until he could wait no longer. He decided to ask directly.

"So you'll accept the mission?"

"If it means that much to the Imam, then I gladly accept."

"You've changed."

"How so . . . "

"You're so enthusiastic."

"I told you that I learned a lot on my last assignment."

"Yes, I remember now," said Hasdai, recollecting the conversation in his office following their last investigation. "About the nature of the world and your own nature."

Hasdai smiled to himself. He felt proud of his younger cousin. The rigors of the previous mission had matured him. His mind reached back to the last time he'd sat on this same couch in this same room. Solomon had returned home to find his small apartment ransacked. Hasdai had come to share with him a change in the mission's plans, and he'd stayed to help return scattered volumes to the shelves of a bookcase left standing. He'd felt tired, exhausted from being up all night. Solomon suggested he rest on the couch. It had been an ordeal for both men.

Hasdai now looked over to those very shelves and his eyes beheld a leather-bound copy of the Torah and a silver *yad*, a small-stemmed instrument made in the shape of a hand with an outstretched finger and designed to insure the parchment wasn't touched by the person reading it. This prevented the letters from being smudged and destroyed over time.

"I see you haven't abandoned us altogether," Hasdai mumbled under his breath while assessing his cousin's religiosity. "You still keep the holy book nearby." As *Nasi*, Hasdai remained concerned about Solomon's faith or lack thereof. He decided this wasn't a good time to talk about it so he kept his thoughts to himself as he turned back to Solomon, but not before chastising himself for losing his focus and forgetting the compelling nature of his visit.

"I'm giving you full rein," he began. "There are no suspects at this time so question whom you like and go where you must. The Caliph will spend whatever is needed to recover the sacred arm bone. It's priceless. Not just its material worth, but its intrinsic spiritual value is incalculable."

Solomon nodded, indicating he understood.

"We must hurry," Hasdai added with an unmistakable urgency in his voice. "The annual display of the sacred arm bone is to be during the next full moon and the Imam is waiting for you as we speak."

Hasdai stood, removed a gold signet ring from his finger, and handed it over to Solomon who gazed down at the royal seal etched into soft metal. It hadn't proven helpful during his last assignment, but one never knew.

"Will I be needing this again?"

"Possibly. We're not sure who we're dealing with here. Men who would involve themselves in such an abomination are capable of anything. No doubt they're armed and dangerous."

Solomon slipped the ring onto his finger. A plan of sorts was taking shape in his mind. He thought about the timing of his meeting with the holy man and those he wished to question. It might take him the better part of the morning.

"Anything else I should know?"

"Just remember that this may be an attempt to sow discord and disappointment, a thinly veiled effort to undermine the legitimacy of the Caliphate. Somebody wants to discourage and demoralize the Muslim faithful and to damage and discredit the Caliph."

"And our future hangs in the balance."

"Hurry, Solomon," implored Hasdai. "There isn't much time . . . "

CHAPTER 2

Solomon reached the Great Mosque just as the sun rose in the eastern sky, long before the perfume sellers and spice merchants arrived to set up their booths on the perimeter of the square. Vendors offering more malodorous goods were consigned to an area further away so their wares wouldn't deter the devout and diminish attendance at prayer services. They hadn't arrived either.

This square, located at the mosque's primary entrance, had taken on an elevated importance because the Supervisor of Markets plied his trade here and important funeral rites were conducted nearby. At this early hour the square appeared deserted.

The site of this Great Mosque had a history. It had sustained a Roman temple dedicated to the god Janus, and a Catholic Christian church dedicated by the Visigoths to Saint Vincent. The building was divided between Muslims and Christians after the Islamic conquest. At this location Emir Rahman I chose to raise his Great Mosque. He generously offered to buy the Catholic church and the plot of land. He could've taken it by force. Under terms of the transfer, Christians were permitted to rebuild a ruined church formerly dedicated to St. Faustus, St. Januarius, and St. Marcellus, three revered martyrs. This set the stage for an ongoing, positive relationship between the two religions in Andalusia. A condition that would last for centuries.

The Córdoba structure was later extended south towards the river by Emir Rahman II and his son, Muhammad. On its north side, Caliph Rahman III would soon construct a new minaret after demolishing the existing tower, built sometime during the late eighth century. The footprint of the structure continued to expand in proportion to the rapid rate of conversion of the populace to Islam so the Great Mosque remained a work-in-progress.

The evolving structure was a visible symbol of Umayyad legitimacy in Andalusia. This claim took on added importance, in 929, when Rahman III reestablished the Umayyad Caliphate.

From the time of the Abbasid massacre of the Umayyad family and Rahman I's miraculous flight, from Damascus, to establish himself as Emir of Andalusia, one of the keys to establishing the legitimacy to rule was the possession of sacred relics. Two in particular. The holy arm bone of the Prophet Muhammad and four bloody pages of the Quran that Umayyad Caliph 'Uthman ibn Affan was reading when assassinated in Medina, Saudi Arabia in 656 CE. 'Uthman was a second cousin, son-in-law, and notable companion of the Prophet.

Now that validity appeared to be on shaky grounds.

Solomon hurried through the Great Mosque's square, walking past a fortress-like edifice with forty-foot high outer walls finished in cinnamon-colored, unadorned stucco. He had always heard the inside of the unprepossessing mosque was breathtaking in contrast to its nondescript exterior. As a non-Muslim, he'd been never allowed the opportunity to see for himself. At least not until now.

He entered a courtyard of olive trees.

He approached the main entrance and found four uniformed guards posted outside. Their swords hung from scabbards resting at their sides. They weren't a part of the Slavic Guard, also known as the Silent Ones. They all appeared to be Arabs and this made perfect sense. Only Muslims could enter the Great Mosque, so these men could venture inside the mosque if circumstances required it.

Solomon approached one of them and offered a curt smile.

"I am here at the Imam's request."

"And you are?"

"Solomon Levy," came the response. "The Imam is expecting me."

"Wait here."

The guard spoke with one of his comrades. This man soon disappeared into the interior as the others waited outside. Solomon paused to collect himself. He decided to wait patiently with no preconceptions of what to expect.

The guard returned, bringing the Imam with him.

A bearded holy man, dressed in the traditional *Abayah*, a high-collared white coat, stepped outside into the early morning shadows along the Mosque's western wall. His head was covered with a short rounded skullcap, also white, called a *tagiya*, The Imam's face glowed like polished alabaster. Illuminated from within, his eyes seemed to be infused with the light of wisdom and understanding.

Solomon had experienced a sense of peace and well-being in his presence at their first meeting. This time something felt different. A bit unnerving. The old man wasn't smiling on this occasion.

"Solomon Levy," intoned the Imam. "I knew you would come. Please, enter this sacred ground."

Solomon knew that he was being accorded a rare privilege. Few non-Muslims had ever been allowed inside of the Great Mosque.

"You're sure it's all right?"

"The Caliph has made a special dispensation, and I believe Allah is in agreement," the holy man answered. "You are being allowed to enter a sacred sanctuary so please be reverent."

Solomon stepped inside and looked around in wonderment.

"Behold the majesty an infinite intelligence can inspire."

No walls separated the hundreds of columns inside from the treed patio. The northern side of the mosque opened out to the courtyard to create a continuous space with the trunks of the olive trees and the marble columns forming a single visual line. The entire effect, open and accentuated, allowed light to penetrate through the columns (some made from marble, others of jasper and still others of porphyry) and the rows of courtyard trees.

Solomon felt himself surrounded by what appeared to be a forest of columns with no focal point. This created a sensation of intimacy and one of limitless space. He had entered a spiritual oasis in which hundreds upon hundreds of columns repeated themselves to infinity, like a mirror of creation whose center moved according to the location of the viewer. This is a labyrinth without walls, he said to himself.

Nothing claimed his attention. No statues, paintings, sarcophagi, or pews. Only patterns woven out of pillars intended to liberate the mind and free it for prayer and meditation. Oil lamps hung from the ceiling.

For Solomon, the real secret of space in the mosque

derived from double-tiered arches alternating red and white masonry. They reached outwards above the columns creating a visually striking canopy above him with the lower arches, horseshoe in shape and the upper more semi-circular. The space between them produced the impression of an endless forest pierced by light and air.

The investigator stood transfixed. He'd never imagined such a wondrous place existed in the entire the world. He became so enamored of the magnificent interior, in his soulful experience of aesthetic arrest, that he almost forgot about the investigation.

The sensitive Imam allowed time for him to absorb impressions before reminding him of the reason he'd been allowed this rare opportunity to enter the interior of the mosque.

"Excuse me, Solomon," said the Imam, interrupting the poet's rapture. "We have grave matters to discuss."

A deep sigh and then a response:

"Yes, of course . . . I'm sorry," the investigator apologized. "I never thought such a place could exist."

"Even more wondrous is Allah's paradise," the Imam assured him.

"I'm sure it is," agreed Solomon.

"Allah chose the right person for this mission."

"But you chose me."

"I am only an instrument, like the Prophet Muhammad," acknowledged the Imam. "A lesser light, but I also strive to fulfill the will of Allah."

"I see . . . "

He said the words like he had understood the sentiment, but Solomon didn't really comprehend how one can consider oneself a humble servant of God.

"Shall we return to the subject of the stolen relic?"

asked the Imam.

"The Prophet Muhammad's arm bone."

"Precisely," the Imam replied. "I'll lead you to its last known resting place. Please, come this way."

The Imam led Solomon down a row of columns and arches towards the mosque's *midrab*, an extraordinary niche rising from floor to ceiling and set into the far wall to identify the direction of the *qibla* wall of the Kaaba, in Mecca. This was the prescribed direction for the offering of prayers.

The Iman stopped to pause, in front of the *midrib*, at an enclosed area called the *maqsura*.

"This area is reserved for the Caliph and his family," he told Solomon before pointing overhead so the investigator didn't miss seeing the stunningly decorated ribbed vault above his head.

The small dome contained filigreed abstractions, Kufic script, floral motifs, and a cascading sunburst radiating from a tiny central star. All this enhanced by light filtering through eight latticed side windows.

Solomon smiled in appreciation because he couldn't find words to describe what he felt at that moment.

They continued on and soon arrived at their destination, the deeply recessed, shell-hooded *mihrab* niche. Armed guards stood posted at two smaller, flanking openings. The guard on the right held a bundle in his hands. The Imam acknowledged the guards, and then he veered towards the right, leading Solomon into a series of chambers.

One guard followed them inside. Solomon imagined the guards were under orders not to allow the Imam out of their sight. The stealing of the sacred relic might be part of a larger operation. One that might even endanger the life of the Imam. The final room, an area the investigator estimated to be about fifteen square feet, turned out to be the mosque's treasury. In the middle of this room stood a carved wooden table.

"Our most precious relics are stored here in this room," the Imam informed Solomon.

"Where was the sacred arm bone kept?"

"Right on top of this table," came the reply. "It lay inside a rectangular reliquary comprised of a gold frame with glass panels."

"And that was taken, also?"

"Yes."

They'll sell the reliquary for its gold value, thought Solomon.

A gilded chest lay on the floor beneath the legs of the wooden table.

"What's inside the chest?"

"Four bloodied pages of the Quran that Caliph 'Uthman was reading at the time of his assassination, in Medina."

"They weren't taken in the robbery?"

"No."

"Any idea why they were left behind?"

"Their value is mostly symbolic," the Imam surmised. "They establish the legitimacy of the Umayyad Caliphate and connect it back to Medina, the home of Muhammad, and later to Damascus. 'Uthman was a close friend of the Prophet and the one man who devoted himself to collecting all the words of the Messenger of God into one book."

Solomon reflected upon these facts for a few moments. He found it hard to imagine these bloody four pages, sitting inside the chest at his feet, just collecting dust. Whatever dust might make its way into that gilded chest.

"So the four pages are stored inside of the chest and never see the light of day?"

"Oh no, that would be a sin!" exclaimed the Imam. "In a manner of speaking they don't see the light of day, but they are shown to the congregation in a candle-lit cere- mony once a year before we lead a procession with our most holy relic."

"I see."

"What you need to understand is that the annual pro- cession is little more than a week away," the Imam said rather empathically. "If the relic is not displayed at this time it may plant seeds of chaos and doubt among our followers."

"When exactly is the annual procession?"

"It takes place after the evening call to prayer a week from tomorrow."

Once he understood that time was of the essence, Solomon found his mind searching for clues. He won- dered how the thieves had seemingly known their way around the mosque. How did they get away with the sa- cred relic? There were only two doorways. One on either side of the *mihrab*.

"The other passage. The one on the left side of the *mihrab*," he wondered aloud. "Where does it lead?"

"It links the mosque with the old Caliphal palace," answered the Imam. "The Caliph only uses it on rare oc- casions. Like the procession of 'Uthman's Quran and the Prophet's holy relic. We rarely see Rahman III since he built his beautiful new mosque in al-Zahra."

Not likely they would attempt to escape using that route, thought the investigator. The old palace was still heavily guarded. This suggested that the thieves knew the floor plan of the mosque. Someone familiar with the layout must have aided them.

The desecration appeared to bring with it a bone-wearying sadness because the Imam looked shaken to the core. He'd once exuded an essence of serenity, but now he was visibly upset. His sense of grace seemed to have deserted him.

"You seem agitated," observed Solomon. "The loss of the sacred relic is reason enough, but is there something more?"

"The writing on the wall."

"Yes, I was going to ask you about that next."

Both men turned to face the south wall where a message had been written in Arabic script. Solomon read the message. A message written in blood: "Taken by command." He wondered why the robbers would resort to using blood and what they were trying to communicate. Is there a hidden message, he wondered. A clue to the motivation of the thieves. He turned to the Imam.

"What do you make of it?" he asked. "Taken by command."

"It's uncanny," responded the Imam. "A similar message is associated with the return of the Black Stone."

"I don't understand."

"Of course not. You've probably never heard the story of the Black Stone. I think it's important that I share it with you, but I'm not sure where to begin," confessed the Imam. "Perhaps I should share with you the story of my own journey, when I was a much younger man than I am today, because it may shed some light upon our current ordeal and aid you in your quest to recover the sacred arm bone of the Prophet Muhammad."

CHAPTER 3

The Imam gazed directly into Solomon's eyes.

There had been a time, he remembered it wishfully, when life had brought an amazing adventure into his life.

"Little more than two decades ago, while I served as the assistant Imam here at the Great Mosque, my predecessor decided that it was time for me to embark upon the ritual of the *Hajj*.

This pilgrimage to Mecca, to walk seven times around the Kaaba in a counter-clockwise direction, is the duty of every Muslim unless they are prevented by disease or other extreme difficulties from making the trip during their lifetime.

I was fortunate. I enjoyed good health and the Caliph paid for all the expenses associated with my journey to Mecca.

Before leaving Córdoba, the Imam prepared me spiritually for my encounter with the Black Stone. It's black color, he told me, symbolized the virtues of detachment, a willingness to accept poverty, and the need to extinguish all selfish thoughts as requirements for making progress towards Allah.

He taught me that the Black Stone is the eastern cornerstone of the Kaaba, the ancient stone building toward which Muslims pray, in the center of the Grand Mosque of Mecca. This sacred stone fell from Heaven during the time of Adam and Eve. Its landing spot marked the place for them to build an altar and it's been venerated at the Kaaba site ever since that time.

Once, when a major fire partly destroyed the structure, the clans of Mecca renovated the Kaaba, but not before temporarily removing the Black Stone to facilitate the work of rebuilding. When it came time to replace the stone, the clans could not agree on which of them should have the honor of setting it back in its original resting place.

They decided to wait for the next man to come through the city gate and ask him to decide for them. The individual happened to be thirty-five year old Muhammad, some five years before his revelation. He asked the elders of the clans to bring him a rug and to place the Black Stone in its center.

He asked each of the clan leaders to hold the corners as they carried the rug to the correct location. Muhammad kissed the stone, and then he set the stone in place, satisfying the honor of all the clans. Already we see his special destiny at work as he, with his remarkable wisdom, arrived at a fair and equitable solution."

The Imam paused to consider how he should proceed.

"I'm sorry, I digressed," he admitted. "I shall return to the story of my personal journey. From the moment I arrived in Mecca, I knew that Allah guided my steps.

Two days later, I joined with thousands of Muslim pilgrims circling the Kaaba. By then I had purified myself in hopes that I might be one of the lucky few who would succeed in stopping and kissing the Black Stone, the sacred object the prophet Muhammad had kissed. If I failed to reach the stone, as most do, I would content myself with pointing in its direction on each of my seven circlings of the Kaaba.

I had walked around the holy shrine six times, each time attempting to get closer to the stone. On my seventh and final circuit I was blessed by Allah. I had approached the eastern corner when two strong men who had just kissed the Black Stone suddenly pushed back the large crowd. The backward surge created an opening and I took advantage of it by running to the stone.

"Praise be to Allah!" I shouted as I placed my hands upon the sacred stone and pressed my lips upon it. The stone glowed and thousands of silver stars flashed before my eyes. I felt something stir deep down inside of me. Time stood still for a brief few seconds before I realized I'd been pushed away by the guard. I quickly regained my wits so that I might complete the final circling.

This will always be the most memorable experience of my life.

But there's more to this story.

The most important part of what you need to know.

Qarmatians stole The Black Stone almost two decades ago and took it away to their holy place in Hajar. The leader of these tribes, Abu Tahir al-Qarmati, displayed the stone in his own mosque, the *Masjid al-Dirar*. His misguided intention was to redirect the Hajj away from Mecca to his newly established site. He failed, of course, as devout pilgrims continued to venerate the spot where the Black Stone had been originally placed.

Earlier this year, the Abbasid Caliphate received a ransom request and were forced to pay a huge sum of gold for the stone's return. This unholy act was followed by one even more despicable. The stone was wrapped in a sack and thrown into the Friday Mosque, in Kufa. Its abduction and removal damaged the stone, breaking it into seven pieces. The custodians of the Kaaba wanted to protect the shattered stone, so they commissioned a pair of goldsmiths, in Mecca, to build a silver frame to surround it.

Here is the one detail that frightens me the most.

Inside the sack, with the Black Stone fragments, they found a note that read: "By command we took it, and by command we have brought it back."

As I read the message written on the wall of this holy treasury, I felt a stab of pain in my heart for it read, "Taken by command." Can this be a coincidence, I asked myself. Is there a ruler or people so desperate they would steal our sacred relic for their own purposes?"

Solomon entertained the possibility that a radical Muslim sect from North Africa might be responsible for the theft. It was no secret that many of them considered the Umayyad approach to Islamic tradition too secular with its embrace of art and science. Whoever it was, they were familiar with the legend of the Black Stone. He had no doubts about that. It was highly unlikely the words of the message scribbled on the wall were coincidental. Perhaps one of the sects wanted to emulate the Qarmations. He realized this was only idle speculation at this point so he changed the direction of his inquiry.

"How did the Great Mosque acquire the sacred arm bone?"

"As I told you, 'Uthman and Muhammad were very close. After the Prophet passed from this world and entered Paradise many of his body parts were taken as relics. In this way Muslims could continue to cherish him. It also helped to assuage the pain felt when contemplating his death."

"I need for you to be more specific," coaxed Solomon.

"How did that particular relic find its way here to this mosque?"

"When the Umayyad Caliph Marwan was assassinated and eighty-two members of his family massacred by the Abbasids, Abd al Rahman I made a miraculous escape from Syria. On his journey across North Africa, and his crossing the straits into Andalusia, he brought the precious relics with him in a trunk. The same chest sitting beneath this table."

"I understand now."

Solomon appreciated the story of Rahman I's escape from Damascus with the relics, but he didn't think it offered any clues that might help him determine who had committed the crime.

"There's more that I need to share with you," claimed the Imam. "A guard tried to chase down one of the perpetrators of this desecration. In his haste, the thief left something behind. Something that might be of interest to you."

The old man motioned for the guard to approach with the bundle.

Solomon had been waiting for this moment. Hasdai had mentioned the sandal. Finally, a clue. Something that might prove helpful in helping him identify one of the robbers. It wasn't much, but there seemed little else of substance.

The Imam took the bundle from the guard and placed it on the tabletop. He began to unfold the material.

"I'd like to take it with me," Solomon requested as he watched the Imam continue to unwrap the bundle.

"Of course."

"Anything else I should know?"

"Judging from the size of the sandal, this man is a

giant."

"A giant?"

"You may judge for yourself," replied the Imam. "My eyes do not deceive me."

The uncovered sandal lay upon its wrappings. It was massive. Both in length and width. The investigator had never seen such a huge foot size. He felt a pang of guilt for underestimating the old man's acumen. The Imam was visibly suffering from this turn of events. The last thing he should be doing is questioning the man's judgement He reproached himself. We have to concern ourselves with the message. Yes, the message. Maybe the shoe was left behind on purpose. Why? To throw them off the track. Had the sandal really fallen off during the flight of the giant?

Solomon took a closer look at the sandal. He turned it over and studied the sole and he observed how the back of the heel had been worn down on the inside. He wasn't quite sure if this fact was helpful so he handed the sandal back to the Imam.

The Imam wrapped the sandal back inside the cloth material and handed it to Solomon.

"May Allah guide your steps and keep you safe during your investigation," he said. "We have little more than a week. If you have not recovered our sacred relic before its display at the annual procession, I fear the Caliphate will be put in mortal danger."

"I would like you to prepare a new reliquary for the holy relic; and, I would like it to be a replica of the one stolen. I'll need it waiting in this exact spot when I return."

"I will do as you wish."

Solomon's heart felt heavy. Like the Imam, he also felt

weary albeit for a different reason. His recent journey to far-off Galicia had taken a physical and emotional toll. He sighed as he searched for the bravery this new assignment would demand. He needed to summon up the energy to be of service to the Imam and by extension to the Umayyad Caliphate and all its peoples.

The sensitive Imam sensed the investigator's state of mind.

"There are people who, pardon my profanity, want to profit from the sacred relic. Yours is a difficult path. May Allah give you the strength and courage you need to return the Prophet's holy arm bone safely home."

"I'll do everything within my power to recover the sacred relic."

"Praise be to Allah."

CHAPTER 4

Solomon usually enjoyed walking through the neighborhoods surrounding the Great Mosque on his way to the doorstep of the one house in all the world he loved arriving at.

He had traveled this same route more than a dozen times since returning to Córdoba from his previous mission in search of the missing Galician woman, Lia, in the northwest corner of the Peninsula, an area which he'd referred to as the savage north. He was, in fact, visiting Lia's old roommate. Sara had become his new girlfriend. They'd met and felt a mutual attraction during his investigation.

Solomon felt troubled on this occasion. As much as he looked forward to being with Sara again the circumstances were difficult. He was being asked to place his own life in danger to help insure the continued existence of the Umayyad Caliphate and he would have to tell his inamorata. He feared this wouldn't go well.

The investigator maintained a brisk pace as he passed the covered market, the *Alcaiceria*, where vendors busied themselves trading silk and other textiles. He next made his way through a lively area of makeshift stalls and craft workshops.

As he continued his walk he entertained thoughts about the theft of the sacred relic, the bone relic. Maybe the massive sandal he carried, in the bundle under his arm, had been left to make it seem like an Andalusi committed the crime. Was the thief working for himself or others, for money or religious purposes? The message scrawled on the wall of the mosque indicated the latter, but that could have been a clever ruse. Was this the work of an individual fanatic or part of an organized subversion designed to destroy the legitimacy of the Caliphate?

He entered a maze of twisting streets, teeming with locals, where the merchandise of the walled city's ground-floor shops spilled out into the streets. He pushed his way through the crowd, keeping his bundle tight against the side of his ribs. So far, it was the only real clue he possessed. He wondered if the relic might be subject to a ransom. The Caliph would pay a fortune for its return.

Solomon walked on through this warren of narrow, cobbled streets, angling northeast before leaving the walled city through the New Gate. He soon found himself in the *Ajerquia*, the oldest extension of Córdoba outside the walls. This suburb, also known as the Eastern Wing, covered an area larger than the walled city itself. A population of Arabized Christians, called Mozarabs, made their homes here. Sara was one of them.

His thoughts returned to more immediate concerns.

Not going to see Sara to tell her the reason for his absence from her life for an unspecified time wasn't even an option. In this city of Muslims, Jews, Catholics, and others practicing a degree of religious acceptance, their relationship was the exception to the rule. Sara had made the challenge clear to him from the very beginning, but it hadn't prevented them from creating a satisfying relationship. Although Solomon was an Arabized Jew and Sara an Arabized Christian, their mutual attraction came from a deeper, more mysterious part of themselves, a kind of shared subliminal oasis of the soul.

Solomon entered a neighborhood he had come to know quite well. An area of deteriorating streets and dilapidated houses. A place where commercial enterprises tended to be less significant: vinegar making, soap making, cobblers, and plasterers. Solomon kept on past the straw market and the mat market.

The meandering streets led him to his destination, and he arrived at Sara's doorstep.

He looked around. He always looked around when he reached her house. Ever since that first visit when he'd spied two misplaced Arabs watching Sara's house from a shaded doorway on the far side of the street. He'd felt a twinge of paranoia on that occasion.

Nowadays it was just a mild apprehension. He never did find out who they were or if they were following him. He hadn't seen them since, but he always looked around until he was satisfied he wasn't being shadowed.

No time to dwell on the past he told himself as he stood before a brightly painted blue door. No flecks of dried blue paint lay at his feet. Times had changed. He had recently scrapped off the old, blistering paint and applied two new coats to the surface. Helping Sara in this way, given her limited financial resources, gave the poet a new-found sense of fulfillment.

Solomon took a small sliver of clove from his pocket and dropped it on his tongue. He then chewed on the fibrous pulp's outer layer releasing a sweet yet pungent flavor to freshen his breath. Solomon knocked on Sara's door. Three knocks, followed by two of shorter duration. The door opened. He drew the woman into his arms and gave her a heartfelt hug. He could feel the warmth of her body against his and smell the herbaceous scent of lemon oil in her hair. They kissed and then kissed again before he drew back from her.

"We have to talk."

Sara's body tensed as she felt an urgency in his voice. He stepped inside and she closed the door behind him. She led him over to the once seemingly forbidden couch where they sat and turned to face one another. He put the bundle on the floor next to him before turning back to Sara. Their eyes soon met. Hers irises were amber with specks of green and brown. His the color of overcooked peas. She might have passed for an Arab woman or a Jewess with her olive-toned skin and dark hair, but her heritage linked her back to the original Ibero inhabitants of the Peninsula.

"What is it?" she wanted to know. "Is something wrong?"

"Hasdai has a new assignment for me."

"I knew this would happen eventually." Sara couldn't hide the look of displeasure on her face.

"It's not his fault," explained Solomon. "The Imam of the Great Mosque made a direct plea to the Caliph requesting my services. I couldn't refuse."

"Can you tell me what's happened."

"Thieves stole a sacred relic from the Great Mosque. The theft could threaten the legitimacy of the Caliphate."

"It's that serious?"

"Yes," he replied with conviction. "It's the arm bone of the Prophet Muhammad."

"Oh my God," she shrieked. "Such a blasphemy."

"Now you see why I have to be away for a while."

Sara shifted her body to get a good look at the bundle that lay at Solomon's feet. He followed her eyes as she gazed down at the cloth wrapping and then back at him.

"What's that?"

"A huge sandal," he told her. "One of the robbers lost it while making his escape. At least that's what we think. It's the only clue I have so far."

An uncomfortable silence.

"You're disappointed," Solomon stated matter-of-factly.

She caressed his forearm with her hand and offered him a warm smile.

"Yes, I am. But I'm also concerned about your well-being, Solomon. These missions, or assignments, or whatever you call them are dangerous. So, yes, I am disappointed."

"Imagine my disappointment, Sara. I was finishing up the Aristotle translation and hoping to work on a new poem when Hasdai showed up."

She took both of his hands into her own and gave them a gentle squeeze.

"A new poem. What's it called?" she asked with a new enthusiasm in her voice.

This is what he loved about Sara. Her genuine curiosity about matters that were important to him and her excitement in learning more about them. And he realized that her interest wasn't limited to his activities. There were mysteries of shared physical, emotional, and spiritual attraction at work.

"It's called *Waves of Wind*."

"*Waves of Wind*," she repeated. "Oh, I like that."

Layla, his longtime confidant, always encouraged him to continue writing poetry between assignments, but she'd never shown this level of attention. The courtesan acted more like an older sister trying to support and perhaps even embolden him.

"What's it about, Solomon?"

"Currents of air, I suppose," was the best response he could offer. " I'm not really sure yet."

"Oh, that's how poetry works," she laughed before thinking about the tenor of her comment within the context of their conversation. "I'm sorry. I didn't mean to sound frivolous. It just seems like you're telling me that you drift wherever the current takes you when you write poetry."

"It's an organic process. Sometimes . . . oftentimes . . . it's full of surprises," he responded before turning the conversation back to the reason he'd come to see her. "I'm working against time. I only have about a week to find that relic before it's supposed to go on display in front of the entire Muslim congregation and pilgrims who will soon be arriving from all over the Islamic world. I'm sorry, but I can't stay longer."

He expected to see a frown on her face, but she nodded her head in agreement, and he knew she was ready to lend him her complete support.

"I think you should go see Bishop Racemundo," she ventured. " He knows a lot about the history of the church and I'm sure he could share some insights on the importance of relics."

"That's a good idea," he agreed as he stood to leave. "I'm going to miss you so much."

"I'll be here waiting for you. You know that, right?" she asked. She needed to know. She needed reassurance.

He hoped to convince her that he felt the same way.

"Yes, and I'll be back with you as soon as I possibly can."

Sara gazed at him with a deep yearning in her eyes. She moved over on the couch and drew him closer. She opened her mouth, and he did the same, fitting his lips to hers. With mouths slightly open, they kissed. Their breaths co-mingled. Solomon heaved a heavy sigh.

It was time to depart.

He reached down and retrieved the sandal, his only clue linking this mystery to the physical world. The world of the senses. He cradled it in his arms as he walked to the door. Sara followed behind and they turned to one another. She brushed his forearm with her fingers. A private joke shared between them alone. She'd done this unconsciously the first time they met and every time thereafter. It had become a ritual. A hidden code like those only lovers share.

"I'm not sure when I'll see you again," he told her.

"May you be safe from every harm," she said as he opened the door to leave. "I'll pray for your safe return."

Solomon left the house and Sara closed the newly painted door behind him.

The weather had changed since he'd entered the house. Sunshine and blue skies had given way to dark clouds and cooler temperatures making the aqua sky disappear; massive swirls now hid the sun. They seemed to mirror Solomon's darkening mood.

Something else struck him as odd. He experienced what felt like an eerie coincidence. Once again he was leaving Sara's house and would soon be on his way to visit the Muwallid businessman, ibn Hafsun. Chance or destiny? He wasn't sure. He only knew that the situation felt familiar. Like an emotional pattern playing itself out and repeating itself. Two threads woven into the mysterious tapestry of his life.

He hoped his next meeting with Hafsun would prove more successful than the first.

CHAPTER 5

Solomon's route took him back through the old walled city into one of Córdoba's long established neighborhoods.

This locale, bordering his own Jewish Quarter, consisted mainly of two-storied, white-washed houses nestled below red-tiled rooftops set behind pleasing interior courtyards filled with fragrant citrus trees. Most of these well-cared for homes belonged to families who'd inherited them, passed down for generations dating back to the Roman occupation of the city.

Many local citizens knew where ibn Hafsun lived. This scion of Visigoth counts was one of Córdoba's most prosperous merchants.

Solomon had learned the location from his previous assignment, long before he too had become a man of means. Perhaps he would also live in a neighborhood like this someday, he reflected. An optimism growing out of his newfound regard for his present and future circumstances.

As he walked along, Solomon reflected on the mathematics of the walled city and its suburbs, and how Jews and Christians each lived in one quarter of greater Córdoba while the Muslim victors possessed one half. His people's share hadn't changed since Roman times. The Christians, on the other hand, had basically been displaced, losing three-quarters a city during the fateful invasion of 711 CE. However, the boundary lines weren't that rigid so there was a good deal of intermingling going on. Arabs, like the Visigoth conquerors before them, never constituted more than one-tenth of the population.

Solomon wanted to talk with Hafsun, only this time not under orders from Hasdai. On this occasion he wanted to follow a hunch of his own. The first time he'd interviewed Hafsun, the Muwallid offered little in the way of help. Maybe this time things would be different. Hafsun mentioned there were some, living in Córdoba and al-Zahra, who wanted to overthrow the Caliphate and bring into power an Arab aristocracy to rule over Andalusia. Perhaps he would be willing to elaborate.

Solomon arrived at his destination and found the courtyard gate unlocked. He'd found that unusual on his first visit. Now he realized this neighborhood was the beneficiary of more police foot patrols than those throughout the rest of the city. He also suspected that Hafsun kept private security lurking somewhere out of sight.

He entered, closed the gate, and walked past a gurgling courtyard fountain. The sound of water added a soothing background ambiance, one the investigator sorely lacked at his own place of residence. One that he never failed to appreciate. Orange and lemon trees grew in pots set back along the walls.

Solomon used the brass door knocker to announce his presence.

The door opened and he found himself staring at the familiar face of a silver-haired man servant. Once again the man wore a black cotton tunic. Seeing anyone dressed in black was a rare occurrence in the lands of the Umayyad rulers who favored the color white or any other color, except for black. The Abbasids, who assassinated Marwan and massacred the entire family excepting Rahman I, were wearers of black clothing and fliers of black flags.

It occurred to Solomon that the man might be a spy or a sympathizer. He kept his suspicions to himself since they had no real basis in fact.

"I'm here to speak with ibn Hafsun," he told the servant.

It appeared the servant didn't recognize Solomon on this second visit. Solomon raised his hand to display the signet ring of the Foreign Minister. This must have jogged the man's memory as he rushed off to inform his master without saying a word.

A short time later, Hafsun came to the door. Solomon observed him closely. A dark haired man, he looked younger than the servant, probably in his late forties or early fifties. But the investigator already knew this from his previous visit. Hafsun wore another lavish silk tunic, this time a long and flowing brilliant blue garment with wide sleeves and a loose fit decorated with orange floral designs. The fabric ended just above leather ankle boots. Solomon remembered the boots. Made of the finest Córdoban leather, he assumed.

"Levy, isn't it?" asked the Muwallid. The way Hafsun expressed himself made it seem more a statement of fact than a question. "What does the Foreign Minister want of me this time?"

"Actually, I need to speak to you."

"Very well," agreed Hafsun. "Would you care to come inside?"

Hafsun's steely blue eyes were well-trained in revealing little of his emotions. The Muwallad smoothed his tunic as the hint of a smile creased his lips. Solomon weighed the options. Time was of the essence, but he might learn more if he accepted the invitation.

"Please, I insist."

"I'm honored."

"Follow me."

The gracious manners. The investigator wondered how much of this was a result of Hafsun's upbringing or just a practiced deception. Solomon remembered questioning the man during his previous investigation. His great uncle had been a chieftain and the political and military leader of rebellious Muwallids. These were descendants of Visigoth Christians converted to Islam.

Great uncle Hafsun was a longtime enemy of the Umayyad rulers. For more than thirty years he ruled a broad swatch of southern and eastern Andalusia from Granada to Málaga and Cádiz to Seville. He renounced Islam and his conversion to Christianity attracted many Mozarabs, but he eventually lost most of his Muwallid followers. He'd hoped to gain military support from Alfonso III of Asturias. When this ploy failed, he pledged allegiance to the Fatimid Caliphate of North Africa. This brought down the full wrath of Rahman III and eventually led to his demise.

As they made their way through nephew Hafsun's lavish home, Solomon realized he'd been overly impressed on his first walk through the house. He now observed that the furnishings hadn't changed since that visit: the lavish reception area lined in the round with carved wooden benches, the exquisite wool rug, the cream-colored floor tiles, and the stucco cupola surrounded by half a dozen stained-glass window panels. This is a man who's comfortable living the conventional life of a successful businessman, thought Solomon.

The two men entered an elegant sitting room. Once

again, the investigator found everything as it was on his last visit: the two oversized, upholstered chairs still sat facing each other on either side of a round table made from deeply grained imported wood. There were no crucifixes or religious pictures on the walls, nothing to suggest that Hafsun wasn't a convert to Islam. Perhaps an intended effect.

Solomon found that he wasn't as impressed by the trappings of wealth this time around. Since he'd been rewarded handsomely by the Caliph, after his last mission, he'd had time to reflect upon his values. And it all came down to him and Sara and the future they might share together. They talked about finding a place of their own since both were still renting. They didn't want to rush into anything despite their strong feelings for each other because both knew that moving in together would take their relationship to a new level of commitment. This appeared to have been a wise choice given the present circumstances.

"Please, sit down," said Hafsun.

The two men sat simultaneously and then faced one another. Solomon kept the bundle on his lap. He didn't offer an explanation for its presence and Hafsun ignored it. A gracious host never insults a guest by prying into their business.

Hafsun went to a side table and picked up a bell-ringer and rang it. Before they enjoyed an opportunity to converse the silver-haired man servant entered the room and walked over to stand before the master of the house.

"Will you join me in coffee?" asked the host.

"No thank you," answered Solomon declining the invitation. "I don't have time."

"Very well."

Hafsun held up one finger and the servant, understanding his orders, quickly disappeared from the sitting room. Solomon remembered the first time he'd spoken with the businessman in this room. He'd learned that Hafsun traded pick-ups, fabric made from silk trimming, for spices. He also maintained a luxurious second home in Alexandria, Egypt. The investigator also recalled that Hafsun summoned his servant on his first visit by clapping his hands loudly. So the bell-ringer was most likely an improvement upon that arrangement.

"So why are you here, Levy?"

"The last time I spoke with you, when I was investigating Umar abd-Rahman's murder, you told me that some close to the Caliph were unhappy with him. You mentioned his own family and specifically Umar and a clique of Arab elitists. I think you suggested that Umar coveted the throne."

"Yes, I remember our conversation."

"Can you elaborate for me, please."

"I have a friend who tells me things," began Hafsun. '

"A Muwallid?" interrupted Solomon.

"Yes, but I won't divulge his identity. I will tell you that he's told me, on more than one occasion, that a group of elitist Arabs are conspiring to overthrow the Caliph. They're upset with his efforts to create more equality in Andalusia. They cherish their privilege and see it slipping away. I'm not sure where my friend gets his information."

"Did he say who's involved?"

"Umar abd-Rahman, but of course he's no longer with us. I don't recall any other names."

"I'll look into it."

"I would advise you to be cautious, Levy," warned Hafsun. He trained his steely blue eyes directly on Solomon in an effort to reveal the seriousness of what he was about reveal. "These men are ambitious, but they are also quite violent. You might be placing your life in danger."

Hasdai had suggested the same possibility. It was disconcerting knowing that everyone, including Sara, felt a need to apprise him of the dangers of his mission. At least they voiced their opinions out of concern for his welfare. Solomon took comfort in that fact.

"Since you're here I'd like to take this opportunity to thank you."

The servant reappeared with an exquisite silver tray before the investigator found a chance to speak. A single cup of steaming coffee, a bowl of sugar, and a spoon lay upon its surface. The man set the tray down on a side table, bowed politely, and then he exited the room leaving the two men to themselves. Hafsun stood and walked over to the side table. He spooned sugar into his cup and took the coffee back with him to his overstuffed chair. He took a sip and a smile spread across his face.

Solomon had waited, but now he picked up the tread of their conversation.

"Thank me for what?" queried the investigator.

"I owe you a debt of gratitude for interceding with the Foreign Minister on my behalf. For keeping my name out of that sordid affair. Umar's murder and all that. We both know that I wasn't even remotely involved, but a cloud of suspicion might have ruined me."

"Then maybe you can answer some more questions?"

"I'll try."

"Is it possible Muwallids are involved in the conspiracy against the Caliph?" inquired the investigator. "Perhaps they're working in league with the Arab elitists."

Hafsun took his time before answering the question.

He sipped his coffee while giving the matter his full attention: "Anything is possible, but I think not," he responded. "We Muwallids certainly have our grievances. However, most of these complaints are a result of the attitude of those same Arabs you refer to. They resent having to share power."

"It was a case of self-defense," said Solomon changing the subject of the conversation. "I'm talking about the killing of Umar."

"I don't doubt that."

Solomon knew it was time to leave. Learning anything of value from Hafsun had been a long shot, but one he felt worth taking. He could now all but rule out the Muwallids. He rose from his chair, bundle in hand, and it was obvious he was making ready to leave.

"I must be going."

"I'll see you out," Hafsun offered.

Hafsun stood, cup in hand, and went to the side table. He placed the cup down on the tray, turned back to the investigator, and then he guided Solomon out of the sitting room. They made their way back through Hafsun's magnificent home and arrived back at the front door.

"I'm sorry I have no names for you. You might want to talk to the widow," suggested Hafsun. "Umar may not have shared these matters with her, but she's an intelligent woman. I'm sure she has an inkling about what's going on."

"My turn to thank you, ibn Hafsun." replied Solomon. "I bid you good day."

The investigator walked back through the patio as the fountain continued to gently splash its soothing song. He had already thought of questioning Umar's widow, Nuzha. The fact that Hafsun suggested this course of action indicated he was offering his full cooperation. Much different than their first meeting.

Solomon had been careful not to discuss the theft of the holy relic during his visit with the Muwallid. There was no need for him to know that the bundle tucked under his arm, and the robbery at the Great Mosque, were paramount on his mind. He knew it was time for him to go see the one person in Córdoba who might provide some understanding about this mystery.

He smiled to himself as he considered spending time in the presence of his old confidant. It was soon replaced by a frown as he remembered the last time he was with her. Still, he needed her help, and she had proven herself to be a valuable and obliging ally in the past. There was simply no getting around it.

It was time to pay a visit to Layla.

CHAPTER 6

Solomon found the latch unlocked and smiled to himself. Some things don't change. He entered a familiar green courtyard carrying the wrapped sandal under his arm, He hadn't imagined ever seeing Layla again. She had entered into another relationship. Had met someone special. He remembered exactly how she'd phrased it.

As he walked towards her door he passed flowering red geraniums. There always seemed to be new blooms in the terra cotta pots.

He approached a wooden door painted a bright indigo and rapped four times in succession. She had remembered their secret code the last two times he'd been here, but that was some time ago. He had no expectations of a warm greeting. He'd been cured of that assumption on his last visit.

The door swung open.

"Solomon!"

"Expecting me?" he asked.

"Not at all," Layla replied. "Your fame has spread throughout the kingdom, so I didn't imagine I'd ever see you again."

"You know better."

"You need my help."

"Well, yes . . . " he told her. Solomon gestured inside. "Is this a bad time?"

"We're no longer seeing each other," Layla answered.

"So this is a good time."

He entered the foyer, and she closed the latch behind him. He continued on to the well-appointed living room, painted in a popular vermillion hue, assuming they'd take their usual places on the deep-cushioned sofa. Layla had other ideas.

"Let's go into the kitchen."

She led the way as he observed her hips swaying beneath a long, silk indigo-dyed tunic. She walked barefooted as she always had. Solomon gazed down at her left ankle where half a dozen gold chains jingled a subtle rhythm, in time with her footsteps.

Courtesan and confidant. And much more.

He noticed Layla hadn't changed her hair style since the last time he'd seen her. The black strands retained subtle highlights of orange-red henna dye, and she still pulled them back from her forehead. She wove the hair into a thick braid falling down her backside to her waist where a ribbon had been tied around three inches of hair splayed out at the end of the plait.

She turned and faced him.

He studied her face.

Layla's tasteful tattoos, stylized arabesques also painted with henna, adorned her entire body.

The most impressive were intricate, swirling lines dancing subtly across her forehead above dreamy indigo eyes accentuated with black kohl eyeliner. They continued downwards before coming to an end on her prominent cheek bones.

A smile.

"Let's sit at the table," she said.

They sat upon intricately carved wooden chairs at a matching small, but exquisite table. A wide, shallow bowl of fruit lay on top, aesthetically placed in the center and filled with oranges, bananas, avocados, and grapes. Solomon placed his wrapped bundle on the tabletop, off to one side. He eyed the ripe fruit and realized he was quite hungry.

"Help yourself, darling."

Not much escaped her notice.

"Thank you." He smiled while extending his hand across the table to grab a handful of red grapes.

He ate the bunch and reached for more while she watched him closely.

"So why are you here?" she wanted to know.

"Thieves desecrated the Great Mosque." Solomon stopped eating. He looked directly into Layla's eyes and then continued, "More importantly, they stole a sacred relic, the arm bone of the Prophet Mohammad.

"You think I can help you?"

"You don't understand, Layla. I need to talk this out . . . you're a fantastic listener . . . and, you've always been honest with me."

"So what do you know?" The courtesan asked, ignoring his compliments as she held his gaze.

"There was a message scrawled on one of the walls," he told her as he laid out the facts. "It read 'taken by command.' Not much to go on. The Imam thinks the motive for the theft might be similar to the robbery of the Black Stone from the Kaaba, in Mecca, two decades ago."

"The Black Stone!"

"You've heard of it?"

"Yes, I have," she told him. "I grew up in Alexandria and my father was a devout Muslim. The Black Stone was taken the same year he planned to make his pilgrimage to Mecca. He felt so disappointed because he had always dreamed of kissing the Black Stone. He went anyway, but he held on to that hurt and sense of injustice for the remainder of his life. I think it broke his heart."

"The Imam thinks a North African sect might be attempting to copy to Qarmatians."

"That's possible," asserted Layla. "But it might also be the Fatimids or the Abbasids. Perhaps a wealthy religious fanatic. Do you have any physical evidence?"

Solomon reached over the grabbed the bundle. He unwrapped the cloth to reveal the giant sandal.

"Dear Lord!" she shrieked. "This person must be a giant."

"I'm guessing he's close to seven feet tall," he agreed as he handed the sandal to her for a closer inspection.

Layla took it in her hands and studied it carefully, turning over the sandal to examine the sole.

Solomon waited patiently while she considered her response. He knew better than to rush her. The insights she would provide might be the key to unlocking the mystery of this robbery.

She turned the sandal over and then once again. What is she thinking, he wondered.

"Wait here," she said.

Layla rose from her chair and left the kitchen.

Solomon ate more grapes, plucking the juicy morsels from the stems before biting down on them. He felt grateful they were seedless. Less mess for him. He also remembered that he'd once cracked a tooth crunching down hard on grapes with seeds. He continued to munch as he waited, eating until almost all the grapes were gone.

Layla returned holding one of her own sandals in her hand. It was much smaller than the one laying upon the table. That was to be expected and it wasn't the comparison she was about to offer.

"What took you so long?"

"I'm sorry, darling," she apologized. "I probably have a hundred pair of shoes, sandals, boots, and performance slippers; but, I'm not very well organized so it's a lot to sift through."

"Woman and shoes," mused the investigator. "A match made in heaven."

The courtesan placed her own sandal down next to the oversized sandal. A quiet smile. She had discovered a similarity between the two objects. Hard physical evidence. Would it help? She didn't know.

"These two sandals are unique," she declared. "I have no doubt the same shoemaker made them both ."

"How do you know?"

"There is only one shoemaker in all of Andalusia who makes a sandal like these two," she claimed, picking up her smaller sandal to use as an example. "You'll observe that cork on the top side is quite different from the cork on the bottom."

Layla showed him the top first and gave him time to take a closer look. She slowly turned the sandal over to reveal its sole. She waited for Solomon to work it out for himself. It was the soul of the sandal she wanted him to discover.

"The cork used for making the sole is different from the cork on the other side," he perceived. "One is dark and the other a lighter tone. They grow these corks in different regions And I would venture to guess you know exactly where that might be."

"That, darling, is irrelevant," she sighed. "What you need to know is the name of the shoemaker and where he can be found."

Solomon frowned. Of course that's what he needed to know. Wanted to know. He had wandered down a path that would lead him to the source of the cork, but not bring him closer to the maker of the sandals.

"And that name is?"

"His name is Faraj and he can be found in Seville."

"You traveled all the way to Seville to buy a pair of sandals?" laughed Solomon, unable to conceal the disbelief in his voice.

"Not just any sandals, darling," she laughed. "These are considered the finest in all of Andalusia. When cork is stripped from a tree, a new sheath of better quality quickly forms. Not many shoemakers know this. Faraj only uses the finest quality cork for the soles of his sandals."

"I don't get it," Solomon confessed.

"Perhaps the Imam is mistaken," she told him. "The sandals made by Faraj are expensive. They are a status symbol coveted by the Arab elite. And the gullible, like myself. Why else do people travel to Seville to purchase a pair of sandals?"

"You're certainly given me something to think about."

"I should mention that I was already in Seville working with a dance troupe when I had my sandals made," explained the courtesan. "I'm vain, but not so vain as to make a special trip just for a pair of sandals. Even sandals as sought after as these."

Layla seemed eager to help and the investigator appreciated her assistance. He suspected that coming to see her would shed light upon this mystery, never imagining such an unusual coincidence coming to the fore. Now the finger might point back to high-placed Arabs who were dissatisfied with the Caliph.

The picture was still quite murky.

"I know what you're thinking," said the courtesan.

Solomon had no doubts about that. Layla had always had some mysterious sixth sense and he had often thought she was one of those individuals they called a "sensitive."

"Are you going to tell me?"

"You're thinking Arab elitists . . . the same ones who are afraid of losing their long held privilege . . . may be behind the theft of the holy relic."

"Makes sense."

"I'm not so sure, Solomon," she countered. "This could be the work of a wealthy relic collector given to extravagance in rewarding his minions."

"I never thought of that."

Pleased with herself, Layla smiled demurely. "Remember how I helped you the first time we met?"

"You mean by introducing me to those nefarious book dealers?"

Layla ignored the question.

"There are collectors who prize relics: bones, clothing, and sometimes even ashes. I imagine the arm bone of the Prophet Mohammad would be highly sought after."

"Is nothing sacred?" Solomon wondered aloud.

"I think you should talk with a successful relic dealer," advised Layla. She thought for a moment and then said: "I know just the person. His name is Abbas. Down in Seville he's known as the Relic Master ."

"Seville," exclaimed the investigator in surprise. "Seems like an unlikely coincidence; the shoe maker and this guy named Abbas who sells relics."

"I thought you knew that Seville is a hotbed of illegal activity. The police have less control over things than they do here in Córdoba or al-Zahra. Abbas uses his book shop as a front," continued the courtesan. "The legality of his relic business is open to question. The good news is that I can tell you where to find him."

"That's great, but can you tell me where to find the shoe maker?"

Layla thought about his request and then realized she was about to disappoint him.

"I'm sorry, it's been so long," she said in a quiet voice. "I was only there once. That city is such a warren of narrow streets."

"You must remember something," he implored.

"It's about five or six blocks from the main mosque, but I can tell you nothing more."

"Now I've got three possibilities."

"But one solid lead," she reminded him. "Faraj the Shoemaker might give you the information you need to track down the perpetrators of this sacrilege."

"Anything else?"

"I can't think of anything else that will help you," she admitted.

Another longer pause in the conversation. How to say goodbye after all that had transpired between them. Maybe if he knew more about the circumstances of Layla's recent relationship he'd have a better idea of where theirs might be heading. He decided to broach the subject.

"So what happened with . . . ?"

He felt awkward realizing he didn't even know the man's name. Layla had never told him and he'd hadn't bothered to ask. She looked at Solomon with a hint of sadness in her eyes.

"Let's go sit in the living room," she proposed as she stood from the table. "I'll clean up later."

Leaving the grape stems on the tabletop, the investigator rose from his chair, grabbed the bundle of material holding the sandal, and followed his confidant out of the kitchen.

They sat together on the sofa. This time Layla didn't move over to be closer to him. This had only happened once before and that was on the occasion of their first meeting. When they hardly knew each other. After that, she'd always cozied up to him.

Solomon placed the bundle on the tile floor next to the couch, and they turned to face one another so they could make eye contact.

"Zayd wanted me to move to Alexandria, so we could live together. I told him I couldn't because the city holds too many agonizing memories for me. Zayd was painfully honest. He said it was all or nothing. He either wanted me by his side every day or not at all. Zayd told me a long distance relationship wouldn't last, and he was right of course. So here I am just as I was when you and I first met."

Not quite, thought Solomon.

"If you loved him why not move with him to Alexandria?"

"It's a long story Solomon," she let him know. "Still, I feel a need to unburden myself."

The investigator gazed into Layla's eyes, eyes the color of indigo dye. He found in them a sadness he'd never encountered while in her presence.

"I'm listening," he said softly.

CHAPTER 7

L ayla moved over closer to Solomon. Familiar terri- tory. Only this time she did nothing overt. No hips touching his own. Not a hint of a smile. No un- spoken invitation for him to consider indulging in phys- ical pleasure. This time things felt different.

"My father's brother came to Alexandria to open a business when I was a young girl," she began. "He asked my parents if he could live with us while he looked for a place of his own."

Layla lowered her eyes.

Behind her mask of false bravado there existed a bruised and abused woman.

"I remained an only child as a result of a difficult childbirth for my mother. One day when my parents had gone off to the market, my uncle stayed behind. I was at that age where a girl's body begins to develop, but I had not yet experienced my first menses. Anyway, I was sit- ting inside my room reading when I heard my uncle call out to me. I went into the kitchen and found him sitting at the table with his chair pushed back."

"Come here and talk to your favorite uncle," he coaxed me. "Come here and sit on my lap."

"I did as I was told."

"Give me a little kiss, Layla."

"I gave him a quick peck on the cheek."

"Not like that," he told me as he took my face in his hands and kissed me hard on the lips.

"I became confused. I didn't understand what was happening. He took me up into his arms and carried me into the bedroom my parents had so generously allowed him to use. He put me down on the bed, and then he climbed on top of me. He smiled as he pulled my tunic up past my waist and pulled down my undergarments. '

"Scream and I will kill you," he threatened.

"My stomach turned over. I felt afraid I would throw up on him. I didn't want to die. He forced himself upon me. Over and over again as I prayed for the ordeal to end. I cried many tears, but I didn't dare cry out for help. When he finished, he got up and left me there alone, but not before giving me another warning: "If you tell anyone about this, I will murder you and your family."

"I kept my shame to myself. He passed himself off as a devout Muslim. My parents never would have believed me. He would deny it and my sadness would have worsened. Not long after, he found a place of his own and moved out of our house," Layla added before abruptly pausing in the telling of her story.

As he listened to Layla share her deeply personal memories Solomon felt his heart aching for her. Such a beautiful woman in so very many ways. Such an ugly man in every way. What kind of man would force himself upon a young woman?

He sat quietly. He'd imagined the story unfold in his imagination. Layla's ordeal disturbed him, and he didn't feel particularly proud of the male of the species at that moment in time. What could he do to console her, he wondered. He took her hands into his own and held them gently.

"I'm so sorry, Layla."

She offered him a smile before continuing her story.

She seemed intent upon telling the story as if this sharing allowed her to unburden her soul. Layla held nothing back.

"You might think that I would withdraw into myself, but the experience had the opposite effect upon my soul. I realized that life is uncertain and so I became emboldened. Time went on and I excelled in my studies and applied to the University, here in Córdoba. I wanted to get far away from my family and from that house and from Alexandria.

I was accepted by the University and my parents agreed to allow me to continue my education, but only on the condition that we move here as a family. I could hardly refuse their offer."

Layla paused once again, reflecting upon whether she wished to continue with her story as Solomon sat by her side staring into her eyes and listening intently.

"Within a year of the move, my father died unexpectedly. My mother's health began to fail. That's when I pursued opportunities as a dancer. I attended school by day and danced at night. I earned enough *dinars* to keep our modest household afloat. I loved dancing. I lost myself in the movements and it helped me to forgot about my pain. I felt determined never to let any man control my body or my mind. I became steeled in my resolve. I would cherish my individuality and fight for it if necessary."

Solomon sat quietly. At a loss for words, he felt deflated. What could he say given the circumstances? Any words he might offer would prove inadequate. At least that's what he told himself. Layla broke the silence.

"I've never shared this with another soul," Layla confided. "I don't know why I'm telling you now."

"I'm sorry."

"No, I'm sorry. This is not why you came here."

"I don't know what to say," muttered Solomon.

"My mother died of heartache," Layla continued. "I began a new life. I cultivated social relationships with the people who hired me to dance at their parties. I developed many friendships. I'm a good listener and I can be discreet. I learned the secrets of many highly placed individuals. So, here I am . . . here we are."

"Did you tell Zayd about your uncle?"

"No. With some men it is a badge of honor. They want to be the first."

"The only one."

"Exactly," she replied. "I guess that doesn't matter now."

"He might have understood."

"I think Zyad loved Alexandria as much as you love Córdoba, but I could never go back. I wanted to make sure he held on to at least one lover."

They had reversed roles for once. Solomon became Layla's confidant for a brief time. She understood that he could be trusted not to speak about the painful memories she had shared with him.

He would never betray her. Despite her worldliness, she revealed an inexplicable shyness and genuine sense of modesty at times. Solomon had always held a soft spot in his heart for Layla. She'd helped him during his first two investigations and had always encouraged him to continue with his poetry during the moments of his deepest doubt.

"I'm sorry. I got carried away," she said, apologizing once again. "You came here seeking my help. Everything you've told me, and showed me, points to Seville. Perhaps, even beyond."

"Beyond?"

"If somebody desires to smuggle the relic to North Africa I would venture to guess they'll use the port at Cádiz."

"Why not Tarifa?"

"It would take longer for them to get there because it's further away," she answered. "The sooner they get that stolen relic out of Andalusia and on its way to North Africa, the better their chance of success."

"Makes sense."

"Wait here, darling," said Layla. "I'll draw you a map so you can find the book shop."

The courtesan disappeared for a few minutes before returning with a piece of paper folded into four sections. She sat back on the couch and handed the paper to the investigator. He took it with a smile.

Layla's sisterly, helpful side soon gave way to amorous intentions as she moved over on the couch. Closer to him. So close he could feel her hips nudging up to his.

Solomon knew that it was time for him to go. He released her hands and rose to his feet.

"You know you can stay if you like."

Once again, Solomon had to fend off Layla's advances, but he wasn't about to take advantage of her vulnerable state of mind.

"I'm sorry, this is too important for me to put my needs first."

There was more to the equation. Sara now entered into it. And the fact that Layla had met someone special and it hadn't been him. For her part, she sensed that for once he meant what he said. He's changed, she thought to herself. He seems more mature . . . more sure of himself. Layla reached up and took his hand in her own and gave it a gentle squeeze.

"I understand."

"I knew you would."

Solomon helped Layla to her feet before she found a chance to let go his hand. He took her into his arms and kissed her softly on the lips before letting her go.

Layla's deep, contented sigh, the last thing he heard before leaving her home, made him wonder what their future might hold. And, what about Sara? Can a man love two woman at the same time? He wondered. Conversely, can a woman love two men at once? It's possible either way, he reasoned, but it wasn't an easy thing to do. Solomon Levy knew he'd be a fool to think otherwise.

Did the kiss indicate Solomon wasn't ready to move in with Sara anytime soon or was it just his way of letting Layla know that what happened to her in the past didn't change how he felt about her now. He liked the latter interpretation best.

Solomon wanted to thank Layla for offering him the grapes, but he felt this might be misconstrued as insensitive given the *gravitas* of her revelations.

He snatched the bundle from the tile floor and made for the door.

Layla followed and watched as Solomon opened the door, stepped through the threshold, and then turned around with a smile on his face. The courtesan reciprocated before closing her front door and retreating back inside.

As he walked through the courtyard, Solomon realized there were others he needed to question, but they all lived in al-Zahra. He decided to return home first to relieve himself of the bundle before setting off for the Caliph's opulent new city. He turned his attention back to the investigation and a disturbing thought occurred to him.

What if he came up empty-handed and the day of the procession at the Great Mosque came and went with no holy relic to reassure the multitudes that the Umayyad Caliphate continued to be blessed by Allah among all other rivals for the right to rule the Islamic world.

What kind of chaos would be unleashed?

CHAPTER 8

Solomon placed the bundle on his writing desk and carefully unwrapped the cloth to reveal the oversized cork sandal. He soon realized that Layla hadn't told him a thing about the attached leather thong. Maybe it held no significance. Apparently the uniqueness of the two types of cork took precedence.

He was about to sit at his desk to write out some mental notes, the answers to many of the questions he'd asked that morning, when there came a knock at the door. When he opened it he found himself looking once again at his older cousin, Hasdai.

"You've surprised me twice in one day, Hasdai," noted Solomon. "This is unprecedented."

"I was on my way to the synagogue and took this opportunity to stop by," explained Hasdai. "There's been some new developments. Ibn Hawqal is staying in Córdoba. He's been invited to give a lecture by one of the professors at the University."

"That seems very sudden."

"Surprisingly so," the Foreign Minister concurred. "Hawqal is an international trader. The fact that he's well-educated and purportedly writing a book on geography gives him a perfect excuse to visit and observe any number of sites including our army and naval installations. There are many who believe he's a Fatimid spy. The professor at the University may be a sympathizer."

"Do you think he's involved with the theft and desecration at the Great Mosque?"

"The Fatimids have made no secret of their desire to undermine our Caliphate. I've placed our navy on high alert in all the major port cities," he continued. "Customs officials have been ordered to inspect every item leaving Andalusia by ship."

They are subject to bribes, thought Solomon. It's a necessary step, but certainly not foolproof.

"Solomon, I want you to question Hawqal. See if you can find out what he knows, and keep an eye out for him. He might be dangerous. Especially if he shows up when you're searching locations for potential clues."

"I'll try to catch up with him at the University."

"How's your investigation coming along, Solomon?"

"Please, come inside," requested Solomon. "There's something I need to show you."

Hasdai entered and followed Solomon over to the writing desk.

"There are three possibilities so far: a radical sect from North Africa, disgruntled Arab elitists here in Córdoba and al-Zahra, or possibly a private collector of sacred relics."

"What is it you wanted to show me?"

"There's a giant involved in the robbery," Solomon told him.

"A giant?"

Solomon picked up the sandal so Hasdai could get a better look. His cousin's eyes widened and he shook his head in disbelief.

"I've never seen anything quite like that."

Solomon lowered the sandal back into the cloth.

"The man who wore this sandal, and I'm assuming it was a man, must stand seven feet tall."

"Anything else I should know."

Solomon led Hasdai back over to the front door. The Foreign Minister of Andalusia, and personal physician to the Caliph, didn't take offense and soon followed Solomon outside where fresh air and blue skies reigned as their new backdrop. Solomon appreciated his cousin allowing him to take the lead in this investigation. He felt that he had proven his worthiness on his two previous assignments.

"I need to journey down to Seville to question the shoemaker responsible for this monstrosity." The investigator needed to clarify his intentions, so he elaborated upon his course of action. "That is, after I'm through conducting interviews in al-Zahra."

"You'll need an escort."

"I'd like for Jalal to meet me on the far side of the Roman Bridge just after the noontime call to prayer," the investigator told Hasdai. "Tell him to bring horses. We'll need two of the Caliph's strongest."

"You want the Slav?" questioned Hasdai. "Are you sure?"

"Is there a problem with that?" asked Solomon. He had answered a question with a question of his own even though he risked sounding rude or insolent. He already believed this mission would test his mettle and there was only one man in the entire world whom he would trust with his life.

"I'll go to al-Zahra and talk with General Naja," Hasdai informed him. "I'm sure he'll have no problem honoring my request."

Solomon spied a black man lurking a short distance away. He recognized him immediately. He was one of the Caliph's private guards, assigned to Hasdai after the murder of the ruler's nephew, Umar. The broad-shouldered, ebony faced mercenary was still in the habit of resting his hand on the steel handle of a long, curved scimitar hanging at his side.

The guard smiled, a gesture of recognition.

Solomon returned the smile.

"Yusef is still assigned to you?"

"Permanently, it appears. The Caliph doesn't want anything to happen to me. Is there anything else, Solomon?"

"Have you ever been allowed inside the Great Mosque?"

"Yes, but only once," admitted Hasdai. "It's . . . "

"Beyond words . . ."

So why talk about it the two men reasoned as Solomon nodded his head in agreement.

"I'll make sure a galley is waiting for you in Seville and one in Cádiz as well," said Hasdai changing the subject. "They'll be the safest choice for your return when you recover the relic. And don't be afraid to call upon our Customs Officials. They may be able to assist you and they serve at my command."

The phrasing didn't escape Solomon's attention. Hadai said "when" and not "if." After two successful missions they assumed he'd recover the relic, but there was no guarantee and he feared he might disappoint them this time. He didn't possess magical powers and he wasn't a miracle worker. Better not dwell, he thought. Stay focused on this relic business.

"You said developments," reminded the investigator.

"You're right," Hasdai agreed. "You mentioned a radical sect in North Africa. Our intelligence in the Maghreb indicates that the ruler of Sijilmasa fancies himself as a

Caliph and may want to contest Rahman III's legitimacy."

The same situation as the taking of the Black Stone, thought Solomon. That strengthened the argument that a competing Muslim sect perpetrated the theft of the sacred relic.

"I must go, Solomon."

The two men embraced before the Foreign Minister took his leave. Solomon watched as his favorite cousin head off in the direction of Córdoba's oldest synagogue before traveling to al-Zahra to speak with General Naja.

Solomon knew the expectations placed upon him were based on past accomplishments and it wasn't that he lacked confidence in his own abilities. But the message and the sandal, no matter how distinctive, were not a recipe for success.

If anything, this might prove his most difficult investigation.

There was so much at stake.

CHAPTER 9

S olomon walked down a shaded path at the University of Córdoba. He already knew the way to the school's main administration building.

The investigator passed a few undergraduates and marveled at their youth. It had been years since he'd attended his Alma Mater, which along with the University of Montpellier, in southern France, was one of the world's most distinguished centers of higher learning.

Both schools maintained impressive libraries containing hundreds of thousands of volumes. Each institution was at the hub of fact based science in the 10th century, and both possessed the most up-to-date medical schools in Europe.

Some things hadn't changed. The international complexion of the student body being one of them. They arrived in Córdoba from every corner of the world. Both the students and the faculty.

Solomon might have been able to retain his youthful idealism working as a translator and writing poetry on the side, but the investigations Hasdai had cajoled him into undertaking had forced him to experience a darker side of human nature. He felt like a much different person now and often reflected on how a person changed over the course of a lifetime. One evolves in fits and starts, progresses and then digresses, and progresses again. The path to emotional maturity was not a straight line. More like a circling of oneself while experiencing the many facets of one's personality. The good and the bad, and learning to accept one's imperfections as a part of the equation.

Solomon found the building and the office he was seeking. The vice-provost of the University informed him that ibn Hawqal wasn't due to lecture until late in the afternoon on the following day.

The investigator overcame the man's reluctance to give him the address of the Professor whom the geographer was staying with by telling him that it was the Foreign Minister's request that he talk to Hawqal. The man balked so Solomon asked him to take a close look at Hasdai's signet ring.

His cousin had always maintained the ring would open doors that might otherwise remain closed. The vice-provost dipped his quill into a jar of ink and then wrote the address down on a piece of cotton fiber paper.

A short walk later found Solomon standing at the front door of a well-maintained home located four blocks north of the University. He knocked and waited for someone to appear. He assumed the door would be opened by the Professor, or his wife, or a household servant.

He heard someone unbolt the door from the other side. It soon opened and the investigator found himself looking into the brown eyes of a man only a few years older than himself. This surprised him. He had imagined the Professor as an older man with a graying beard. His assignments had taught him never to assume anything. Why must we be always learning the same lessons over and over again, he wondered.

The man wore a tunic made of white cotton, a material that breathed and helped alleviate discomforts created by Andalusia's scorching summer sun.

"May I help you?" asked the man.

"I'm here to see ibn Hawqal."

"I am he."

A second surprise. He hadn't expected the geographer to have free rein of the house. He looked past Hawqal into the interior but there was no sight of the Professor, or his wife if he had one, or any servants. The scene proved a little unsettling, but he didn't have time to dwell on his discomfort. Time to get down to business with this tall, well-built stranger.

"I'm here at the behest of the Foreign Minister."

"Hasdai Shaprut sent you to see me?" the man asked in astonishment.

It was a day of surprises for all involved.

"Yes, he did."

Solomon held up a finger bearing the signet ring. The one possessing seemingly magical powers. The two men briefly introduced one another, a necessary formality.

"Please come inside," motioned Hawqal as he stepped back into the room to allow Solomon to pass.

The geographer closed the door, bolted the latch, and led him down the hallway before turning into a book-lined study. The investigator followed him into the room.

Solomon took a look around before focusing on the bookcase. He studied the titles, most written in Arabic with a smattering in Latin. The room suggested a high degree of intelligence. He saw a few books scattered on a desk on the far side of the room.

Behind the desk, an oversized arch-shaped window provided a view into a lush backyard patio. In the center of the room he noticed a low, round table with maps spread out upon it. Solomon stole a glance at one of them and recognized references to Constantinople, Egypt and the Nile.

"I was expecting the professor to be present," admitted Solomon.

"He's gone to the University," explained Hawqal. "He's hosting a faculty luncheon in my honor, and he desires to insure that it proceeds smoothly."

"And he left you here?"

"I remained behind to work on my book and maps," came the reply. "The professor understands the importance of my work."

"The Foreign Minister is curious what you're doing here in Córdoba."

Hawqal gestured to the maps spread out upon the table.

"I'm here to create maps and descriptions of Andalusia as part of a larger work on world geography."

"There's been some trouble at the Great Mosque," stated the investigator. He said no more, careful not to reveal any details about the theft of the holy relic.

"How does that concern me?"

Hawqal appeared confused by the sudden attention directed his way. He wrinkled his brow and took on the expression of a man searching for explanations. Not finding any, he merely shrugged his shoulders.

"Hasdai Shaprut is known far and wide. We haven't yet met, but his reputation is outstanding throughout the entire Islamic world. And among Jewry worldwide I might add. His role as personal physician to the Caliph is fraught with responsibilities and I must say I've always admired him from afar."

Hawqal sounds like a diplomat, thought Solomon. Is he a well-trained spy or is it just a natural talent?

"I wonder if the Fatimids might be involved."

He waited for the geographer's reply, eager to gauge the reaction.

"I doubt the Fatimids are involved. Their claim is based upon direct ancestry from the prophet Muhammad. The Umayyads maintain their own reasons for a claim to legitimacy. I don't take sides in the matter. I keep friends among the Fatimids and friends among the Umayyads. I'm afraid I can't be of much help to you," the geographer apologized.

A long silence ensued as Solomon waited for Hawqal to consider what he might add to his explanation.

The traveler finally decided to elaborate.

"A lot of Muslims are unhappy with your Caliph. They don't appreciate him allowing Jewish professors and other outsiders from all over the world to teach at the Universities. No restrictions on grounds of religious affiliation or ethnicity. It's the same with his government administrators and the generals of his army. As for his embracing of science and the arts, there are those who don't approve. I myself am not one of them."

The response sounded plausible, but the investigator wasn't sure; and, Hawqal sensed a reluctance on Solomon's part to accept what he'd just told him.

The geographer bit down on his lip.

"Look, I can save us both a lot of time."

"Go on . . . "

"There are those who think that I am a spy. People say many things, most of which cannot be proven. I know many who think that I am a Fatimid spy because I speak highly of them. Those Muslims transformed the island of Sicily with their farming and fishing innovations. They're doing amazing things just as you are here in Andalusia. I've observed how irrigation and employing many kinds of fertilizer have transformed the Peninsula. Does the fact that I admire progress, regardless of the source, make me a spy?"

"Not necessarily."

"Perhaps if you understand my story. How I came to do what I do and go where I go."

"If you think it might help."

"I was not much more than a child when I became interested in books of voyages, explorations, travel accounts, and the ways of life of distant peoples. I started my travels seven years ago, and traveled by many methods, and covered a lot of ground. Much of it on foot. Financed by business interests, I've visited the entire Islamic world and many of the countries and peoples bordering it. I was fortunate to discover new merchandise and also open new markets for Baghdad merchants. After leaving Baghdad I traveled to Syria, Sicily, Egypt, across North Africa, and now here I am in Andalusia. I am now a wealthy man interested in maintaining my integrity and my independence of thought. I am beholden to no one man or any group of men."

Solomon appreciated the background and even found himself admiring the man, but he failed to see how this was saving either of them much time.

"I've traveled far and wide and learned a good deal about different regions and their peoples, but the most important lesson I've learned is . . ."

Solomon waited as the geographer paused for dramatic effect.

Hawqal smiled knowingly as he prepared to enlighten his visitor by sharing with him the wisdom of a seasoned traveler.

"If you are at home in your heart, you can feel at home

anywhere."

Solomon took a moment to reflect upon the sentiment.

"I'm calling my book *The Face of the Earth*."

He's certainly loquacious, thought the investigator. But it's not helping me.

"How about the Professor," Solomon inquired. "Would you consider him a Fatimid sympathizer?"

"The Professor and I are broad-minded individuals," he replied. "You may draw your own conclusions. Now, if you'll excuse me. I mentioned that I have a previous engagement to attend. I really shouldn't be late for a luncheon being given in my honor."

Solomon also had a previous commitment. To meet with Jalal just after the noontime call the prayer. No need to linger when it was apparent Hawqal was too intelligent to divulge any information that might be of help in the investigation. He excused himself.

"I'll see myself out."

He quickly left the book-lined study, retraced his steps through the Professor's home, and soon found himself outside where the absence of clouds compounded the effects of the sizzling summer sun.

What had he learned from his brief encounter, he asked himself. The geographer wasn't going to admit it if he were a spy. Though he had suggested otherwise he'd been very circumvent and hadn't come right out and denied it. What was it he had said: "You may draw your own conclusions." The only conclusion Solomon could draw was that he couldn't possibly draw any conclusions from his questioning of ibn Hawqal.

CHAPTER 10

Solomon arrived at the ancient Roman Bridge, an engineering marvel spanning the Guadalquivir River and its waterway linking Córdoba to the Atlantic Ocean and beyond.

The bridge's roadway, supported by sixteen solidly constructed arches, was a part of the Via Augusta, a five centuries old route Solomon and Jalal would soon use to travel to Seville. A road which had also been constructed by enterprising Romans to facilitate trade and military movements on the Peninsula.

Surprisingly, this vital Roman Bridge required rebuilding by the conquering Muslims, two centuries earlier, to renew commerce across the river. The Visigoths had made the city of Toledo their Iberian capital, and, lacking interest they allowed superior Roman ingenuity to fall into disrepair.

As he strode across the bridge, the wide river flowing below him, Solomon felt a deep sense of anticipation at meeting up with his escort Jalal once again. Their mission to Galicia had ended with success. Though they hadn't parted on intimate terms, after their many experiences together, they had grown very close during that time. The investigator remembered fending off robbers together, being attacked in Santiago de Compestela, and sharing the sunset at the known end of the earth. These weren't so much visual memories he could revisit in his imagination, though they were that also, but more importantly a shared subliminal symbiotic bond.

Jalal stood waiting on the far side of the bridge holding the reins of two heavily-muscled geldings. These powerful horses, equine eunuchs of the finest breeding, came directly from the Caliph's stables. The soldier wasn't wearing his military attire. Solomon requested he be allowed to use civilian clothing. Otherwise, they'd be too conspicuous and this might make them easy targets if someone wanted to prevent their movements.

So both dressed in a half tunic, cut tight in the body and sleeves along with cotton pants tucked into tall riding boots made from oiled leather, a kind of leatherwork made famous by Córdoba's boot makers since before the arrival of the Romans. The mercenary didn't wield a scimitar, but rather a broad, heavy sword of tempered steel whose blade rested in a protective scabbard covered in purple velvet.

A smile spread across his face when the Slav discovered Solomon approaching.

"I didn't think you'd request my services again," Jalal said.

"Why not?"

"I almost got you killed in Galicia."

"You also saved my life," Solomon reminded him.

"Well, yes. I'd forgotten about that," the self-effacing Jalal replied, keeping a tight grip on the reins of the horses as well as his own emotions. "I was just performing my duty."

Solomon took a moment to study his friend. Jalal still wore, and was allowed by his superiors to wear, his blond hair down to his shoulders. The tanned face, more ruddy than brown, gave evidence of a great deal of time spent outside. He hadn't changed much since their return from the savage north.

"Any word on your manumission," Solomon inquired.

The frown on Jalal's face, in response to the question, didn't bode well.

"General Naja required me to prepare a written report outlining the details of the events that transpired during our mission," explained Jalal. "I believed it was necessary to be completely honest."

"So you told him about the attack in Santiago?"

"He knows that I let my guard down."

"I'm sorry," Solomon sympathized. His feeling was sincere and from the heart, so he tried to think of something that might ease the soldier's obvious pain.

"I'm sure it's just a matter of time."

Even though their mission to Galicia had ended successfully, the soldier hadn't gained his freedom, his manumission. And he knew why. Required to report in writing to General Naja, he chose to give a true account of events regardless of the consequences.

He mentioned the attack in Santiago and his lapse in attention. If he hadn't, and it was discovered later, he'd never have a chance to secure his freedom. It stung, not earning his freedom after the hardships he'd endured, but he had failed both his escort and the Army by his lack of diligence. Solomon proved to be more forgiving than the General.

"So why am I here?" he asked.

"A new assignment," the investigator told him as he directed his attention to the horses. "I'll tell you about it on our way to al-Zahra."

Solomon reached out and Jalal handed him the reins to one of the geldings. He grasped them, mounted in a single fluid motion, and watched as his escort did the same. He settled down into his saddle until he found a comfortable riding position, and then he took the lead. The two men rode west and soon left the old Roman Bridge in the distance. A turn to the north took them along the west side of the walled city.

"You haven't forgotten how to ride," observed Jalal, teasing the investigator.

"It's a good thing," Solomon countered in a more serious tone. "We have a lot of miles to cover."

Jalal realized his mistake when he heard Solomon's somber response. He knew it had something to do with their new assignment, and he suddenly understood the urgency of their mission meant the Caliphate was somehow in danger. Where would this mysterious undertaking take them, he wondered.

Solomon's changed, no doubt about that. The reluctant investigator, the one who'd searched out opportunities to get sidetracked, now seems determined, even eager, to confront the challenges ahead.

Jalal realized that he had no clue what was going on.

Solomon and Jalal rode through al-Zahra's double-walled entrance as the sun reached its zenith. This new center of government, seven miles west of Córdoba, displayed a lavish opulence befitting the most influential empire in Europe: bustling markets, cobbled streets, public lighting, gardens, fountains, aviaries, and even a zoo.

This palatial city was built on three tiers, monumental terraces cut into a huge natural spur of the Sierra Morena mountains, east of the fertile Guadalquivir river valley. The upper tier housed the Caliph's unparalleled palace complex and the nearby army headquarters as well as clusters of luxurious Umayyad family villas and those belonging to members of the Arab elite.

The middle tier consisted of lavish reception halls, the offices and residences of government officials (including a house used by the Foreign Minister) as well as gardens, orchards, fountains, and ponds.

On the lower level were the mosques, public and private schools, libraries, hospitals, pharmacies, public baths, parks, and the homes of the city's artisans and laborers.

The verdant city, clothed in lush green foliage, had sprung to life watered by a ten-mile long system of underground pipes and aqueducts whose source lay in the mountains to the north. It was laid out in a rectangular shape, stretched a mile and a half from east to west and almost two miles from north to south.

Caliph Rahman III chose the name Madinat al-Zahra for his fairytale like city. Contrary to popular belief it was not named after one of his favorite wives. It meant "The Resplendent One," paradise on earth, and was intended as a modest precursor of the heaven awaiting all true believers of Islam.

Nonbelievers were meant to share in the opulence of his earthly bliss. The liberal minded Caliph, following in the footsteps of his Umayyad predecessors, strove hard to maintain a fair and just society. Remain loyal--whether Muslim, Jew, Christian, or some other persuasion--and this magnificent world is yours to enjoy.

Solomon led the way along the upper terrace, knowing Hasan's stables lay a mile east of the Caliph's less modest training grounds and enormous stalls. He had questioned Umar abd-Rahman's brother twice during his previous investigation.

In the distance, also on the third and highest level of the city, the Caliph's magnificent white palace overlooked the city. It dominated the upper terrace along with the villas of his family and the most successful merchants.. White flowers blossomed in unbroken rows of almond trees planted along the top of the mountain, and their scented blossoms created a white carpet along the ground where they'd fallen. The effect was dazzling to the eye.

The investigator knew he'd find Hasan at his stables. He had made it clear in the past that his first love was his horses. "The most beautiful thing in Allah's entire creation." This is how he had described them.

The last time they were in each other's presence, inside Hasdai's office when five murder suspects were undergoing questioning, Hasan had become so irate that he had spit on Solomon's shoe out of disgust. Umar's brother soon found his own tunic used to wipe off the splat of saliva. There was no love lost between these two men. Nor, apparently, between Hasan and his brother, Umar. The investigator believed men like Hasan and Umar, with their attitude of ethnic and familial privilege, were a curse to the world.

Solomon and Jalal rode into the stables and soon located pear-shaped Hasan. He stood leaning on a fence, gazing out to the track where riders took half a dozen Arabian horses through their paces. The investigator remembered how the brother's garlic infused breath overpowered, so he remained sitting atop his mount.

Hasan heard the horses approaching. He turned his head around to see who it might be. His bulging eyes and sun-burned skin looked much the same as during their last encounter. His love of horses hadn't changed either, because the equine enthusiast couldn't help but admire the two chestnut-colored geldings.

He studied their conformation and realized all the

elements combined pointed to exceptionally fine blood-lines. Hasan had a hard time taking his eyes off them as he unconsciously licked his lips. He had no doubt the two geldings had come from the Caliph's stables. When he finally pulled himself away to look up at Solomon he couldn't help but frown.

"I thought I was done with you."

"I thought the same . . ."

"So why have you come here, Levy?" Hasan asked as he looked up past the investigator to his escort.

"I have a few questions to ask you," the investigator replied. "It shouldn't take long."

"I told you before that I don't need to answer your questions."

"No, but this time you'll be answering to the Caliph himself if you don't," threatened Solomon.

"Very well, Jew," came the half-hearted response.

"I've learned Umar may have had designs upon the throne," Solomon began. "There are some who suggest a faction of elite Arabs are unhappy with Rahman III and would like to dispose of the Caliph."

"I'm not going to give you any names if that's what you're after."

Jalal looked over to gauge Solomon's response and heard a smirk.

"Hmmmph," grinned the investigator as he motioned to Jalal before pulling on his reins and turning his horse around to leave. The soldier followed his lead and the two men rode out of the stables without exchanging another word.

Why had he expected cooperation? Solomon wondered. He should have known better. Maybe he'd changed since his last investigation, but some people never change. That was a pity in the case of Umar's brother.

Jalal rode up alongside.

"That was a waste of time."

"Not really," Solomon enlightened him. "Hasan told me he wouldn't give me any names, but he didn't deny there's a plot against the Caliph. In fact, he's all but admitted it. That's all I needed from him."

"Are you going to have him arrested?"

"No, I'm going to try to find out who's the leader of this cabal and if they know anything about the break-in at the Great Mosque," Solomon answered. "Our first order of business is to find the stolen relic."

Rumors of the conspiracy against the Caliphate had reached Solomon's ears much too easily. He reasoned Hasdai would already have been apprised of the machinations of the Arab elitists and was probably having suspected plotters watched by the police. Hasan would have been among them.

"Where are we headed next?"

"We're going to visit to the widow of Umar abd-Rahman."

CHAPTER 11

U pon his death, the luxurious white villa that once belonged to Umar abd-Rahman had become the property of his young son, Ali. Two eunuchs stood guard outside the domed domicile and Solomon soon realized that he'd been mistaken on his past visits.

During that investigation he'd assumed the eunuch guards were a part of the Caliphate's army because of their military uniforms. He now realized they were private security. This made perfect sense given the vulnerability of the Umayyads. It would have made less sense if they didn't take such precautions.

Solomon and Jalal dismounted.

"Would you watch our horses," Solomon asked the shorter of the two guards.

"Yes, Sir."

He handed the reins to the eunuch and Jalal did the same.

The taller of the two eunuch recognized Solomon from his two previous trips to the villa and once again led the way down a long walkway towards a front entrance built in a style favored by Umayyads, a horseshoe-shaped archway. He found the once green foliage along the footpath yellowed further since his visit earlier that summer.

They entered a reception area that opened up inside into a light and airy interior with an expansive sense of space. Arched portals led deeper into the seraglio's guarded apartments where, the investigator knew, the concubines and children of Umar lived lavish and well-cloistered lives.

The tall eunuch disappeared through an archway on the far side of the room, leaving Solomon and Jalal free to gaze at regal splendor. Jalal seemed awestruck. The soldier had never been invited inside such a magnificent dwelling.

Solomon studied the walls while he waited. Their surfaces were painted a soothing aquamarine, but something was missing. The brilliant gold lettering, an elegant calligraphy rendered in stylish Arabic script. He remembered reading words arranged from right to left, written in the same direction as his native Hebrew. The sentiment paid homage to Umar abd-Rahman.

Its distinct script revealed the graceful hand of the compositor. Solomon remembered his initial reaction to the refined Arabic calligraphy. A blissful gratefulness for the writing's sheer rhythmic beauty. No wonder Andalusi's call the practice of calligraphy "The Golden Profession," he'd mused on his first visit.

Now it was gone.

The elegant calligraphy, an homage to Umar abd Rahman, had been painted over. He winced. Such a shame, but he thought he understood the motivation behind the act. Nuzha was no doubt attempting to protect her son, Ali. The writing on the anteroom wall projected an idealized image of the man who was his father, an image that would not serve the boy as he grew to manhood. It might undo him if Ali were to later discover the true nature of his father. Or, he might deny the reality of that truth.

He turned his attention away from the wall just as two women, both clad in floor length tunics, entered the room from an arched doorway. The Eunuch followed them across the room before taking his leave.

One of the women, dressed in red silk, stepped forward.

"Solomon ben Levy," she declared. "I didn't expect to see you again so soon. At least not here at the villa."

The investigator had last seen the attractive widow at the fateful encounter in the Foreign Minister's office when he'd brought together five suspects to reveal which of them was responsible for Umar's demise. She hadn't changed since then. At least not physically. The delicate nose and full sensuous lips. The long, luxuriant black hair still cascaded down the sides of her neck. Only now she seemed more comfortable inside of her skin with its texture as smooth as the finest porcelain.

"You remember Fatima?" she asked, motioning to the woman standing next to her. The former concubine gave the investigator a welcoming smile.

"Yes, of course,"

"This is my escort, Jalal."

Jalal stood in an at-ease position, sword hanging conspicuously by his side. He gave the two women a brief nod, but he didn't say a word.

The two woman assessed the mercenary. His blond hair suggested he might be one of the Silent Ones even though he dressed in civilian clothes. Impossible to tell from appearances.

"May we speak privately, Solomon ben Levy?"

Without waiting for his answer, the widow led Solomon over to one wall of the reception area where she sat on a marble bench decorated with chenille pillows. They left Jalal and Fatima to fend for themselves.

"How's Ali taking his father's death?" Solomon asked in a voice barely above a whisper.

"I retained Ahmad to tutor him," she responded. The widow also kept her voice low. She picked up one of the pillows and held it on her lap, pressing down on it as a way of relieving her anxiety. "Losing his father was difficult enough. I didn't want to compound his loss."

"Seems like a wise decision."

"Knowing the circumstances will make it easier to talk with my son when he's old enough to understand.," she continued. "I owe you a debt of thanks, Solomon ben Levy. I thought I didn't care who killed Umar, but I discovered I was mistaken. You've given me closure."

Nuzha looked over at Jalal who appeared engaged in polite conversation with the concubine. She turned back around and gazed directly into the investigator's brown eyes.

"Why are you here?" she wanted to know.

Solomon wondered how much he should share with the widow. It wouldn't do well for him to mention the break-in at the Great Mosque or the theft of the holy relic. He could avoid that subject and still find out what he needed to know.

"Rumors are circulating that a group of high-ranking Arabs are dissatisfied with the Caliph."

"Yes, I've heard these rumors."

"We have reason to believe Umar was one of the leaders," he told her. The investigator watched her closely. Nuzha didn't flinch or reveal any emotion at this disclosure. In fact, she didn't seem surprised.

"That's why I'm here to see you. I need to know if you possess any information about Umar's close associates."

There came a long pause.

Solomon began to feel uneasy, suspecting that the widow might have decided not to cooperate with him.

Looking into her eyes, he remained silent but raised his brows in a questioning gesture.

He waited for her to respond.

"I tried to stay out of my husband's affairs."

Solomon found her response less than convincing. He couldn't help but wonder which affairs the widow was referring to given Umar's reputation as a philanderer. Maybe she was attempting to circumvent his question. Give him a truthful answer, but not the one he was looking for.

Time to apply a little moral persuasion.

"The Imam of the Great Mosque finds himself in a delicate situation and he assured me that you would be willing to help us."

Nuzha took her time before deciding that it might be in her best interests to cooperate. If the Imam were involved it meant that Allah could be looking into her heart and listening to her response.

"He does have a friend named Malik," she sighed.

"Do you know where I can find him?"

"Malik lives in the villa at the end of our road," she explained. "Just travel east as far as the road takes you."

"What can you tell me about Malik?"

"Unlike Umar, he takes care of four wives and maintains a harem of concubines with many offspring."

"That's all?"

Nuzha ran her hands up and down the pillow. She appeared ill at ease and Solomon wondered if she might feel threatened by Malik.

"Umar's friends formed a secret political group. These dissidents are united in a plot to overthrow the Caliphate to reestablish strict Arab rule in Andalusia. That's all I know. I merely overhead bits and pieces of conversations."

No reason not to believe her.

The investigator decided this was a good opportunity to follow up on the dead man's brother.

"Do you think Umar's brother, Hasan, might know something?"

"I doubt it."

"He might have let something slip."

"They weren't very close," she confided.

There was little more Nuhza could do to help him. He decided to cross Hasan off his list of suspects for the time being so he could concentrate on the man named Malik. Nuzha must have sensed as much because the widow took the pillow from her lap and placed it back down on the marble bench.

Solomon stood to leave.

"I appreciate your help, Nuzha."

She rose and the two of them returned to find Jalal and Fatima lost in their own private dialogue. They were laughing at something one of them had said. When they saw the widow and the investigator approaching their embarrassment brought an abrupt end to the conversation.

Solomon turned to Umar's widow.

"I know the way out," he told her.

"I would be grateful if you didn't mention my name when you speak with Malik."

"I understand."

Solomon waited inside yet another vast reception area. He'd left Jalal outside with the horses. He didn't want it to seem like anything unusual was going on and the presence of one of the Slavic Guard might tip off the owner of the villa. A female servant greeted him at the door and invited him inside after he'd stated his business. The servant disappeared through an open archway.

The walls were painted in the same aquamarine hue as the walls of the previous villa. Only this time he observed exquisite gold lettering on the wall identical to the calligraphy Nuzha had hired someone to paint over. He read the stylized Arabic words from right to left. It described the virtues of Abd al-Malik, just as Umar had been the subject of his own villa's script.

Same calligrapher, same theme. Solomon began to suspect that Umar and Malik shared a lot in common. They both held a high opinion of themselves along with the vanity and means to hire one of the finest artisans in all of Andalusia. The investigator wondered how many wealthy Arabs decorated their anterooms in like manner.

The young servant girl returned and waited patiently as Solomon completed his visual inspection. His smile indicated that he was ready to move on, so she guided him back through an open arched doorway leading them to one side of the residence. They arrived at another arched doorway, only this one had been fitted with an oak door. The door stood closed so the servant knocked quietly three times in succession.

Malik didn't come out to greet Solomon upon his arrival.

"Enter," came the command.

The servant girl opened the door, allowing him to pass through. The door closed behind him and the investigator, looking across the room to where a man sat at a richly carved desk, found himself staring at Malik's backside. He observed that the man was writing something and that he wrote left-handed. He expected some courtesy, but this Arab, with his clean-shaven head, continued to write without turning around to bid him welcome.

Solomon looked around the well-appointed study with its impressive library. All of the books appeared to be written in Arabic. Not surprising since this was the principal language of Andalusia.

In one corner, he spied an ornate silver hookah with a glass basin. As he continued to wait for the man to acknowledge him, he couldn't help wonder if Malik's rudeness had been intentional.

The Arab put down his quill and spun around. He followed Solomon's eyes over to the hookah.

"I'd share some shisha with you," he said as he found Solomon eyeing the hookah. "But you're a Jew."

"I don't smoke tobacco."

This was not a good beginning. Malik had already placed an emotional chasm between them, and he'd made it obvious that his rudeness was intentional. Solomon felt his stomach tighten, a pang of discomfort. Don't overreact, he told himself. Attempt to remain composed.

"I'm very busy, but my servant said you came here at the request of the Foreign Minister."

So he'll take a little time out from his busy schedule to insult me, Solomon groused as he held up his hand to display the official signet ring.

"So why has Shaprut sent you?"

"There are some questions I need to ask you."

Malik stroked his dark beard while considering how to respond. His continued silence created a palpable tension in the room. Solomon stared into the Arab's dark eyes letting him know he was refusing to back down. Not a word passed between them. The stare down continued until the investigator decided to take the lead.

"You were friends with Umar abd-Rahman," Solomon began. He found himself tapping his foot nervously on the marble floor and quickly ceased the movement in case it made him appear anxious. "Were you close?"

"Umar was like a brother to me," confessed Malik. "I was closer to him than Hasan."

Solomon wondered if he should mention Ahmad. Did Malik sleep with both men and women? Did he know about Umar and Ahmad? Surely he must have. Focus, Solomon told himself. His sexual proclivities had little bearing on the matter at hand.

"Did Umar ever share with you his feelings about his uncle, the Caliph?"

"The Caliph is a mongrel," Malik uttered with disdain.

Solomon knew the Arab was testing the limits of his loyalty to the Caliphate. Baiting him into agreeing was a ploy to increase his own leverage in the conversation. The investigator had no intention of compromising his own integrity. He chose to remain silent while he thought about how best to proceed.

"Then so was Umar," asserted Solomon.

This time the Arab remained silent. The investigator had thrown out something for him to consider. A devious smile creased the edges of Malik's mouth as he realized that he had unwittingly shared a sentiment best kept private.

"It's not Rahman's background that I take exception to," he said. "It's this idea that Andalusia should be governed based upon loyalty to the Caliph above all else. Our kingdom, founded by Arabs, should be ruled by Arabs. That's what I mean when I say the Caliph is nothing more than a mongrel."

"Did Umar agree with you?"

"Of course," replied Malik. The Arab looked surprised that Solomon was asking a question with such an obvious answer. "And there are many others."

Solomon wanted to delve further into the subject, but he had heard enough to know that the rumor he'd first heard from the Muwallid, ibn Hafsun, had just been substantiated. Malik might share his opinions about the Caliph's approach to governance, but he'd never admit to a conspiracy to overthrow the Caliphate of abd al-Rahman III.

"The Caliph has many weaknesses," the Arab contended. "Don't you agree?"

A wan smile. You don't really expect me to respond to that question, do you? wondered Solomon. It was time to turn his attention back to the reason for his visit. Maybe he could coax Malik into admitting his complicity in the theft of the holy relic. He couldn't mention the break-in. However, a clever ruse would do the trick.

"There's a legend about the Black Stone . . ."

"Never heard of it!" exclaimed Malik, interrupting the investigator. He rose from his chair, his face reddened from anger. Like Umar, the Arab was a tall, powerful man. He took a step forward, an intimidating step. Solomon moved one hand behind his back and clenched his fist. The fist with the signet ring.

"I won't answer any more of your questions, Jew."

"I don't have any more questions for you," admitted Solomon.

"Then you may see yourself out," sneered the Arab elitist.

Solomon relaxed his fist and turned on his heels. He pushed open the elaborate door and retraced his earlier route through the open archway and back to the reception area. He found it deserted. Breathing heavily, his heart pounding and his chest heaving, he stepped outside into the afternoon heat.

The investigator walked angrily down the outside walkway. He was fuming as he passed a young man traveling in the opposite direction. Someone heading inside to spend time with Malik, he guessed. He shot a quick glance at the newcomer. The young man carried himself with an air of superiority. Shaved head like most Arab men, but his beard wasn't full. It had grown in sparsely. He gave Solomon a dismissive look as he proceeded up the walkway.

Jalal and the geldings were resting in the shade of a cypress tree.

It was time to put the two horses to the test.

Time to travel to Seville.

CHAPTER 12

Solomon had already planned the necessary steps. He told Jalal to return the horses to the Caliph's stables for boarding overnight. They would both pack twin saddlebags. Best to travel light since they had a lot of territory to cover in a short time.

This would also make it easier on the geldings. Jalal would retrieve them in the morning and meet Solomon on the far side of the Roman Bridge after the first call to prayer.

The investigator's mind filled with thoughts as he lay down to sleep. There seemed no way to fend them off, the accumulation of a dramatic and unexpected change in his life. He marveled at how a single day could alter the course of one's life, for good or bad. He hadn't seen it coming.

Finish his translation of the writings of Aristotle, continue to write his poetry with hopes of publication, and most of all savor the wonder of his relationship with Sara. That was his new life. It had changed with the appearance of Hasdai earlier that morning. So many unexpected developments coming to the fore.

A vision of the holy relic appeared before his mind's eye. The arm bone of the Prophet Muhammad, from the wrist bone to the elbow joint, resting horizontally in a glass reliquary framed in gold. Even in his imagination the holiness of the object resonated with a powerful charge of energy. This was no ordinary object of the material world he told himself. Unique? Special? These were only words. A poor attempt to describe its numinous nature and how this particular bone suggested the presence of divinity.

The Imam had been shaken to the core. And, rightfully so. What kind of people would perpetrate such an act? The kind who dislodged the Black Stone from the most sacred site in all of Islam. Radical extremists willing to go to any lengths to further their cause. A viewpoint that seemed like an error in perspective, as if they didn't see the world clearly. A rigidness willing to impose itself upon others. A desire born from an unacknowledged deep uncertainty in regards to their own cherished beliefs.

Solomon decided to follow Sara's suggestion. He would seek out Bishop Racemundo to see if the Catholic clergyman could help him understand the motivations behind worshiping relics and just as importantly, stealing them. This would have to wait until morning. It meant one additional stop, and one brief delay. But the investigator felt it might prove helpful. The Basilica of St. Acisclus lay on the road to Seville. Otherwise, he might not take the time.

What next? the investigator asked himself.

Travel to Seville was the obvious answer. Should his first order of business be to search out the Relic Master or the shoemaker? He mulled it over and decided upon the shoemaker. The huge sandal was the only piece of physical evidence in his possession. It offered him the opportunity to make a connection to a real person. One who had committed a still unsolved crime. The Relic Master could wait.

His mind continued its unrelenting flow of thoughts. Be silent chameleon mind, he told himself on this occasion, just as he had many times in the past. The admonition wasn't working, so he decided to get up and pack his saddlebags. The same ones used on his travels to Galicia, earlier in the spring.

The first thing he packed was wrapped in its original cloth.

The gigantic sandal.

So far his only real lead.

Once again, Solomon found himself preparing to leave his small apartment. This assignment from Hasdai, his third and hopefully last mission, might require yet another lengthy journey. How long might he be gone? This no longer mattered to the investigator as long he found the sacred relic and returned it to the Imam in time for its annual procession before the faithful. It certainly couldn't be as long as his journey to Galicia's savage north to track down Lia. Perhaps a bit more time than he'd needed to recover the lost manuscript.

This dwelling, his familiar home, was no stranger to emptiness. The land's previous rulers, the Germanic Visigoths, passed harsh laws against his people. Jews had property seized and they were subjected to economic servitude. Foreign trade and commercial ventures were forbidden them. Everything done to keep them living in squalor.

Like many of their neighbors, and fellow Jews living in towns and cities throughout the Iberian Peninsula, this abode's occupants fled Córdoba. In this case, they probably lacked the funds necessary to relocate to Italy or southern France. If they chose the nearest possible destination it meant North Africa. At least that's what his landlord had told him.

Had they joined Tarek's army during the fateful invasion of 711 CE. Many Jews had returned back across the Straits of Gibraltar with the Arab led Berber armies. One of the principal divisions of this army was commanded by a Jew.

Jewish guides had escorted Muslim armies along the highways of a country unfamiliar to the conquerors, furnished information on Visigoth army movements, disclosed the whereabouts of Visigoth military supplies and hidden wealth, and taken command of conquered cities while the Muslim forces drove deep into France.

The apartment would survive just fine without Solomon's presence.

The leather saddlebags were packed with dried fruits bought at the marketplace as well as a change of clothes, soap and of course, the sandal.

He added one additional item at the last minute. A copy of Muslim historian Ahmad Razi's book on the early history of Andalusia. He'd been browsing in one of Cordoba's hundreds of bookstores when he'd discovered the slim volume two weeks earlier. He also purchased a companion piece. A history by the elder Razi's son, Isa Razi, that began with the ascension of Rahman III in 912. This he left behind.

He simply couldn't imagine having nothing to read on his journey, but his interest in Andalusian history included the Visigoth and Roman eras of which he would learn nothing in the younger's work. He'd already begun reading Ahmad Rizi's history a week earlier not suspecting that he'd be embarking on a journey that the book might help illuminate.

Hasdai had provided rather detailed notes for his mission to far-off Galicia. This time he'd offered nothing.

Solomon believed this wasn't an oversight. Time simply hadn't permitted it and the route they were taking was more obvious. Most students had been exposed to the history of the Via Augusta, the kingdom's most important roadway, if they'd attended the University of Córdoba and taken one of the prerequisite history courses.

The investigator slung the saddlebags over his shoulder and went out through the front door.

Solomon turned the door key counter-clockwise inside an iron lock. He tucked the key into his vest pocket and walked out through the patio. Turning around at the iron gate, he gazed fondly at the dwelling that had served as his home for the last five years. He'd alerted the landlord of his absence. This consideration wasn't required of him, but one he felt a matter of courtesy.

While walking through the narrow streets of the ancient Juderia, on his way to the Roman Bridge, Solomon felt a gentle breeze on his face. The morning air, still cool and fresh, awakened his senses. He spied a couple of feral cats searching for food scraps down a deserted alley. He continued on and soon the bridge came into view. Solomon looked across the wide roadway leading to the far side of the river and found Jalal holding the reins of the two geldings as he waited for the investigator's arrival.

Solomon and Jalal rode along the thousand-year old Via Augusta, a road known to them as *al-Racif*, as they made their way towards Bishop Racemundo's Catholic Basilica of St. Acisclus.

Within Córdoba's city walls were numerous Christian churches such as the church of St. Cyprien; but, the main Christian places of worship lay beyond the city walls in suburban districts, like Sara's eastern *Ajerquia,* with their large populations of Arabized Christians, the Mozarabs.

The Catholic Basilica of St. Acisclus, in existence since the sixth century, lay beside the road to Seville in the suburb known as *Rabad al-Rakkakin*, west of the city walls. This made it a slight, but convenient detour for an investigator determined to visit the prelate to see if he could provide some insight into the widespread desire for sacred relics.

The church was named after a fourth century Christian martyr who, along with his sister Victoria, suffered persecution when he was beheaded at the order of the Roman Governor Diocletian. Before the decapitation the Governor taunted him, "Think about the beauty of your youth, lest you perish." Victoria was killed by arrows and the prosecutor cast the siblings into a fiery furnace. Their home became a shrine and later a church. One ninth century Christian martyr, the priest Perfectus, once served at the Basilica of St. Acisclus.

As he approached the church, Solomon realized he hadn't even thought about what day of the week it was. Fortunately, he wasn't traveling on a Sunday or the Bishop might have been busy inside the Basilica. It was still early in the morning, a bright and sunny Tuesday morning, so Bishop Racemundo could be found at the Parish House. The investigator decided to leave Jalal to keep watch on the horses so he could be alone with the cleric.

Solomon hoped the Bishop could shed some light on the shadowy world of stolen relics. Something that might lead to his successful recovery of the sacred bone relic.

CHAPTER 13

Racemundo suggested they take a walk around the centuries old church grounds, so he and Solomon set out, at a leisurely pace, along a shady lane lined with olive trees.

As they strolled, the tall, bearded and imposing figure, struck the ground with a crosier, a curved wooden pastoral staff. A piece of linen cloth was attached to the staff just below the crook. If he'd dispensed with the handkerchief, he would have looked an Old Testament patriarch.

Bishop Racemundo wore a hooded black cloak. A gold, pectoral cross hung down from his neck on a long chain. An impressive circlet of gold, a ruby set into its center, surrounded the fourth finger of his right hand. Every time Solomon saw this ring it reminded him of another ruby ring. One worn by Bishop Sisnand of Galicia. He concentrated on the present moment to keep his mind from returning back to unpleasant memories.

"Why have you come to see me, Solomon?"

"I need to know why some believe in holy relics," replied the investigator. "And why some might choose to steal those relics."

The Bishop reflected as they continued their walk along the tree shaded path. They came upon a stone bench, just off to one side of the path. It had been strategically placed to take advantage of the shade offered by a massive olive tree.

"Let's sit," suggested Racemundo.

The two men sat on the bench as Solomon waited for the Bishop to enlighten him on the nature of something he'd never given much thought to. He wasn't sure the delay would be worthwhile, but he was hoping for insights he could use to track the thieves.

"Some believe praying to relics might induce a saint to intercede on their behalf with God."

"They're praying to relics instead of offering their prayers directly to God?" asked Solomon. "Isn't that blasphemous?"

"Quite the opposite."

"Well, you've enlightened me before when I entertained mistaken notions."

"I have?"

"Remember when you told me that refusing to eat in prison is an act of courage and strength and not an act of weakness." Once again, Bishop Racemundo had been required to educate Solomon on spiritual matters. Most recently during a detention center hunger strike.

"Oh, yes," said the Bishop smiling. "I'd almost forgotten about that."

Solomon watched as Racemundo rested his staff against the side of the bench, making sure it felt balanced before he continued.

"So back to these relics. It was considered unseemly for ordinary mortals to appeal directly to God for miracles. People believed God would perform a miracle only for a saint out of admiration for the saint's virtues, not for the supplicant. So you see, the request for a miracle could only be addressed to an intermediary whom God admired. To make the appeal in the presence of the relic of a saint--clothing or body parts like fingers and teeth, or ashes--increased one's chances of having their prayers heard. Objects placed near relics are thought to absorb their power. More important is to see and touch them because saints will respond to prayers uttered only in the vicinity of their relics."

Although it seemed a convoluted mental arrangement, the investigator saw there was a certain logic to the belief. But only if one believed they needed a miracle.

"What type of miracles are they praying for?"

"Cures for illnesses, divine protection from natural disasters like drought and plagues, and belief in the possibility of gaining access to supernatural powers as a defense against a terrifying universe," elucidated the Bishop, rattling off the list as though it were committed to memory. "Mostly it's a general desire for relief from disease and suffering. The prevailing view among our faithful is that physical disease has spiritual causes."

Racemundo paused and waited for Solomon's response. When none was forthcoming, he continued with what began to amount to a monologue.

"One thing I admire about Jews and Muslims is your search for the nature of diseases and how you choose to employ physical remedies," admitted the clergyman. "Our church is somewhat negligent in that regard. We offer no real medicine. So, the faithful believe in the exorcism of evil spirits as a cure for physical maladies. Or, pray to a saint in the presence of their relic in hopes God will intercede. I'm afraid there are many charlatans among the priesthood."

"I think I understand what you've been telling me," said Solomon. His statement didn't sound convincing, and he admitted to himself that he still felt somewhat befuddled as he sat with his hands in his lap, twiddling his thumbs. Something gnawed at him, and he knew it to be an important element in his search for the thieves who stole the holy relic from the Great Mosque.

He was still missing half of the equation.

"So why steal a holy relic," he asked. "Surely the saint will look upon the thief with disfavor, even condemnation."

The Bishop let out a hearty laugh. Shaking his head, he couldn't hide the widespread smile on his face. It was time to enlighten the young investigator once again. He placed his hand over his mouth in an attempt to stifle the sound of his laughter.

"I'm sorry, that was rude of me," confessed Racemundo. "It works like this . . . stolen relics are the most prized of all. They are thought to have special powers so they are especially valuable. Abbeys and Monasteries that come by relics legitimately go to tremendous lengths to claim they were actually stolen."

"Where's the logic in that?" Solomon wanted to know.

Bishop Racemundo fingered the cross hanging around his neck, rubbing it unconsciously. He wondered how many of his personal thoughts he should share with the investigator. He had already helped Solomon in the past on two notable occasions.

The first time was when the manuscript of the *De Materia Medica* was stolen from Hasdai's office and the Foreign Minister pressed his poet-translator cousin into service because he knew that he could be trusted to keep the theft a secret while attempting to recover the priceless document.

Then, in late spring, he accompanied the investigator to the prison to visit with two Galician murder suspects, Lia, and her brother Roi, held during an investigation into the murder of the Caliph's nephew, Umar abd-Rahman.

The cleric continued to finger the crucifix.

Solomon's cousin was Hasdai Shaprut, a man the Bishop both admired and respected. Both men, leaders of their respective religious flocks, navigated the same waters, attempting to keep their religions viable under Muslim rule. The Caliph supported their efforts, but there existed others not so inclined. Still, Racemundo and Hasdai remained trusted members of the Caliph's inner circle. They were on intimate terms. For these reasons, he believed he could trust Solomon to be discreet.

"Saints *allow* their relics to be stolen from a prior shrine," explained the Bishop. "It's a sign the saint is displeased with the previous site and prefers their earthly remains to be moved to a new site. For the faithful, the dead saints are still very much alive in their hearts and minds and souls. No saint would allow their relic to be relocated unless they felt in agreement with the site of the relocation. Relics bring pilgrims and pilgrims bring gold and silver. You can see why there is strong competition for them. I don't condone the practice, but I do understand its attraction."

"It seems a bit cynical and greedy, but I guess it's a matter of survival."

"Exactly," agreed the Bishop. "I call it justified avarice. The churches aren't alone in this business. There are individual collectors and they employ professional relic hunters. These collectors allow the faithful access to their relics, but they charge a fee."

It was Solomon's turn to laugh. He couldn't help himself. The thought of charging pieces of gold and silver to touch an object, even one purported to be sacred, seemed a strange notion.

"I believe I've told you all I know on the subject," said the Bishop. "I think it's time we go back."

Racemundo took up his staff and planted it firmly in front of himself. He used it to steady his balance as he rose from the bench.

The two men said little as they walked the pathway back to the Parish House.

Once they'd arrived, a disturbing thought occurred to the investigator. Solomon wondered if he should ask about it, but he knew Bishop Racemundo, as a trusted member of the Caliph's inner circle, would already know about the theft of the sacred relic from the Great Mosque.

It hadn't entered into their conversation, but Solomon was certain that Hasdai, or the Imam, or perhaps the Caliph himself had told the man of God about the break-in and the writing on the wall. Solomon decided to trust his instincts. He might be wrong. If so, he would soon find out. Racemundo's expression wouldn't be hard to read.

"Do you think Bishop Sisnand of Galicia would steal a Muslim relic?" he asked the cleric.

"From what I've heard of his enmity towards Andalusia, and his lack of Christian charity and compassion, it's a possibility."

"Maybe he's attempting to create a war between us and the Fatimids to weaken us so that he can attack Andalusia?"

"Perhaps, but the writing on the wall suggests someone familiar with the history of Islam," the Bishop pointed out.

Solomon's instincts had proven trustworthy. The Bishop's mention of the writing on the wall confirmed what he'd already suspected. Every member of the Caliph's inner circle had been apprised of the theft of the holy arm bone from the Great Mosque. Time had come to remove one more possible suspect from the list.

"So Sisnand doesn't seem likely?"

"I don't think so."

"Thank you for your time, Bishop," said the appreciative investigator.

"I wish you Godspeed, Solomon," Racemundo said in a quiet voice as he offered his blessing. "The future of Andalusia may depend upon your recovering that sacred relic."

CHAPTER 14

Solomon and Jalal returned to the Via Augusta and rode south towards Seville. They began their pace at a trot along the most important road in the Iberian Peninsula, once called Hispania by the Romans who used the term to describe the territories of Spain, Portugal, Andorra, and the southern-most part of France.

When Emperor Augustus went to Hispania between 16 and 13 BCE, his ambitions included the establishment of new towns and roads to connect them. He ordered the construction of the Via Augusta and it became the longest and most important route on the Peninsula. This imperial road formed a major link in a chain of roads connecting Rome with the oldest city in Europe, the port of Cádiz on the Atlantic Ocean. Its strategic importance was due to its dual nature as a military and commercial thoroughfare.

"It's a long ride and we're in for a long day," announced Jalal as he rode up next to the poet turned investigator. "Are you sure you're up to this?"

"Don't worry about me," Solomon answered.

Although there was nothing to worry about, Solomon still felt a bit fatigued from the arduous journey the two of them had undertaken a couple of months earlier. He had decided not to share this fact with Jalal. He didn't want the soldier making allowances for him since he was determined to summon strength from within himself to meet the challenges that awaited them. He simply refused to entertain any thoughts of tiredness.

They eased the horses into a relaxed canter as they entered a gently rolling countryside dominated by olive groves and vineyards. The geldings moved beneath their riders fluidly and effortlessly. Jalal, as the more experienced rider, set the tempo or rather he allowed his horse to set the pace at an easy canter for a couple of miles before slowing to a walk while the horses caught their breath. Then they trotted some more.

The day wore on. The dry heat of the Andalusian summer slowed their progress, but only slightly. Jalal had chosen the two Arabian geldings carefully, making sure to pick smaller, light framed horses with lean, streamlined muscles. Nothing like the sturdier, bulkier mares they'd ridden earlier that year in the mountains of the Sierra Morena and Galicia.

Occasionally, they'd see a patch of grass or a source of water and take a break to refresh themselves. On one such stop, while their well-trained steeds grazed nearby, Jalal's curiosity began to get the better of him.

"We're not bringing tents or a pack mule with supplies on this assignment," he began, stating the obvious.

"We don't have time to be setting up and taking down tents," replied Solomon. "We'll find accommodations along the way."

"Can you tell me what this is all about?" the soldier asked. "General Naja wasn't very forthcoming."

"I'll tell you, but you must understand that we're sworn to secrecy."

"It's that serious?"

"Nothing less than the survival of the Caliphate is at stake," warned Solomon. "This could get very dangerous."

"Which is why I'm here."

"Yes. "

"What are we dealing with, Solomon?"

The investigator proceeded to explain the situation to his escort in great detail: the theft of the holy relic, the monstrous sandal, North African sects, Arab elitists, and unscrupulous relic sellers. After he had finished describing the assignment, Solomon's gaze turned towards the horses. Jalal understood the nonverbal cue and knew that it was time to resume the ride.

The landscape flattened and the olive groves and vineyards became interspersed with fields of barley and wheat and sunflowers as they neared the small settlement of La Carlota. A mosque, a public bath, a solitary caravanserai, and a scattering of sun baked houses left little doubt that this area existed primarily for agriculture.

They found livery for the horses and took time to enjoy a three-course meal inside the village's lone inn before continuing west towards Éjica where they intended to spend the night. They had agreed upon how they would proceed. Jalal would continue to set the pace, but it was Solomon who determined what seemed to the soldier an ambitious itinerary.

Jalal sensed a change in the personality of the investigator. This wasn't the same man he'd accompanied to Galicia. The one with the aggravating lack of focus who was always looking for excuses to sidestep their mission. This changed Solomon Levy stood single-minded and resolute, but there was also an authentic aura of humbleness about him. The soldier felt honored to be serving him, and he vowed to do everything in his power to help him succeed in his mission.

Whatever the cost.

As they approached Écija they noticed first the crumpled Roman walls. Jalal seemed shocked, but his companion knew the story behind the now defenseless city and he shared it with the soldier courtesy of al Razi.

"During the fateful invasion in 711, the Islamic army met strong opposition, in Écija, from the local population while on their way to Córdoba. After a six-month long resistance, the former Roman and Visigoth city capitulated. The original Roman walls stayed standing at this point to protect a city that served as a center of immense agricultural productivity. The land yielded several harvests a year from fields of wheat, barley, and sorghum, and the city provided food for both Córdoba and Seville.

Sometime, early in the tenth century, the city walls were demolished in retribution for local support for the rebel leader Umar ibn Hafsun, the great uncle of the Hafsun whom I questioned only yesterday. The threat of an insurgent army lurking so close to the capital city of Andalusia was too much to bear so the walls remain in their deteriorated condition as ongoing punishment, but they also serve as a warning to other cities of the consequences of revolt."

"A visual reminder not to underestimate the power of the Umayyads," Jalal stated in a matter of fact tone.

"Exactly."

Solomon and Jalal rode on towards Écija under a deepening twilight sky. They had made good time during this leg of their journey as both horses and riders enjoyed cooler temperatures during the evening hours.

The city's urban nucleus had always been situated on the left bank of the Genil River. Solomon wisely chose to steer clear of the river. He wanted to avoid the hordes of mosquitoes breeding near the water during their peak season. Instead, he selected a location on the outskirts of the city in an area dominated by the ubiquitous caravanserais.

They entered a welcoming caravanserai and relished an opportunity for rest and recovery from the day's journey. They rode through the thick-walled exterior and soon found themselves in an open courtyard.

Travelers and merchants mingled in the cool shade of the caravanserai.

The inside walls of this enclosure had been outfitted with a series of bays and niches and stalls accommodating all: merchants and their servants, animals, horses and camels, and a wide array of goods for sale. After arranging for bedding and feed for their mounts, the two men replenished their dwindling supplies. They decided upon separate rooms and Solomon looked forward to retiring in peace, alone to reflect upon personal thoughts.

They strolled the grounds, glad to be out of their saddles and on their feet for a change. They had a bite to eat, but it had been another long ride, so they retired to their quarters shortly after the muezzin sang out the final call to prayer.

Solomon's room didn't amount to much. A plain wooden table set back against one wall upon which he immediately placed his saddlebags. A single bed, barely big enough for one person to comfortably sleep on, stood in the middle of the room.

But it was a bed with mosquito netting surrounding the frame. Precautions had been taken to prevent untold grief and lack of sleep. The owners didn't want their patrons attempting to doze off to sleep only to be kept awake by an annoying buzz in their ears. Or be subjected to a constant itch upon awakening. The netting compensated for the sparse furnishings and the investigator assumed Jalal's room was furnished in a similar manner.

As he lay in bed, safely ensconced inside his netting, Solomon thought about his previous assignment. Upon his return, he had soon realized that the immaturity of his previous attitude had compromised his mission to Galicia. He was fortunate that the outcome had been successful. Still, he felt ashamed of himself as he recognized that his cautious approach might have meant devastation for his people. Not just the Jews, but all the peoples of Andalusia and the Umayyad Caliphate. This time he would do all within his power to make sure he didn't repeat his previous mistakes.

In the past his thoughts, a kind of ceaseless and meandering internal monologue, would have occupied his mind at this late hour. Now he felt determined not to dwell upon the thoughts that came to him. He felt tired and his body ached. Not quite to the point of exhaustion, but he welcomed a good night's sleep. One that would revive him for another hard day of riding. One that would bring them a day closer to recovering a sacred relic whose annual appearance at the Great Mosque would ensure the future of all the religiously tolerant people of Andalusia.

They would begin their adventure once again in the morning. One day, one more important step bringing them closer to recovering the holy relic.

That was Solomon's last thought before his head sank down into a soft pillow for a night that brought him a series of wild and uncontrollable dreams.

Upon waking, he didn't remember most of these dreams. He tried to imagine short segments of scenes, but none had stayed with him. None that had any influence on his waking mind. Except for one. The sword fight. The last scene before awakening to the day, an experience charged with an energy created by its own light. One in which he felt his heart pounding in his chest.

He was somewhere in the middle of a dark dungeon. He knew not where. The cavern dimly lit by a couple of torches set into the walls. He found himself wielding a sword and engaging a menacing red-caped adversary. They thrust and parried, but neither could gain the advantage. The sharp, metallic sound of swords clashing. Dueling on until neither man had energy left to continue the fight.

The struggle finally ended. Stalemate. No advantage. The black-haired swordsman, sweat dripping from his brow, grinned as he took one step back and raised his blade in a gesture of salute.

It suddenly occurred to Solomon, right in the midst of his dream, that his foe was also his comrade and that the most courageous thing he could do was befriend this shadowy figure. They were no longer enemies. The two had become of one mind as the morning call to prayer echoed over the rooftops.

A new day had dawned.

The dream, illuminated by some mysterious interior source of light, lingered in his consciousness as he lay in bed preparing himself inwardly for the day ahead. Then he drew aside the netting and rose from his bed eager to resume the quest for the stolen sacred relic.

Solomon discovered Jalal outside in the courtyard of the caravanserai. The sun hadn't yet risen above the walls; they stood in shade. The soldier wielded a long sword as he rehearsed different strokes with deft precision. Solomon found the coincidence, his dream and the soldier's practice, curiously pleasing. Like those times when the stars align and destiny feels like its unfolding as naturally as we came to be upon this earth.

Our intrepid investigator continued to observe his Slavic escort, one of the Silent Ones. Only Jalal was unlike most of his fellow soldiers from Eastern Europe. Most of these Slavic soldiers chose to live apart, demonstrating little interest in learning the Arabic language or assimilating themselves to the dominant Muslim culture. Jalal took a keen interest in learning the language of Andalusia. He reasoned this path would aid his rise through the ranks and the achievement of his ultimate goal, attaining the status of a free man.

So he still spent weekends with an Ibero-Muslim woman, a convert to Islam. And she graciously tutored the warrior, teaching him the rudiments of reading and writing Arabic script. And they ventured out into the markets for a little practical application. His desire to learn the language was one reason he'd been chosen by General Naja to protect Solomon on their mission to Galicia. That, and his fearlessness and unparalleled skill with a sword.

The soldier continued with his practice until he sensed someone watching him. He turned to find Solomon staring in appreciation. He slowed his swing and lowered the sword to the ground, placing the blade next to an empty sheath. Next to this lay another sheath, this one holding a second sword.

"I brought two swords with me," Jalal informed him. "One is for you."

"For me?" asked the investigator, walking up closer to the soldier to get a better look.

"You do know how to use a sword?"

"I took a class at the University."

Jalal frowned.

"Don't look so worried. The instructors are among the best in the world," Solomon assured him.

The soldier didn't look convinced.

"Unfortunately, I've never put what I learned to use," admitted Solomon.

Jalal smirked as he leaned over and bent down at the waist. He picked up the sword he'd been practicing with and handed the hilt over to Solomon.

"Show me something."

The investigator grasped the sword, felt its heft, and practiced a few slashing moves. Then he executed a quick sidestep and pretended to fend off an attack. The moves were coming back to him because he had subliminally stored memories in his muscles that hadn't been forgotten. Memories subject to recall through the senses. It was like learning to play a musical instrument, putting it down for years, and then picking it up again to play melodious music.

"I want you to use my sword," Jalal said as he generously offered his favorite weapon to the investigator.

"Are you sure?"

"You might need it to save your life," the soldier told him. "You said this mission could be dangerous."

Solomon knew he was holding a valuable object. A sword of this quality possessed many merits besides its material value: a weapon offering physical protection, one creating spiritual power through the necessary strong body-mind connection needed to wield such a blade, and an armament capable of yielding a sense of deep emotional security.

"It won't disappoint you."
"I'm sure it won't."

CHAPTER 15

Solomon and Jalal arrived at the Muslim version of Carmona.

There had been many versions before this.

Thirty thousand years earlier nomadic hunter-gatherers arrived in the area. They evolved into agricultural peoples forming loose confederations of villages about five thousand years later. Phoenicians, seafaring traders from the Middle East, made contact with the indigenous Tartessian peoples in the eight century BCE, but this trade network collapsed two hundred years later during the mid-sixth century.

Enter the Tudetani culture who built their city in the fifth century over the remains of old Carmona while expanding its boundaries. Three centuries later, Carthaginians turned Carmona into an important enclave. They made the mistake of engaging the nascent Roman Empire in a series of wars. They lost the island of Sicily, the Iberian Peninsula, and then watched in horror the sacking of the entire city of Carthage, its population slaughtered and the site demolished enabling Roman expansion into North Africa.

All this occurred before the birth of Christ. All these different peoples, their cultures, and ways of life having taken root here. Generations of people living in the region of Carmona for tens of thousands of years.

Carmona prospered for six centuries until the collapse of the Roman Empire.

The invading Visigoths, who constituted only a tenth of the population, ruled over a local population superior to them economically, socially, and culturally. The conquerors were advanced only in the exercise of arms, but this allowed the newcomers to maintain their dominance. The land suffered.

All this changed with the arrival of Islamic culture in 711 CE.

The city signed a Treaty of Capitulation regulating the relations between the conquering Muslims and the local populace. The agreement allowed for co-existence with peoples of the occupied city, giving residents permission to maintain their own laws and customs, retain property, and practice their religion in return for paying a special tax.

These treaties were much the same throughout the entirety of Andalusia.

Carmona had evolved into a thoroughly Muslim city by the time Solomon and Jalal gazed up at the massive walls of the Córdoba Gate. This gate led into the eastern portion of a city that was virtually impregnable with its forty foot high walls and two-storied towers and lateral access walls. The main arch and side pillars of the alcazar stood formidable and evoked their admiration after the crumbled walls of Éjica.

The two men sat quietly astride their horses.

They had little idea what they'd discover once they passed through that portal.

Carmona felt familiar. As rich and varied as the twin cities of Córdoba and al-Zahra. The Via Augusta led them towards the center of the prosperous city. The streets appeared almost deserted, most citizens taking refuge inside from the scorching summer sun of Andalusia. They passed libraries, schools, an outdoor market, a hospital, luxuriant gardens, and fountains fed by a Roman aqueduct whose source was far away, in Seville. Below the street lay a sewer system also engineered by the Romans.

They halted their progress to have a look at the Arsenal.

This structure, designed to house a variety of armaments and explosives, was built in response to Viking marauders who sailed down the Atlantic Coast, and then up the Guadalquivir River, to launch a surprise attack on the city of Seville. On October first, 844 CE, when most of the Iberian Peninsula was controlled by the Emirate, eighty Viking ships arrived in Seville and attacked it for seven days.

The Emir Abd al-Rahman II, prepared a military contingent to meet them. The results were catastrophic for the invaders, who suffered a thousand casualties. The Vikings made another incursion in the year 859, but were again rebuffed. These raiding parties, though eventually repelled, led to a major expansion of the Umayyad Navy and the development of port facilities along all the Andalusian coastlines.

Solomon and Jalal continued on until they reached the mosque with its marble columns and stone archways. An impressive minaret stood in the middle of the city. They found the public baths, heated by a still functioning underground furnace designed by the Romans, another long block away.

Solomon could have used the Foreign Minister's signet ring to gain entrance to the Governor's Palace, the city's next impressive sight, and perhaps even secured lodging for the night for both him and Jalal. He chose not to because invariably there'd be questions about his presence in the city. Questions he wasn't prepared to answer. He ruled out this option since he didn't want to resort to lies if it came to that. He knew that the person in command was an Arab and, as such, Solomon felt wary. No telling how far the influence of al-Zahra's Arab elitists had reached.

They passed by the Palace. Spreading out from here, subdivisions of houses stretched block after block.

Solomon and Jalal continued on through the city. The investigator wanted to stay the night somewhere near the Seville Gate entrance to the city. This would save them time in the morning. It would also place them in the Arabized Jewish quarter, a neighborhood which didn't literally constitute a physical quarter of the city.

It's possible that Jews first arrived in Carmona with the Phoenicians centuries earlier. They likely remained during the Roman occupation and under Visigoth rule until the Council of Toledo took away their rights and property. They finally returned to the city as did Jews throughout much of Andalusia. Many a Jewish trader earned his livelihood along the Via Augusta.

Solomon knew of a small Lodging catering to these Jewish merchants and traders. Hasdai had referred it because he believed this location would ensure their safely on the route to Seville.

After Solomon and Jalal found livery for the two geldings, they lugged their saddlebags to an Inn which had once been a typical Roman villa comprised of a variety of buildings--the kitchen, the dining rooms, bedrooms, and baths--arranged around a courtyard or atrium with a terra cotta tiled roof which allowed rain water to flow down into the atrium to be collected, decanted, and stored in underground cisterns. The villa had once fallen on hard times, but it underwent a renovation in the Arab style with refurbished bedrooms serving traveling guests.

Nothing extravagant.

A hearty dinner, harmless banter with Jewish traders, and a good night's sleep.

The harmless banter included a description of local sights. The Roman necropolis was by far the jaded traders favorite venue, even eliciting witty anecdotes regarding the dead, comments that might be considered by some to be in poor taste.

Jalal listened intently.

When the two men found themselves alone again, the soldier shared his thoughts.

"Remember when you insisted we visit the Roman Theater when we stayed in Mérida?"

"When you protested vehemently?"

"Yes," admitted Jalal. "Before you told me that you have a proclivity for finding things that have gone missing."

"Where's this leading, Jalal?"

The soldier leaned in closer so he could make eye contact. Solomon gazed directly into the Slav's blue orbs, but the investigator couldn't hide the amused look on his face. Jalal definitely seems intent upon something, the investigator thought to himself. What might it be?

"I actually found myself enjoying the experience," he revealed. "Especially the Coliseum and the gladiator ring. I never imagined such a world existed in the past."

"And what?"

"I wouldn't mind visiting the Roman Necropolis those

men talked about."

"I'll have to think about it, Jalal," said Solomon, in a noncommittal tone.

He didn't want to make any promises. Promises he might regret in the morning. It seemed to Solomon that he and Jalal were reversing roles. He had unwittingly unleashed a more curious side of his companion's nature on their journey to Galicia, but he felt determined not to indulge this aspect of his own personality. Still, the ride to Seville was the shortest of the three days. Solomon had pushed hard to get this far this soon. He wasn't sure what his decision should be.

He didn't want to disappoint Jalal. Mostly because he had been so insistent, almost to the point of rudeness, in Mérida. And also when they had reached the *Finnisterre*, the end of the earth in Galicia. He had been adamant that they go experience the furthest point in the known world.

Solomon decided to wait until they reached Seville before taking time to enjoy the relaxation afforded by public baths. He reasoned one more day wouldn't be too much of an inconvenience. He had brought along one fresh change of clothes, but he reckoned that could also wait another day. Until after he bathed.

Tired from the long day's ride, he excused himself and returned to his room. The investigator climbed on the bed and lay his head down into a soft pillow.

He fell asleep with the matter unresolved.

The following morning, after retrieving the geldings, the two men walked the horses towards the Seville Gate on the city's exposed western flank. Over the centuries this location received the most attention since it had always been Carmona's Achilles' heel. Here, they encountered another massive fortress surrounding the portal.

They mounted a short distance from the gate.

Jalal rode along with Solomon and he remained suspiciously quiet that morning. He'd barely uttered a word during their breakfast of coffee and breads and fruits. He appeared uneasy to the investigator, not his usual outgoing self. Solomon decided not to engage in conversation. He'd wait patiently until the Slav felt ready to share what was on his mind. It didn't take long.

"Have you given the matter of the necropolis further consideration?" he inquired.

"It means that much to you?"

The soldier shrugged, but it was not one of those noncommittal signals. His constituted an apologetic affirmation. Travel had stoked the fires of his imagination and expanded his idea of what the world had been, what it now was, and what it could be.

"This will be our shortest, easiest day of riding?" Solomon asked as his horse continued towards the gate at a slow walk.

"Correct."

"All right, but I won't be taking time to scribble notes for future poems, and you won't be doing any sketching."

"Agreed."

The matter appeared resolved and both men seemed pleased with the outcome.

The Seville Gate loomed before them.

Another impressive two-storied Alcázar guarded the city at this entrance. Here, on the always vulnerable west side of the city, catapults were placed along the tower's platform to defend Carmona in case of attack. The Roman walls and gates, improved upon by the Muslims, created the sense of a nearly unassailable stronghold.

The two men continued to walk the horses as they left the city through the massive stone portal.

Jalal felt pleased with himself.

Solomon still harbored doubts.

CHAPTER 16

A short ways outside the city wall, as they continued on the Via Augusta, they came upon the ruins of the Roman stadium dedicated to public spectacles back in its heyday.

Adjacent to this was the better preserved Roman necropolis with more than six hundred family tombs dating from the 2nd century BCE to the 4th century CE. Enclosed in subterranean chambers hewn from the rock.

The tombs often contained frescoes and niches housing limestone funeral urns, many inscribed with the names of the deceased. Some larger tombs bore entrances lined with stone benches for funeral banquets and it wasn't uncommon to see carved family emblems.

Solomon and Jalal would not be viewing much of this.

That much had been agreed upon.

They reined their horses off to the right, onto a dirt path that diverged off the main road. A short time later they arrived just outside the entrance to the necropolis where they found livery for their animals. It wasn't much. A few simple stalls fashioned from wood. Solomon didn't balk at paying the exorbitant price that the old livery hand demanded. The Caliph will pay the price of admission to this deathly venue, he reasoned. Why shouldn't he?

They found black-skinned youth hanging around outside the entrance looking to find work as guides. Solomon watched one of them as he made his advance.

They seemed to be taking turns approaching visitors. The youth couldn't have been older than fifteen. His white tunic contrasted sharply with his dark black skin. The investigator wondered if this boy was a North African. He appeared undernourished though he might have been naturally thin. He carried himself with confidence and his sparkling brown eyes suggested a bright mind dwelt behind them. He didn't wear a veil like many North African men. It would've been a hindrance in his line of work.

Solomon entertained a moment of doubt. The presence of these young black men reminded him of his mission and his promise to find and return the sacred bone relic. He would have to keep this short, but how could he deny Jalal?

He now considered his escort a friend. How could he not after all they'd been through together. And Solomon didn't have a lot of friends. Mostly his fellow poets, both men and women, who felt as passionate and dedicated as he about taking Hebrew out of the synagogue and using the language to describe a wider world of love and gardens and daily secular life.

They met occasionally to share their progress and perceptions, always taking leave of one another to go back to work on their craft. The spirit of their times empowered them to continue these efforts in the face of the stiff opposition of Arabized Jews who clung to the status quo. Theirs was a lonely song sung by the wind.

Solomon had spent more time with Jalal during their previous assignment than with anyone else since living at home with his parents and sister, so he wanted to honor their shared existence. He dismissed the lapse in Santiago even though it might have ended tragically. They survived it and the investigator found that forgiveness came easy. The soldier had saved Solomon's life and offered to protect him with his own.

The investigator also admired his traveling companion. Jalal may have been considered one of the Silent Ones because he was one of thousands of Slavic soldiers, mercenaries working for the Umayyad Caliph Abd al-Rahman III, many of whom were brought to Andalusia as children or slaves. Not content to remain silent and apart like his compatriots, he committed himself to learning Arabic as an avenue to help him achieve his overriding goal of gaining his freedom. This revealed his dedication and resolve.

General Naja, the supreme commander of all the Caliphate forces, had accomplished this seemingly impossible task. He remained the exception. He served as the example of what could be accomplished. Although unlikely, it might still be possible. Jalal convinced himself that his destiny included manumission. He knew the Arabic language would aid him in his ambition so what might be considered arduous to some became a labor of love to the soldier.

Solomon wasn't content to have the Hebrew language confined to the precincts of the synagogue. His reading and translation of the work of the Greek philosopher Aristotle gave him a decidedly secular bent. And he wanted Hebrew to encompass this world. So the two men shared a similar trait. Each desired to use language as a means of expanding their world. Both in a personal and a social sense. There was much more that they shared in common, but they hadn't yet discovered what that might be.

The future would reveal these mysteries.

The boy walked up to Solomon as if he had already chosen which of the two men he would approach. As he came closer, the investigator took a closer look at his face: blemish free, smooth black skin; brown eyes shaped like almonds; and curly black hair. He appeared quite handsome until he opened his mouth to speak. Crooked and discolored teeth not only ruined his appearance, but left little doubt he led a poverty-stricken life.

"My name is Abdul and I offer my services to guide you through the graveyard," he blurted out with an undisguised enthusiasm in his voice. "I know many secrets about this place, and I'm willing to share them with you for a small fee."

He certainly makes it sound enticing, thought the investigator.

"We don't have much time," Solomon told the youth quite honestly, knowing the boy would be disappointed because his small fee had just grown smaller. "We'll have to settle for the highlights."

"That will be no problem, Sir," agreed Abdul. "I will show you the Sevillia, and you will be amazed. There is none like it in all of Andalusia."

"Then lead the way . . . "

"Yes, Sir," came the enthusiastic reply.

The young man led them into the necropolis grounds, past a well-preserved circular tomb that resembled a low hill but was actually a vaulted chamber carved out of rock with niches for urns.

Solomon appreciated the sentiment behind the creation of such a structure, but he wondered if the Tomb of Sevillia would prove a disappointment. We could be on our way to Seville, he thought.

They continued walking through an open area accentuated by a scattering of cypress trees until they arrived at a monument built to resemble a complete Roman Villa.

Its vast courtyard, lined with marble statues, contained a deep well built with stone. Beyond lay a massive portico giving access to the tomb. Solomon stopped at the closest statue, that of an attractive young woman, to read the inscription on its pedestal. Ever the translator, he assumed correctly that it was written in Latin.

Jalal followed him over to the statue so that he might listen.

"To Serviliae, daughter of Lucius, wife of Publius Marius, from her mother," read Solomon, translating the words from Latin into Arabic.

The youth stood wide-eyed with amazement at hearing these words translated for the very first time: "Serviliae," he repeated to himself.

"Yes, Serviliae," said Solomon. He'd overhead the young man enunciating the syllables and wanted to reinforce the correct pronunciation. He knew his guide was memorizing the woman's name for future reference.

The boy smiled and then he made a beeline for the portico. The two travelers followed him through the entrance into the funeral grounds, gaining access to a doorway and a small antechamber with a vaulted roof which in turn led into the burial place itself. Frescoes, painted in floral designs and geometric patterns, covered the walls and ceiling of the massive mausoleum. There was an altar and niches for the cremation urns as well as stone tables, each surrounded by three stone benches used for funeral banquets. Another doorway led into, of all things, a bath.

"I did not lie?" asked the boy.

"No, this is quite remarkable."

"Follow me," their guide insisted.

The youth led them into another room, a small sanctuary carved into the mountain. Here they found a marble statue of its namesake, Sevillia. Solomon grew entranced by the man's clean-shaven face: wavy hair parted straight down the middle, unusually long eyebrows, the classic Roman nose, and full lips. He appeared more youthful than one would expect of a successful merchant or politician. Perhaps the sculptor played to his vanity.

"There's more."

Back through the main structure and out through a rear door. They emerged outside, squinting as their eyes adjusted to the bright sunlight. Their guide led them over to a crematory excavated in the rock.

"This is where the funeral pyres stood and where the bodies were cremated."

The blackened rock gave proof to the assertion. Not that Solomon doubted him.

"There's much, much more," their guide promised. "I can take you to the Tomb of the Elephant."

Solomon looked to Jalal and was met with raised eyebrows. The kind that expressed anticipation.

"This is fascinating," admitted Solomon. "But I'm afraid we must be going now."

The investigator couldn't help but see the looks of disappointment on both of their faces. As much as he wished he could comply, he understood that it was out of the question. He'd given in once, but not again. Their mission took precedence no matter how interesting it might be to continue with the tour of the tombs.

Solomon withdrew a leather pouch from his pocket, opened it, and took out a shiny gold dinar which he handed to the boy. A bright, appreciative smile indicated the guide's satisfaction with the generous payment. Much more than expected for leading such a brief visit to the vast necropolis.

"Now, if you'll lead us back out."

"Yes, Sir."

They returned to the Via Augusta on well rested horses.

Feeling the hint of an early morning breeze led Jalal to increase the geldings' speed to a brisk canter. Best to make good use of the time before the hot Andalusia sun slowed them down. That and a twinge of guilt for taking time off from their assignment to visit the Roman necropolis though he'd found the experience fascinating.

This would be the shortest day's ride on their journey to Seville. Only twenty-one miles. An easy ride through a slightly rolling to flat landscape past more fields of grains. The same type of terrain encountered all along the way. Nothing to distract them. Nothing to interfere with keeping their focus on the ride. The horses appeared to be in high spirits. Did they intuit the shorter day's ride, wondered the investigator. Maybe Jalal had talked to them that morning. Would he ever know the answers to most of his questions, especially the most outlandish ones.

They resumed their journey and put distance between themselves and Carmona and it wasn't long before an entirely new element entered into picture. Solomon noticed that Jalal kept looking behind himself as they continued the ride. He didn't think much of it. He knew from experience how the soldier always kept himself on guard. Always on the lookout for unexpected surprises, most importantly the ones that arrived as threats to their well-being.

"We're being followed," the soldier informed him.

"What does it mean?"

"It means we're on the right track," replied Jalal.

"Do you think they're professionals?"

Solomon's mind still retained memories leading it back to the frontier zone. To the five riders who followed them until riding off towards León. The soldier had been convinced those riders looked professional. Their behavior indicated as much since they slowed down or sped up the pace to keep in time with the investigator and his escort.

"I don't think so," asserted Jalal. " Whoever they are, they seem incapable of keeping a steady pace. I have no idea why."

"What should we do?"

"I think we should try to put some distance between us," suggested Jalal. "What do you say?"

"Let's ride . . . "

Solomon and Jalal rode the two Arabian geldings at a full gallop.

The investigator marveled at their phenomenal power, their long, smooth muscles striding out to full length and their large nostrils sucking in air to fuel their flight. At least that's how it felt to Solomon, like they were flying across the plains of southern Andalusia They continued to ride at a gallop for almost half an hour before Jalal slowly slackened the tempo to a lope as he began the process of cooling the animals down. They trotted for a while and finally returned to a walking pace before stopping altogether to give the animals a rest.

The soldier looked behind them. Their pursuers were nowhere in sight.

"I think we've lost them," he announced.

"We'll be in Seville far earlier than I planned."

"Don't be surprised if we see them again," warned Jalal. "Whoever they are."

He's right, thought Solomon. If they were being followed it was only a matter of time before their pursuers, however inept, caught up with them in Seville. That is if they could find them. A Jew traveling with a Slav wouldn't be that difficult to spot on the streets or to make inquiries about. So there was a good chance their whereabouts would be discovered.

The investigator wondered who these men might be. If he and Jalal were chasing the thieves who'd stolen the sacred relic, who were the men chasing them and why? What about Seville? Would the Shoemaker or Relic Master reveal something that might help them recover the holy arm bone of the Prophet Muhammad?

CHAPTER 17

They entered Seville through yet another gate built into one more city wall.

After boarding the horses they headed for the center of the city carrying their saddlebags over their shoulders. The sweltering summer sun burned down on them, and they were sweating by the time they reached the city's main plaza with its impressive mosque, built over the foundations of a Visigoth Christian Basilica. They found an even more impressive quadrangular shaped Alcázar, located at the far end of the plaza.

The Alcázar served as an armed fortress complete with a Governor's palace set amidst fragrant flower gardens and orchards of fruit trees. Fountains, ponds, pools, and irrigation channels, all fed by the waters of an aqueduct running parallel to the city walls.

It was built in 913 by order of Rahman III, sixteen years before he declared himself Caliph, soon after the city had nearly capitulated to the rebel ibn Hafsun. The fortified castle became known as *Al-Qasr al Muriq*, The Verdant Palace.

Solomon chose to resist the luxurious accommodations the Governor surely would've offered them. He wasn't sure how widespread the network of Arab elitists might extend and Seville had a long history of resistance to Umayyad rule. He didn't want to risk the success of his mission for a night or two spent in relative comfort.

So they rested in the shade of an orange tree, one of

dozens in the deserted courtyard of the mosque, knowing they wouldn't be allowed inside the Muslim house of worship since neither man was a convert to Islam. However, Jalal was considering adding his name to those fueling an ongoing, steep increase in the curve of conversion.

"Tomorrow this courtyard will be packed, because Friday is the Muslim day of worship."

"Good timing," agreed Solomon. Having grown up in Córdoba he had long known the calendar of the three main religions of Andalusia and also their days of worship: Friday for the Muslims, Saturday for the Jews, and Sunday for the Christians. He might have shared this bit of knowledge with Jalal, but he didn't want to seem like he was taking on airs.

"My woman has been telling me about the teachings of the Prophet Muhammad."

"You always refer to her as 'my woman.'" Solomon pointed out. "Does she possess a name?"

He might have asked does your woman possess a name, but that wording might have been mistaken for disrespect. Anyway, the investigator felt certain that Jalal had not meant "my" as possessive, but rather in a familiar sense like in an intimate relationship.

"Her name is Bahja," cooed Jalal. He sounded pleased with his answer and Solomon sensed there was something more he wanted to share. The soldier smiled to himself with a far-away look in his eyes, picturing *his woman* in his mind's eye. "It means beauty."

"She must be lovely."

"She's beautiful," sighed the soldier, not realizing the obviousness of his choice of words.

The holy relic, thought Solomon. All this chatter is interesting, but there is more important business to attend to. He left Jalal to his daydreaming while he reached over into his saddlebags and withdrew a map with an address written upon it with an arrow indicating the investigator's route lay to the northeast in the direction of the old Jewish Quarter of Seville.

He nudged Jalal in the shoulder to bring an end to the soldier's reverie.

"We'd better be off."

They turned to leave the courtyard just as a familiar face entered it.

Solomon recognized Ibn Hawqal immediately. The intense brown eyes and his tunic made of white cotton because the material breathed, helping to alleviate the discomforts created by the afternoon sun. The geographer didn't take on airs. His world travels dictated he take a more practical approach to dress. Comfort preferred over style. The man seemed lost in thought as he walked towards the orange trees.

"Ibn Hawqal," said the investigator in a loud tone that registered somewhere between normal speech and a shout, one that conveyed his surprise. Once he had the man's full attention he didn't hesitate to come directly to the point.

"At first I wasn't sure I recognized you," he began. "What are you doing here?"

The geographer looked up and his brown eyes opened wide. It appeared obvious that he also felt a victim of surprise.

"Hello, Levy," said Hawqal, greeting the investigator like a long lost friend. "How are you?"

He didn't answer my question, Solomon noted. He's charming and polished and diplomatic All the traits of a successful spy. Best take a similar approach.

"Imagine encountering you here, in Seville."

"I'm going into the mosque to pray."

He's good, thought Solomon. He has avoided the question twice already. This wasn't going to be easy, but two can be circumvent just as easily as one. It was the investigator's turn, and he hoped he could be just as skillful as the geographer.

"The lectures didn't go well in Córdoba?"

A pause as Hawqal considered his response before offering it. This indicated a man who thought before he spoke.

"Actually, quite the opposite," he bragged. "They were a resounding success. I only hope my presentations at the University of Seville are received with such enthusiasm."

Maybe Solomon had misjudged the man.

"You're lecturing at the University of Seville?"

"Yes, it's one of a series of lectures I'm offering here in Andalusia," Hawqal responded gleefully. "I'll be off to Cádiz after this."

"We wish you every success, Ibn Hawqal."

"That's kind of you."

"Please, don't let us keep you from your prayers."

"Thank you, prayer is very important to me," said Hawqal, revealing a spirituality Solomon found quite refreshing. "It helps me remain grateful and humble for all the blessings in my life."

The conversation ended on a tonic note. Hawqal smiled and continued on into the orange trees in the direction of the mosque while Solomon and Jalal left the courtyard and walked out to the cobblestone street. They turned and headed for the Alcazar.

Solomon couldn't help but wonder about Ibn Hawqal's presence, in Seville. Such an unusual encounter.

Was the geographer following them? Was he really delivering a lecture at the University of Seville? Perhaps the lecture tour had been arranged at the last minute. Maybe it's a convenient cover for a Fatimid spy.

The investigator didn't have time to follow up on any of this because he remained obsessed with one overriding goal. They must find the thieves who'd stolen the holy relic from the Great Mosque. They must remain focused.

They passed by the fortified walls of the fortress and entered a warren of white alleyways and narrow streets with beautiful homes whose patios remained in bloom year round. They turned down another street which led them to a small plaza with shade trees and a gurgling fountain. Solomon stopped to consult the map.

"We're getting close to our destination," he advised Jalal.

They continued down another narrow street. Solomon felt awkward carrying a sword by his side while for Jalal it felt like an appendage, just another part of his body. With saddlebags slung over their shoulders they turned down another alleyway before veering off to arrive at their destination.

They entered the front patio through an unlocked iron gate and discovered a fountain lacking water along with empty flower beds. It didn't seem promising and the investigator wondered if he had been given the correct address. Jalal shrugged his shoulders and shook his head. He was wondering the same thing.

Solomon went to the front door and rapped on it.

"I'll be right there," promised a voice from the other side.

They waited.

The door opened slowly.

"May I help you?" asked an old man peering at them suspiciously.

"We were given this address by Hasdai Shaprut," declared Solomon.

"Hasdai Shaprut," repeated the old man. "Easy enough to say the Foreign Minister gave you my address."

Solomon showed the skeptical old man the signet ring. The man's eyes widened with a look of recognition. He gazed fondly at the ring for a moment before opening the door wider so that the two men might enter.

"This way please," he beckoned.

They were led into the old man's dwelling and were surprised to find fresh cut flowers in vases, scattered throughout the living room, vases set down on tables and on the tile floor. Solomon glanced over to his companion. Jalal's expression registered disbelief. They both looked back to their host. The old man smiled at them as if he knew what they might be thinking.

"My housekeeper brings the flowers," he explained. "Please be seated and rest yourselves. You look like you've traveled a long distance in a short time."

Is it that obvious, wondered Solomon as he took his saddlebags off his shoulder and rested them on the floor. Jalal did the same before taking off his sword and laying it over the saddlebags. Solomon followed his lead.

Like the vases of flowers, large pillows lay scattered around the room. The travelers plopped themselves down on a matching pair while their host remained standing.

"I am called Samuel."

"Solomon Levy and this is my friend, Jalal."

"I see you are armed," the old man pointed out.

"The Foreign Minister told us we are on a potentially dangerous mission."

"May I offer you some water or perhaps wine?"

"No thank you," replied Solomon politely. He studied the old man's wrinkled face. Crowned with gray hair, and covered by a gray beard, it exuded an aura of world weariness offset only by sparkling blue-gray eyes. There was a softness in those eyes and a gentleness in his voice. His simple cotton tunic appeared well-worn, but clean. Probably laundered by the housekeeper. She, or he, was nowhere in sight. But, the old man had said the word "brings."

"How is young Hasdai?" Samuel asked.

"Why did the Foreign Minister send us here?" probed Solomon, ignoring the question.

"Because I am in his employ."

"You work for him?"

"I am an old man so people pay little attention to me as I wander about the city," he told them. "I hear idle bits of gossip and pick up snippets of information as I make my rounds."

"You're a spy?"

"I like to think that I'm a friend of the Foreign Minister," came the old man's response. "His interests and my own often coincide."

Solomon didn't venture a guess as to what those interests might be. Instead, he shifted his weight in an attempt to get comfortable on the worn out, threadbare pillow.

His thoughts turned towards cousin Hasdai. So much he still didn't know about the man. The extent of his power and widespread influence. Who he knew and who he "employed." This old man for one. He watched as the informant finally sat himself down in worn out padded chair . Apparently this was a sign that it was time to get down to business.

"We're looking for a shoemaker named Faraj."

"The name sounds familiar, but I don't know where you might find him. I think we should go to the mosque this evening," Samuel suggested. "There'll be an outdoor market and food stalls. I bet if we ask around we might get lucky."

Jalal had remained quiet the entire time, allowing Solomon to dominate the conversation. He decided to speak his mind.

"Seems we don't have a choice."

Always stating the obvious, mused Solomon. A soldier through and through.

"You're going to join us?" asked the investigator.

"I am the eyes and ears of the Foreign Minister here in Seville."

The sweet aroma of grilled vegetables wafted in the air surrounding the mosque of Seville. Solomon and Jalal felt famished so Samuel led them over to his favorite food stall where the threesome ordered couscous with vegetables. Solomon paid for the dinners and the three proceeded to devour a meal accompanied by ceramic goblets of water. Fresh, clean water brought into the city by the ancient Roman aqueduct.

The investigator looked around the vicinity of the mosque. Merchants had set up their booths, displaying their wares on tables and rugs. Spices, silk, nuts, fruits and vegetables, and carved ivory boxes. An amazing hodgepodge of goods. He gazed down at the saddlebags sitting by his side. Tucked securely down inside it lay the gigantic sandal.

Once they'd finished eating, Solomon felt eager to begin his quest.

The old man sauntered off to see what information he could glean, talking up the merchants while feigning interest in their goods. Solomon and Jalal took a different approach. They went around asking people at random if they knew of the shoemaker and where they might find him. They all came up short. Many had heard of his reputation. Nobody knew where to find his workshop.

Solomon wasn't about to give up. Yes, they'd had a difficult time. It had been a disappointing search. Still, he felt determined to continue. At least for a time. If people knew the location of the shoemaker's shop nobody was admitting to it.

Then he saw a young Arab man walking with two young women, perhaps his girlfriend and sister, or two girlfriends, or two sisters. He decided to take a chance since he'd come up empty so far.

The investigator approached the trio with a friendly smile.

"I'm looking for a shoemaker named Faraj," he told them.

"He's my uncle," said the young man, much to Solomon's surprise.

He'd gotten lucky as Samuel had phrased it. He might have reflected on the nature of getting lucky, but there wasn't time.

"Can you take us to his shop?"

"Follow me."

Samuel saw them and began to walk in their direction with the intention of joining them. Solomon waved off the old man. Didn't need him tagging along. He might slow them down. A wan, knowing smile as Samuel quickly turned and walked back towards the mosque as the youth marched off, leaving the two young women to fend for themselves.

He led the way down a busy side street. He wasn't walking to the northeast. Not in the direction of the Jewish Quarter. He led them in the opposite direction into a neighborhood where Arab Muslims, Muwallids, Mozarabs, Berbers, and Jews lived in co-mingled harmony, somehow managing to live and work side by side in relative peace.

They passed yet another street market, only these merchants worked breaking down their stalls and packing up for the day, so they had to sidestep their way through the chaos. The young man set a brisk pace. Down a narrow side street, and then another. Sidewalks made of cobble stones until they arrived at a door one step up off the street. There existed no sign out front indicating a shoemaker's shop.

The young man knocked on the door and it was opened by an older woman.

CHAPTER 18

The youth explained to his aunt that the two men who accompanied him to the front door were intent upon talking with the shoemaker. Both assumed, and quite naturally, that the men were interested in purchasing custom-made sandals.

"My aunt will take you to see Faraj," he told them. "I'll wait outside for you."

Solomon and Jalal entered what appeared to be the family's living room. They followed the woman into a back room, a simple kitchen and dining area. A large woolen rug had been spread out upon the floor for communal meals. Nothing pretentious, nothing to suggest the shoemaker had acquired wealth or was highly successful at his craft.

At the rear of the dining space this dwelling opening out into a large shop area where cork and leather stood stacked in piles. To the right of the enclosed space, they discovered the shoemaker's workshop. The lady opened the door for them and allowed them to enter. She didn't follow them inside or explain their presence to the shoemaker.

"May I help you?" he asked, opening his mouth to reveal several missing teeth.

"Mind if we have a look around?" asked Solomon.

"Please, be my guest," he invited with a lilt in his voice. "Or, should I say guests."

Solomon walked around the shop. He found a handful

of letters, all written in Arabic script, tacked to the walls. Testimonials from appreciative customers. He recognized the names of several of Córdoba's Arab elite. Apparently Layla hadn't bothered to write a reference for the shoemaker.

Beneath the written endorsements were a couple of shelves, attached to the wall, with samples of the shoemaker's art. All possessed the telltale signature of the artisan, the two different colored corks. Andalusia had emerged as one of the world's few consumer cultures over the past decades and this man surely benefited from the kingdom's wealthy connoisseurs.

The shoemaker took time out from his work to observe his customers. Their dress didn't suggest that they were affluent, but he didn't want to insult them, so he remained quiet. Solomon returned to the shoemaker holding his bundle, unwrapped the cloth which he handed to Jalal for safekeeping, and then he held up the gigantic sandal for the shoemaker to view.

"I believe you made this sandal."

"I'll have to take a closer look," asserted the shoemaker. "There are many imitators these days."

The investigator handed him the sandal for further inspection. The man studied it closely, turning it over two or three times.

"Two men came into the shop together," began the shoemaker. "One was a giant of a man. A black-skinned man. He wore a veil so I didn't get a look at his face. I can tell you he would stand out in a crowd."

"And the other man?"

"An Arab. He didn't wear a veil, but he did have a hood on his tunic, and he pulled it up over his head."

"You didn't see his face?"

"Just a long nose," recalled the shoemaker. "And, blue eyes. I remember his eyes because the color surprised me."

"You made them sandals?" inquired the investigator.

The shoemaker inspected the huge sandal once more just to be sure he wasn't mistaken. He rubbed his fingers along the edges feeling for a slight bevel. He placed the sandal back on his workbench once he felt convinced that it was his work.

"Just the giant. He asked if I could repair his sandals," the shoemaker finally answered, looking up from his bench. "I told him they were beyond repair, but I would be happy to make him a new pair. A better pair. He said they were in a hurry to get to Córdoba. I offered to put my other work aside and I told him I would give him a good price. He consulted with his companion. The other man nodded his assent."

The shoemaker paused.

"Go on," prodded the investigator.

"I've never crafted a pair of sandals that big in my entire life," the shoemaker said. "I should have charged him twice my normal fee, but I wasn't thinking. His friend seemed pleased that we were able to conclude our transaction. He paid me and thanked me politely and then they left the shop."

"And the giant left wearing the sandals?"

"He was grinning from cheek to cheek," said the shoemaker proudly. "I thought that was the end of it. That I would never see them again."

"They came back?"

"Yesterday."

Solomon looked to Jalal and the soldier's raised brows indicated he'd been listening to the shoemaker's story as well. Yesterday meant they were close on the trail of the thieves and stood a good chance of recovering the sacred relic.

"Morning or afternoon?"

"Late afternoon."

"What happened yesterday afternoon?"

"They returned to the shop for another pair of sandals," announced the shoemaker. "They claimed the first pair had been stolen, but I had my doubts. The Arab said he'd wait and again they wanted them immediately. I looked up at the giant. You don't argue with a man of that stature."

"I'm sure you don't," agreed Solomon.

"The giant came into the shop barefooted so I measured his feet, and they waited for me to finish a rush job on the sandals. I don't usually like to hurry my work, but the Arab insisted. He claimed it was urgent. They seemed to be in a rush again. This time I made sure to charge a hefty premium."

"I would like to keep the sandal," declared the investigator.

The shoemaker picked it up from the workbench and handed it back to Solomon.

So the two thieves--at least one of them was a thief-- had been to this shop.

"Did you see them carrying anything with them?"

"The Arab kept a small package tucked under his arm."

The investigator assumed this package contained the sacred relic.

"Anything else you can tell us?" Solomon wanted to know.

"No, I'm sorry."

"Thank you for your cooperation."

The shoemaker came out from behind his workbench and showed them the way through the house, to the street, where the young man waited patiently to take them back to the center of the city. Solomon gave their guide a gold dinar as a reward for his help, and they followed the youth back through the now deserted streets.

They reached the vicinity of the Mosque as twilight began to darken the sky and discovered that Samuel had waited for them to return. He offered them shelter for the night and the threesome made their way back through the Jewish Quarter's warren of alleyways and streets until they reached the old man's home. Few words passed between them. Hasdai's informant friend may have been curious, but he also knew how to be discreet.

Samuel offered them his bed, but they weren't about to inconvenience the old man.

They moved pillows together on the living room floor to create makeshift beds for themselves. Certainly not the luxury afforded by the Alcázar, but it offered a safe haven for the night. And Solomon knew he wouldn't be sleeping anytime soon.

The investigator lay on the pillows savoring in his good fortune. Now to make some sense of it. The thieves traveled through Seville on their way to and from Córdoba, and they stopped at the shoemaker's workshop on both occasions. Of that much he was certain. The artisan had no reason to lie to them.

Why had they chosen that particular shoemaker? His sandals were expensive and sought after. Perhaps the blue-eyed Arab was one of the cabal of elitists who wanted to overthrow the Caliph. Maybe he wanted to impress his giant companion. Maybe the obscurity of the shop's location is what appealed to him. Maybe the man wasn't an Arab.

The shoemaker might have been mistaken. There existed blue-eyed Berbers with mixed bloodlines coming from Roman and Visigoth occupations of North Africa and Andalusia. Perhaps he was a Muwallid. They claimed ancestry from Visigoth royalty. Hard to say. Did the answer to these questions make any difference?

What he knew for sure was that the thieves had a day's lead on him.

"Looks like we've reached a dead end," Jalal exclaimed, piercing the darkness with his baritone voice.

So the soldier couldn't sleep either.

"Not yet, we haven't" ventured Solomon. "My friend Layla suggested I see a man called the Relic Master. It's a possible lead. We'll need to follow it up in the morning so we should get some sleep."

"Good night."

But Solomon found sleep impossible as his thoughts turned to Sara.

He hadn't realized how much he would miss her presence in his life. They had been together almost daily since his return from Galicia. Yes, this mission was necessary, even vital to the continued existence of the Caliphate, but that didn't lesson the pain of separation. Her tenderness had made his world a sweeter place and he couldn't wait to return to her waiting arms.

Hoping to dream of the woman he loved, the investigator finally fell asleep.

Three men sat outside around a patio table tucked into one corner of the courtyard.

Solomon hadn't noticed the table and chairs upon his

arrival at Samuel's house. That's odd, he thought. He imagined himself to be quite observant. Maybe he'd been a bit preoccupied by the day's events? Then again, he needed to pay more attention to his surroundings.

The unlocked iron gate suddenly swung open and an attractive young woman entered the courtyard carrying fresh cut flowers in her arms. She seemed surprised to find Samuel entertaining visitors, but quickly regained her composure. She offered the three men a sweet smile as she approached the table.

"Good morning, Rebekah," said Samuel, greeting the young woman by name. "Would it be possible for you to bring us some food?"

"Of course, Samuel," she replied good naturedly.

Rebekah's presence had taken Solomon and Jalal by surprise. They'd assumed the old man's housekeeper was a middle-aged or even older woman. This dark-eyed young Jewess, with her long flowing tresses, was completely unexpected. Solomon chuckled to himself. Hadn't he told himself more than once that the only thing one can safely assume is that one can't assume anything.

While they waited for breakfast, Solomon took the time to conclude one final piece of business. He reached down into the saddlebags sitting at his feet and pulled out a bulging leather pouch. It was small, tied tight by a long leather strip. He held it up for all to see, and then he handed it across the table into Samuel's open palm.

"Your friend, the Foreign Minister, said that I should give this to you."

"After all . . . what are friends for," laughed the old man.

His smiling face gave him the appearance of someone ten-year's younger, and Solomon had no trouble imagining him donning disguises as part of his informant's repertoire. What a chameleon, he thought to himself as Rebekah returned to the table with a plate of fresh fruit: figs, dates, grapes, bananas, and watermelon.

Had the investigator and Jalal actually seen Samuel's kitchen they would have known that it was well-stocked with food and provisions. The housekeeper placed the plate in the center of the table and left to attend to her flowers.

"Thank you, Rebekah," Samuel called out after her.

The threesome ate with their fingers until they felt well nourished, fortified for the day ahead.

"It's been a pleasure, gentlemen," Samuel said as he stood to take his leave. "I'm sure you have important business to attend to." There was a twinkle in his eyes when he said the words. Perhaps he knew more than he cared to share with them. Before they realized what was happening, the old man disappeared into the interior of his house.

They knew they'd never lay eyes on Samuel the Informant again.

CHAPTER 19

Solomon and Jalal entered what appeared to be a book store.

They found it down a long, narrow street barely wide enough for the two of them to walk side by side. The address coincided with the one Layla had provided and she'd remembered the exact location, unlike with the shoemaker, so she was able to provide a sketch of the neighborhood.

Books, all written in Arabic, lined the shelves of the dusty little shop. Their appeared no apparent organization of the titles. Nothing alphabetical. Neither by author nor title or even subject matter.

Working as a translator and poet, the investigator found occasion to frequent dozens of Córdoba's book stores and libraries (there were hundreds), but he'd never encountered such confusion. Then he realized that the book store was really a front. He was there to see a man named Abbas. A man known as a Relic Master.

Jalal picked a book up from a table display and began to browse through its pages. Solomon found it difficult to feign interest, so he cleared his throat loudly and waited to see if there would be a response.

It wasn't long before a man emerged from the back of the shop. As he approached, Solomon observed that his hair and beard were unkempt. He smelled of coffee and tobacco. The man smiled. His teeth were stained a dull yellow and his faded silk tunic was splattered with stains.

He may be a master of relics, but he's not a master of hygiene, thought the investigator. There was important work to do, so he tried to overcome his aversion to the man. Detach himself from his personal feelings. Proceed like the situation was nothing out of the ordinary.

"You're Abbas," Solomon said, in a matter of fact tone.

"And you are?"

"Solomon Levy," answered the investigator. "Layla sent me . . . "

"Layla," said the man arching an eyebrow.

Solomon observed Abbas closely. He'd remained composed at the mention of the courtesan's name. The investigator reasoned that the Relic Master did business by reference only. The phony little book shop was just a convenient front.

"That's a name I haven't heard in a long time," said Abbas in a low, hoarse voice. "How is Layla?"

"She's doing very well," replied Solomon. "She sends you her regards."

"So what is it I can do for you?" asked Abbas as he returned the conversation back to matters of business. Not the business of books. They'd quickly moved beyond the bookstore ruse and into the illicit trade of stolen relics.

"I'm curious about the availability of a special relic," admitted Solomon. He didn't identity the arm bone of the Prophet Muhammad as the source of his interest. He wanted to see how Abbas would respond.

"Please, follow me."

Solomon complied with the request while Jalal remained behind in the bogus book store to ward off any possible intruders. Neither man could imagine an actual customer coming into the fake shop.

Abbas led Solomon to the back of the shop and

through an open doorway. They entered a cavernous workroom lined with display cases clearly marked and filled with a variety of relics arranged by type: hair, teeth, bones, bits of clothing, and even small bowls of ashes. An emporium of every kind of relic one might imagine. It appeared highly organized. Not being inclined towards the collecting of relics the investigator found it all quite amusing. He decided to take a more serious approach and conduct himself in a businesslike manner.

So he walked down the aisles perusing the goods on display and feigning interest.

"This is quite a collection," he observed.

Abbas stationed himself behind one of the displays. Having seen his own collection many times, he wasn't about to spend time following a potential customer down the aisles. He didn't employ the hard sell. The fawning salesmen wasn't a part of his repertoire. His cool detachment had always proven the most successful marketing demeanor.

"I enjoy access to much more," bragged the Relic Master. "Much, much more."

"I'm impressed," lied Solomon as he continued down another aisle making his way closer to the display case hiding the lower half of Abbas' body.

"My scouts are currently working in France and Italy."

"Still, I imagine you're not quite ready to compete with the Pope," joked Solomon.

"Not quite yet," agreed Abbas. "I'm working on it."

Solomon stopped and turned so that he could look the Relic Master in the eye. There came a long silence while the two men appraised one another. Both were good at superficial banter, but this was not why either of them were there in the Relic Master's lair. Both men knew that it was time to put the pleasantries aside.

"In my line of work one never knows who to trust," claimed Abbas.

"I imagine not."

"You mentioned that you're curious about one particular relic," Abbas stated in no uncertain terms. "Would you care to explain yourself."

The question felt like a challenge. Solomon had no doubt about that as he walked to the end of the aisle and went over to join the Relic Master. Behind the display case, concealing half of the Relic Master, a many colored rug with a floral design lay spread upon the floor. A hookah sat placed strategically in the center. Abbas motioned to the set-up and the two men sat choosing opposite sides of the rug.

Time to put aside all pretenses.

"I'm interested in the arm bone of the Prophet Muhammad."

"I assure you nobody has come to me to offer such a treasure," Abbas asserted. "It's value would be priceless. I can think of some who might be prepared to offer a steep price to possess such a marvel."

Solomon observed the Relic Master licking his lips. An unconscious habit, wondered the investigator. Was he itching to get his grubby hands on such an invaluable relic? Had he succeeded? If not, did he know the identity of the thieves who'd stolen the sacred relic from the Great Mosque of Córdoba?

"I procure authentic religious relics for many kinds of patrons," continued the Relic Master. "Some are wealthy collectors who succumb to a passion for collecting a vast array, the kind of collection that might outshine one of their competitors. Most of these individuals are obsessed.

For them, collecting relics is like a rare disease. Some of them charge others for the privilege of venerating their holy relics."

Solomon cleared his throat.

The Relic Master paused and looked disturbed by the interruption. Had something he said caused it?

"Sorry," apologized the investigator as he cleared his throat a second time.

The Relic Master continued, "These collectors are not alone in desiring to get their hands upon these treasures. Many of my clients are clergymen who engage my services in acquiring relics. I try to oblige them as long as they don't ask too many questions. I sometimes have to engage the services of associates."

Church robbers, thought Solomon. Abbas doesn't employ scouts. He hires church robbers to stock his inventory of desirables. The investigator raised his hand in a gesture that indicated he'd heard enough. And, he certainly had. Bishop Racemundo had explained the nuances of church competition for the legitimacy of their relics.

"I consider mine a sacred calling . . . "

"And Muslims?" asked Solomon. "Do you get many requests from them?"

"Occasionally, but not as often," reflected the relic seller. "They're harder to come by and not as sought after. You might search for a bone dealer. There are some who specialize in specific objects. I myself cast a wide net."

Solomon felt a tightening in his stomach. It grew out of his frustration at not making progress in finding the holy arm bone. He suspected that the Relic Master had been attempting to deceive him. A sacred calling my ass, he fumed. This man only lived to turn a profit from exploiting unsuspecting and guileless clergymen and relic collectors.

No wonder he plied his unscrupulous trade in Seville. He'd have been arrested long ago in Córdoba or al-Zahra. In his anger, the investigator began to understand how Hasdai, in his role as Foreign Minister, sometimes felt it necessary to resort to using pure political power as a means of gaining a legitimate and noble end.

Solomon raised a finger, holding the signet ring up for inspection. This singular gesture left no doubt that he was charged with defending the honor of the Umayyad Caliphate. Abbas leaned in closer to get a better look and his face suddenly contorted. He looked crestfallen. Like one whose world had come to an unexpected and abrupt end.

"You're going to tell me the truth," the investigator demanded. "Otherwise this enterprise will be shut down and you'll be going to prison for a long, long time. And that's not a threat, it's a promise. Cooperate with me and I'll turn a blind eye to your . . . sacred calling . . ."

There was no mistaking the animosity in his voice as his eyes pierced through those of the Relic Master. Abbas, in turn, sighed deeply while considering his options which amounted to none.

"What is it you want to know?"

"I'm looking for two men. One is a giant of a man and the other possibly an Arab," began the investigator. "They stole a holy relic from the Great Mosque and I need to find them. Did they come here to your shop? I want the truth."

"Yes, they came to see me yesterday morning," acknowledged the Relic Master. "The Arab showed me the arm bone and explained its significance. He asked if I was interested in purchasing such a relic. I told him yes and I made a lucrative offer, but he quickly rejected it. He claimed that he really didn't want to sell it. He merely wanted to determine its value."

"Is that all?"

"No, he wanted to know if I knew how he might smuggle the arm bone out of Andalusia without being detected," replied Abbas. "I asked his destination and he said it was North Africa. I told the man that I have a friend who owns a music shop down the street. Three doors down."

"A music shop," interrupted Solomon.

"We share other interests in common."

Solomon guessed they were illegal activities, but he decided not to pursue the matter further.

"Go on."

"I told them my friend might know of a way for them to smuggle the arm bone out of the country."

Layla had suggested that Solomon visit the Relic Master. Sometimes she possesses a mysterious knowing, he thought. Almost medium-like powers. He recalled her connection to dubious characters and an underworld of illegitimate occupations. Maybe she'd been a spy in a past incarnation.

Was this another coincidence or was destiny at work as if everything had been planned down to the last detail? The investigator wasn't sure and he didn't want to dwell on the question. There was a holy relic to recover and time was of the essence.

The Relic Master's story sounded plausible. Solomon would question the owner of the music shop to determine its veracity. He'd find out which side of the street, and then he and Jalal would pay a visit to the music shop. He stood and looked down at the relic dealer, a sad and dejected looking man. At least to appearances. Solomon had met too many good actors during his assignments for the Foreign Minister to believe that he could tell when someone was acting and when they weren't. Still, he had to play the game.

"You better not be lying."

CHAPTER 20

They found the music store three doors down and located on the right side of the street.

A large, black, musical signature was painted on a white tile and mounted above the front door. In a clear window, 'uds, both four and five stringed, were displayed to entice interested musicians into stopping in for a closer look, or rather a closer listen.

They saw more 'uds inside the shop. A wide variety hung along the inside walls at varying heights. Solomon took a quick look at the instruments in the window, but he had more important matters on his mind as he entered the shop.

Jalal didn't follow the investigator inside. He decided to keep an eye on the street. He thought he'd seen someone lurking in the shadows near the Relic Master's place of business. His actions may have been inspired by a brief moment of paranoia. More likely they were a product of a soldier's natural inclination to be extra cautious.

Solomon left his saddlebags, with the giant sandal, in Jalal's safe keeping. His friend remained behind while Solomon went on with his business.

When the instrument maker appeared to help him the investigator didn't bother to look around the shop or pretend to be interested in the 'uds for sale. He came straight to the point.

"I was sent by Abbas."

"My old friend, Abbas," exclaimed the luthier.

Old friend. That description told the investigator all he needed to know about the nature of the man standing before him. Perhaps he wasn't being quite fair. He didn't really know anything about this man or his relationship with Abbas. Then again, the Relic Master sent the Arab and the giant to him and not strictly for his expertise with music.

Solomon wanted to show the man Hasdai's signet ring, but he didn't think the luthier would recognize it so he explained himself.

"I'm here under orders of the Foreign Minister to recover an important relic. One stolen from the Great Mosque," he began. "Abbas told me that he sent two men in possession of such an object to this shop. He told them that you might know of a way for them to smuggle an arm bone out of Andalusia."

Solomon paused to look at the luthier so that he could assess his response. The man was obviously reflecting on what he'd been told. Probably trying to decide whether to cooperate. The investigator decided to make it easy for him.

"Anyone who resists cooperating with my investigation risks their own death," he told the luthier. "It's that simple. Just ask your old friend, Abbas."

This bit of heavy-handed encouragement seemed to do the trick.

"The two men you speak of came to me saying they wanted to buy an inexpensive 'ud," admitted the luthier. "I showed them a four string 'ud devoid of ornamentation. I tuned it and played it for them, but they made the oddest request."

"What do you mean?"

"They asked me to take the strings off the instrument,

They then requested that I create a false bottom. Since I was being paid handsomely, I had no objections. Naturally I was curious, but decided it was best to remain silent and not ask any questions lest I frighten them away. They showed me an object wrapped in cotton cloth. It was an arm bone."

"So you hid the arm bone in a false bottom and replaced the strings?"

"No," replied the luthier much to Solomon's surprise. "I told them I knew a better idea. Once I determined the dimensions of the arm bone, I realized it would be better hidden in a hollowed out fingerboard. They talked it over and agreed."

"How did you manage that?"

"I created a completely new fingerboard for the instrument. Split a piece of wood and hollowed out both sides. I made the fingerboard slightly longer, but to the untrained eye it looked like any other 'ud. "

"That must have taken some time," said the investigator.

"Yes it did, but they had no objections even though they had to wait quite a long time for me to finish the work. They returned to the shop late last night to pick up the 'ud and the blue-eyed man bought a second 'ud. He played a few and selected a five-stringed instrument. It was getting late, but I didn't mind because it turned out to be quite a lucrative day for me," boasted the grinning luthier. "I considered closing the shop today, but those kinds of days are few and far between."

Late last night, Solomon repeated to himself. He and Jalal were hot on their trail. They had undoubtedly left early in the morning. Maybe late last night, but not likely. No time to waste. Time to retrieve their well-rested horses and leave Seville behind. Time to ride to Cádiz and if they were lucky they might overtake the relic thieves somewhere on the Via Augusta.

Solomon didn't think it necessary for him to inspect the backroom workshop. The sacred relic was long gone. On its way to Cádiz, the oldest city in Europe.

"I appreciate your honesty."

Like the luthier had any choice but to cooperate.

Once he was back outside, Solomon shared the gist of the conversation he'd just had with the luthier. His companion marveled at the ingenuity of the instrument maker. The investigator also added one salient detail. He told Jalal how Layla had suggested their visit to the Relic Master. This, in turn, had led them to the luthier.

"Time to go search for two men and a pair of 'uds," said Solomon.

Jalal balked. He left his saddlebags sitting on the ground and turned to the investigator to explain his actions.

"Somebody is shadowing us," he warned. "I want you to wait right here. I'm going to go around the block and sneak up behind them."

"Are you sure?"

"Trust me and you better draw your sword and be ready to use it."

"Jalal . . . "

"They've been following us, or they knew we were coming here and have been waiting for us," claimed the soldier. "Wait here for me."

The investigator turned around, but there was nobody in sight.

Solomon watched Jalal run to the corner, turn, and

disappear from sight. He withdrew his sword, took a deep breath, and attempted to prepare himself mentally for a fight. This wasn't easy. He'd never been in such a predicament. Fencing was merely a sport at the University.

He turned around and looked down the street. Four men stepped out of a storefront and approached him at a measured pace, all with swords pointing in his direction. He swallowed hard and prayed that Jalal was somewhere nearby. He knew he was no match for the four assailants.

"I believe you are looking for me."

Jalal announced his presence loudly in his well-practiced Arabic and the four men quickly turned to see who'd addressed them. The soldier waited until he knew that he held their attention, and then he removed his sword from its sheath. He wasted no time warming up. Smiling confidently, he charged up the street to attack the assailants.

Taken by surprise and now forced to defend themselves against a fierce opponent, the four men had forgotten that Solomon was standing behind them. The investigator heard the clash of swords as the fighting began.

Jalal deftly maneuvered around the four swordsmen until he found an opening. He managed to isolate one of his assailants and made a quick little advance trying to create a response he could capitalize on. A fast movement of his blade created such a reaction and he waited as his overzealous opponent countered the move. The soldier violently turned aside the counter leaving the man open to attack. Jalal's powerful thrust found its mark.

"Ahhhhh ," came the loud, piercing scream as the attacker slumped down to the ground in agony while his three companions renewed the attack.

Solomon, who had been shocked by the violent nature of the attack, realized he was now in a life and death situation and that Jalal depended on him for help. Not knowing exactly what to do, the investigator simply reared back and drove his sword deep into the back of one of the unsuspecting assailants. The man fell face first, straight down onto the cobblestones as Solomon withdrew his blade, ready to join the fray. He never saw the man's face.

The odds were now even.

The two attackers who still remained standing realized they were facing two opponents, one in front of them and one behind. It didn't take long for the two to act accordingly. One continued to face off with Jalal while the second turned to do battle with Solomon. Soon the sound of swords clashing, metal against metal, filled the narrow street with long, loud, ringing sounds as the four men fought at close quarters.

Solomon went on the defensive as his opponent, a man perhaps ten years older than him, sneered and lunged forward thinking he'd found an easy target. The investigator countered the attack, and they disengaged before resuming the fight.

There came another attack by his opponent. He was moving slower than Solomon so the investigator slipped his blade under the attacker's and sent a hard thrust directly into the man's neck. His attacker's eyes bulged out in shock and disbelief. Solomon withdrew the blade and sliced the already bleeding man across the throat.

The assailant dropped his sword and began making loud, gurgling sounds. He grabbed his throat with both hands to stop the bleeding, but it was too late. A look of horror filled his face as he slumped down on the street. It was the look of a man who knew he would soon be dead. His eyes widened for an instant before he closed his lids for the last time.

Solomon turned his attention to Jalal and found him grappling with the last assailant still standing. They fought close up against the wall of one of the shops as the man tried to keep Jalal cornered against that wall with one hand on the soldier's sword, trying to prevent him from using it. He raised a dagger high above his head and it appeared he might be about to stab Jalal.

Without thinking, Solomon pivoted on both feet and swung his sword out in a wide arc, whipping it back around with all his might and driving the blade deep into the aggressor's back. A loud cry echoed between the storefronts as the man collapsed and fell down to the ground before the investigator had a chance to withdraw his blade. Solomon and Jalal both breathed a deep sigh of relief and the blade was pulled out of the dead man's back.

The two men used their opponents' tunics to wipe the blood off their swords before placing them back inside their sheaths.

"They may not have been professional riders, but they certainly were professional swordsmen," Jalal maintained. "You acquitted yourself well, Solomon. I believe you may have saved my life."

Solomon knew his friend was exaggerating, and he had no doubt the soldier would've emerged victorious in the end even without his help. Still, he appreciated the sentiment. "It will protect you," Jalal had told him. In the end, it had protected the soldier.

"Are you all right, Solomon?" asked Jalal. He could see that the investigator was clearly shaken. "You look pale."

"I think so."

Solomon had never killed a man, let alone three in one sword fight. But his instincts had taken over and it was a case of kill or be killed. He chose to live and did what it took to assure that outcome. The experience only served to steel his resolve to recover the stolen sacred relic.

"A well-placed thrust," observed Jalal.

"I wasn't aiming," confessed the investigator. He had been fueled by pure adrenalin and the heat of battle.

"This isn't the University," laughed the soldier trying to make light of the situation.

"No, it isn't," agreed Solomon. Jalal's comment left Solomon wondering if the attack had been orchestrated by Ibn Hawqal. The soldier meant that training to fight and actually fighting were two different things, but it triggered thoughts of the geographer. Was he a Fatimid spy? Perhaps his presence in Seville was no coincidence. He didn't have time to check into it.

"Let's retrieve our things and get out of here."

They picked up their discarded saddlebags and walked hastily up the street in the direction of the livery stables. They would steer clear of the mosque and the city center to avoid getting caught up with the multitudes attending the noontime Friday prayer.

When they'd passed the bookshop on the way up the street, Solomon observed that it was closed to business. That got him to wondering. They continued on a short distance. Then the investigator stopped and turned around to look back down the street where he found Abbas standing outside his front door gazing in their direction.

Could the Relic Master have ordered the attack? Did he possess the kind of power and the types of resources needed to mount such an assault at a moment's notice? Or, were their attackers the men who chased after them on the way to Seville? Abbas waved his goodbye. Perhaps he was just grateful to be rid of them. Solomon didn't reciprocate. He turned back and continued up the narrow street.

The sword at his side no longer felt foreign.

He had made a new friend.

A friend he could trust.

CHAPTER 21

They left Seville just after the noontime call to prayer. They were getting a late start, but felt encouraged knowing that they were close on the trail of the thieves. The horses were well-rested and well-fed so they felt inclined to push the pace, putting an end to the horses' brief vacation. A slow trot, a faster trot, and then an easy gallop along the Via Augusta.

The midday sun forced them to slacken the pace. Not a cloud in the sky, so they took time to stop at a roadside station to water the horses and give the geldings a brief rest. The investigator learned that the Arab and giant had done the same earlier that morning. Much earlier.

Solomon and Jalal agreed to take advantage of their Arabian geldings' incredible endurance. Their goal was to reach the city of Utrera as soon as possible. Once there, they could decide whether to continue on or stay the night. They mounted and rode, and they rode and rode through a level to gently undulating countryside where fields of wheat and sunflowers stretched to the horizon. Few words passed between the two men as they focused on putting the miles behind them.

When they finally found themselves on the outskirts of Utrera, Solomon and Jalal exchanged smiles because there was still a lot of daylight left due to the longer summer days. This would allow them to ride for another four to five hours. They decided to continue on after an extended break in the city.

Utrera shared a history similar to the other towns and cities along the Via Augusta. Settled before the birth of Christ by indigenous peoples, and later conquered by the Romans and Visigoths, it was now a decidedly Muslim city. Much like nearby Seville only on a smaller scale with no discernible Jewish Quarter.

The main mosque was the center of religious life while the markets remained the center of economic life along with agricultural products produced for export. A caravanserai on the outskirts provided all two men and two horses needed. Food, water, and rest for the geldings. Food and drink for the stalwart travelers.

Solomon asked after the blue-eyed Arab and giant, but they had apparently stopped elsewhere. Perhaps inside the city proper. Had they made up time on the robbers? Cut into the thieves' lead? Only the future could answer those burning questions so the investigator and the soldier felt content to fortify themselves for the journey ahead.

They found themselves back on the road in what seemed like no time at all.

The landscape soon changed from wheat fields to mile upon mile of olive orchards. Another change in the scenery as small lakes and marshes came into view. They entered the lower reaches of the Guadalquivir River plains where rice farming took precedence and bird life flourished.

The horses were tiring, their riders beginning to feel weary. They slowed from an easy gallop until they were walking the geldings along the Via. Keen-eyed Jalal, trained from boyhood, pointed out something in the sky overhead. Solomon searched until he spotted an eagle circling upwards in the evening wind currents. They continued on until they saw a city about three miles away.

They wouldn't have seen the city the Arabs called Montújar if it hadn't been built at the top of a hill. By the time they reached it, twilight had transformed the sky into a lavender canvas with a sprinkling of stars. On the lower part of the hill there existed another Roman necropolis. This one paled in comparison to the marvel of Carmona. It mattered not since both men felt too tired to pay much attention to the graveyard.

They left the Via Augusta and guided the horses up a road leading to the highest point on the hilltop city. They stopped about halfway up the hill because it was here that they discovered livery for the horses. After settling the horses down for the night, Solomon inquired about lodging. The stable agent recommended an Inn with a view, but that meant carrying their saddlebags all the way uphill, so they opted for modest accommodations in the same neighborhood.

They settled for an establishment two short blocks away. Two short uphill blocks. There were no options further down the hill. Solomon arranged for two rooms and the two men went their separate ways. They'd meet back up in the morning to resume the mission. What they needed most, after an arduous day of riding, was the renewal only a good night's sleep could provide.

But the investigator couldn't sleep.

He'd never taken another life before, let alone three. He understood it necessary under the circumstances, but he felt like a changed man with no illusions as to what he was capable of doing as a human being. A part of him accepted this need to integrate his own dark side, but another part of him wished that Hasdai hadn't thrust him into a situation where self-defense might be required.

Would he write a poem about this unexpected experience? How to convey that it was unnerving and thrilling and fearful and challenging all at the same time. The rush of emotions. The acting out of pure instinct. A poem? Perhaps one day when he had more time, and could create some distance between the event and the telling.

His thoughts turned to Sara. The last two days had felt like an eternity. Not seeing her and being with her. Not sharing her laughter and good natured conversation. Her interest in his poetry and more. That physical and subliminal chemistry existing beyond what any words could convey. Hint at maybe. Or, maybe not.

He felt homesick and decided it might be best to put thoughts of Córdoba out of his mind.

They still had a mission to accomplish.

He attempted to fall asleep. It was no use. Try as he might, Solomon couldn't give in to slumber. His mind was too filled with ideas and questions, and he knew they'd persist until he acknowledged them, reflected upon their significance.

He began recalling the events of the past few days. It felt so long ago that Hasdai had shown up at his doorstep, in the early hours of the morning, with this new assignment. The stolen holy relic. Would they recover that precious arm bone? A giant's sandal and a message scrawled across the wall of the Great Mosque, "Taken By Command," the only clues.

And now the blue-eyed Arab. He might be a Berber thought the investigator. He knew some of these North Africans possessed mixed blood dating back to the time of the Roman occupation of their homeland. Were Blue

Eyes and the giant taking the relic to North Africa in an attempt to set up a rival Muslim sect? One that might challenge the legitimacy of the Umayyad Caliphate or more likely siphon off Muslim pilgrims and their gold.

Who were they? Exactly where were they headed? Would they succeed in getting the sacred relic out of Andalusia and down to North Africa? Would he and Jalal follow them? Of course they would, but this would jeopardize their efforts to return Muhammad's holy arm bone in time for the annual procession at the Great Mosque. Best to find them before they departed Cádiz. That was the challenge.

The interviews now seemed inconsequential: Hasan, Nuzha, Malik, ibn Hafsun, and ibn Hawqal, and Bishop Racemundo had provided him information, but it had been given over to generalities.

Layla had offered solid hints to assist him in his investigation. Her two leads, Faraj the Shoemaker and Abbas the Relic Master, had actually proven helpful during the investigator's pursuit of the thieves. Had Abbas decided not to cooperate Solomon would have never questioned the luthier and learned how the robbers planned to smuggle the bone out of Andalusia. How clever of the luthier to suggest the fingerboard alternative.

Where were those two robbers now? At the top of the hill sleeping at the Inn with the view? Somewhere along the Via Augusta traveling by moonlight? Further along in the next town? Solomon realized this stream of thoughts and questions was getting him nowhere. He turned over on his side and sunk his head down into the soft pillow. He closed his eyes and allowed his mind to go blank. Embrace the darkness, he told himself. Allow your mind to exist as an empty vessel. Forget the past and don't think of the future. Now is the only reality, he told himself. Sleep the only cure for weariness. The exhausted investigator finally fell asleep.

Nothing could awaken him.

Nothing.

CHAPTER 22

They got back together first thing in the morning. Solomon and Jalal found a place serving breakfast a short block away. A simple, unpretentious place. Only a handful of tables and chairs, but it was already filling up by the time they arrived. The food, as plain as the furnishings, consisted of breads and fruit and cheeses. Both men felt hungry and appreciated the strong coffee that accompanied the meal.

"Sleep well?" Solomon asked.

"Like a rock."

Solomon smiled. Must be nice, the investigator thought. He had slept soundly, but only for half the night. As much as he would've welcomed a full night's sleep, he didn't feel sorry for himself. Quite the contrary. His desire to recover the holy relic, and to return it in time for the annual procession, far outweighed any tiredness he might be feeling.

He felt resolute. Determined to find Blue Eyes and Giant and to recover the holy relic. He'd taken to calling the two thieves Blue Eyes and Giant. He wasn't sure why. Just an easy way to connect to the two strangers. Two robbers whose actions threatened the continued well-being of the Umayyad Caliphate, the fortunes of his people, and the future of all the peoples of Andalusia. There were other, less flattering names he might have called them. He settled for Blue Eyes and Giant.

Solomon was becoming more and more convinced

that the thieves' destination was North Africa and he believed they were part of a Muslim sect, or hired by such a faction, to bring the Prophet's arm bone to a new territory in an effort to establish a legitimate site for the sacred relic.

He remembered the Imam's story about the Black Stone and how that theft failed to come to fruition. Millions of devout Muslims continued to make the holy pilgrimage to Mecca and circle the Kaaba in a counter-clockwise direction. And they attempted to kiss or touch the spot where the Black Stone had been originally set. Kiss the stone in the place it had been and was always meant to be.

Don't think so much, the investigator chastised himself. Eat your breakfast and drink the strong coffee. You have a long ride ahead of you and much ground to cover if you want to catch those two thieves. He reached for a slice of unleavened bread, found his knife, and spread on a thick layer of goat cheese. He took a huge bite and washed it down with coffee.

"There's something I don't understand," admitted Jalal. "Why would they attempt to smuggle the arm bone out of Andalusia in a musical instrument?"

"It's somewhat ingenious, but not entirely original," replied Solomon. "Perhaps they know the story of the Donegal Fig."

"What do you mean?"

"It's a well-known smuggler's trick, but the method has been used too many times in the past to be effective."

"The Donegal Fig?" queried the perplexed soldier. "I've never heard of it."

It wouldn't hurt to give him an abbreviated version of the story. Jalal was probably raised on those plump, juicy

Málaga figs. Everybody loves those figs. They're so delicious they export them all the way to Baghdad. Keep it brief, the investigator warned himself.

"Over one hundred years ago, during the reign of Emir Abd al-Rahman II, an envoy traveled from Córdoba to Constantinople to work in our embassy. His name was al-Ghazal. He saw the fig growing in that city and he admired it. He believed that the Emir would like it as well.

However, it was forbidden to take anything from Constantinople. Al-Ghazal devised an ingenious scheme. He took seedlings of the fig and concealed them among the books that he had wrapped up. He was searched when he took his leave of the city, but his books remained wrapped. When he arrived in Córdoba he removed the seedlings from the wrappings, planted them, and tended them. When they bore fruit he took it and presented it to the Emir. He explained his ruse and the reason behind it and received congratulations on his success. The fig became a cash crop here in Andalusia."

"That's a great story."

"We'd best be on our way," the determined investigator replied in no uncertain terms.

The two men made arrangements to have their leftovers wrapped, and then they packed them at the top of their saddlebags. It was another long ride, and they didn't want anything to slow them down along the way. They could eat when the horses rested without losing too much time. They retrieved the geldings from the livery and soon they rode back along the Via Augusta.

Solomon and Jalal witnessed a caravan of camels and mule drawn carts traveling along the road. They were headed in the opposite direction and accompanied by armed guards because the animals carried gold shipments from Africa to al-Zahra and the Caliphate's mint.

The investigator and his soldierly companion now headed for the place where the crows gathered and it wasn't long before they found flocks of the black birds perched in the trees of a small village surrounded by grain fields. It was little more than a wayside stop accommodating travelers and their animals. The perfect place for a respite since Solomon and Jalal were halfway to their destination of Jerez. A place serving water and food for both horses and riders.

They left the geldings in good hands and walked a dirt trail to a series of outdoor food booths. Their breakfast snacks were long gone, so they ordered pieces of marinated lamb attached to a bladed metal skewer along with bowls of rice. This and cold coffee.

"Did you know that kebobs were first created by soldiers?" asked Jalal.

"No, I didn't know that."

"Soldiers used to grill chunks of freshly hunted animals skewed on their swords and roasted over open fires."

"Sounds reasonable."

A flock of crows suddenly flew off from the trees making a series of loud, raspy caws. They circled overhead for a brief time before returning to the trees. The raucous noise would have made the village a difficult place to spend the night, but Solomon asked after Blue Eyes and Giant anyway.

He learned that they had been seen by many of the villagers the evening before. Giant would always attract attention. They had ridden east in the direction of what was once a large Roman City. It lay three miles away with numerous villas. Many were restored and turned into inns. Although off the beaten path, the area also possessed an added attraction. There were numerous mineral springs to soothe the tired muscles of weary travelers.

The investigator realized that he was only half a day, perhaps even less, behind the thieves. If they had stayed at one of the refurbished villas it meant that they must be well financed. Faraj's sandals and the custom work of the luthier reinforced this belief.

These facts still made it difficult to determine if the sacred relic was being smuggled out of the kingdom to satisfy the needs of a religious sect or an individual relic collector. Did they have a ship or some smaller vessel waiting for them in Cádiz? This possibility seemed unlikely, but he couldn't discount the notion.

For all he knew, Blue Eyes and Giant had already arrived in Cádiz. Where would they stay in the city? How would he find them? By what means would they attempt to smuggle that 'ud across the water to North Africa? There was only one way to find out. He and Jalal would try to catch up with them.

"Let's finish up here."

"Are you in a hurry?"

"Yes," came the enthusiastic response. "We're getting close."

"How do you know?"

"I just know," Solomon declared. "I feel it with every fiber of my being."

CHAPTER 23

They rode the horses at a brisk walk.

The oppressive summer heat required a slower pace, and they wanted to be sure the horses could respond adequately to any threatening situation. Another chase meant another long gallop to escape their pursuers.

So they took precautions. Jalal set the pace accordingly and the investigator followed his lead. They still made good time. By early evening they were passing immense vineyards planted in the chalky soil of southern Andalusia.

Up until then they'd seen small groups of travelers and occasionally a lone individual on their way down the Via Augusta. These and the gold shipment. But the traffic increased as they made their way down to the coast. Small caravans of camels and mules brought imported goods, delivered to the port in Cádiz, up into the interior of the kingdom.

Soon the walls of Jerez rose in the distance under a cloudless, blue sky.

They entered the city through an open gate in the fortified walls, a wooden gate high enough for heavily laden camels to pass under. They followed the paved road to the center of the city where they found a lavish palace and an octagonal shaped mosque in close proximity to one another. The city and its cobbled streets exuded an air of prosperity though they didn't see many people out at that hour.

Solomon chose not to spend the night as a guest at yet another palace. He still wasn't sure which officials might be trustworthy. No telling who might be sympathetic to the elitist Arabs plotting to overthrow the Umayyad Caliphate.

He'd seen a splendid looking caravanserai on the way into the city and decided to backtrack so that he and Jalal might pass the night in relative comfort. Not a palace, but it did offer amenities they hadn't allowed themselves thus far.

The investigator led the way.

They entered the caravanserai. This roadside inn offered a welcome opportunity for rest and recovery from the arduous days of hard riding. They walked the horses into an open courtyard where travelers and merchants mingled in the cool shade provided by arcade galleries.

This would be easy. They didn't have to lug their saddlebags up and down streets after finding livery for the horses. Everything was at their fingertips because a series of bays and niches accommodated merchants and their servants, animals, and a wide array of merchandise. The caravanserai provided drinking water for humans and animals and water for personal hygiene and for the enactment of ritual ablutions.

The dusty duo wanted to enjoy the communal baths before eating and retiring for the night, and these baths proved quite special. They were comprised of three different sections: a cold room, a warm room, and a hot, steamy room. The two travelers opted for the warm room which had underfloor heating like in the Roman baths. Sighs filled the air as they eased themselves down into the warm waters and felt their muscles begin to relax.

"You're really determined to succeed in this mission, Solomon," ventured Jalal as he broke the quietude they had enjoyed during their first few minutes in the bath. They were all alone so he felt safe speaking his mind.

"We have to recover that holy relic," said the investigator rather emphatically. "If we don't, the world as we know it could come to an end. We are the light of Europe, and we cannot and will not allow that light to be extinguished."

Solomon had shared the same message that Hasdai had once delivered to him. Another occasion, a different assignment, but the sentiment remained the same. So did the consequences of a failed mission. No longer would the Jews of Andalusia thrive. They would be lucky to survive. And the same might hold true for all the peoples of the kingdom: Berbers, Muwallids, Mozarabs, and others.

Jalal sensed the *gravitas* of that moment.

"I will do all within my power to help you recover the sacred arm bone."

"I'm getting hungry," said Solomon in a conscious effort to change the subject as well as the tenor of the conversation.

"I'm going to use the cold bath first," declared Jalal. "Care to join me?"

"I'll wait here for you."

Solomon had been quick to respond. He remembered climbing out of a hot thermal pool, in Galicia, and following Jalal's lead when the soldier dove out into the middle of an icy cold river. He smiled at the memory, but it wasn't an experience he wanted to repeat.

"I'll be back shortly," the soldier assured him.

Solomon couldn't remember the last time he'd felt so

relaxed.

He allowed himself a glass of wine with his three course meal that evening. The vineyards they'd ridden past earlier had influenced his senses at some deeper level and this might be his last chance to enjoy a glass. He knew the search would intensify once they reached Cádiz.

Jalal didn't allow himself the pleasure. They found themselves surrounded by chattering merchants and travelers at dinner, so he remained cautious and alert. One never knew who might be observing them. He understood that the investigator needed to unwind a little, but he would remain on duty. He had made a pledge and he intended to see it through. No lapses like in Santiago. There was too much at stake including his personal desire to earn his freedom.

They were about to pay the fare and retire for the night when the owner of the establishment arrived at the table carrying a silver tray with two small glasses filled halfway to the top with an amber liquid. He grinned at his patrons as he sat the tray down at their table.

"I'd like you to sample this liqueur with my compliments," he offered. "I make it myself."

Jalal winced. He knew that Solomon wouldn't dare insult their host by declining his generous offer. In this instance, a refusal would amount to a personal insult given the man's obvious pride in his product.

"Very generous of you," said the investigator. "We'd be honored."

The owner's face lit up as his eyes danced in his head. He turned and left his two customers to enjoy the fruits of what was obviously a labor of love.

Solomon shrugged. What was he to do? He wished he hadn't ordered that glass of wine, but it was too late. He took a slow sip and savored the flavor which tasted dry and slightly nutty and much stronger than his wine. He looked over to Jalal and gave him a nod, a go on now take a sip of your own nod. Jalal peered down at the amber liquid, but he didn't make a move towards the glass.

Solomon waited.

Jalal balked.

The investigator took another slow sip of his liqueur. He then leaned over and poured the remains of his drink into Jalal's glass. The soldier managed a weak smile as the owner of the eatery returned to retrieve two empty glasses. He looked down and gave Solomon a questioning glance.

"I'm so sorry," Solomon apologized. "I forgot that my friend here has sworn an oath of abstinence and celibacy for an entire year."

"And what about you, sir?"

"I would love to indulge in another glass of your liquid sunshine," fibbed the investigator. "However, we must be on our way early in the morning, so I won't be able to follow my inclinations."

"Perhaps you would care to purchase a bottle for your journey?"

"A wonderful idea," replied Solomon. "Thank you so much for suggesting it."

The owner left to retrieve a bottle of his prized distillation. He was grinning from ear to ear. So was Jalal who was also shaking his head in disbelief. Disbelief and relief. He knew his friend to be clever with words, but he found the spontaneity and dexterity of his mind quite remarkable.

"You handled that well," complimented the soldier.

"Thank you, but I'll still have to hold you to your solemn oath," laughed Solomon.

The landscape changed dramatically as Solomon and Jalal neared the Atlantic Ocean.

Sand dunes and marshlands, ponds and wild grasses, and an amazing variety of mid-summer resident birds: larks, orioles, crakes, kites, warblers, pipits, and many more species. But our two travelers barely took notice because once again the Via Augusta became a road with potential danger. No time for observing the scenery.

"I think we're being followed again," announced Jalal.

Solomon turned to look behind them and found a handful of riders back up road at a distance of less than a quarter mile. Who are they this time? he wondered. Reinforcements for those who had met their demise back in Seville? Or perhaps they weren't being followed at all. Maybe the soldier was feeling a bit paranoid.

"Do you think we should try to outrun them?" Solomon asked.

"Only if they make a point of getting closer to us."

"Whoever they are they'll probably catch up with us in Cádiz."

"Exactly."

So the two men began keeping a steady pace, holding the geldings to a brisk walk.

Those following behind made no move to overtake them.

It wasn't long before their noses filled with the tang of salt air. Glimpses of the ocean came in and out of view as the Via meandered its way closer to the ancient city on the Atlantic.

The investigator felt his pulse quicken. He knew that he was getting nearer to the holy relic. At that very

moment the sacred arm bone of the Prophet Muhammad, hidden inside the fingerboard of a rather ordinary
musical instrument, could be found somewhere in the
city of Cádiz. It was in the possession of two thieves who'd
stolen it from the Great Mosque, so Solomon felt certain
that he and Jalal would soon be meeting face-to-face with
Blue Eyes and Giant.

CHAPTER 24

Solomon and Jalal entered Europe's oldest city on Sunday afternoon.

The sun shone down on a town that had become decidedly Muslim. The sun always seemed to be shining here and this section of the Andalusian coastline, extending from Tarifa in the south to the mouth of the Guadiana River, was known as The Coast of Light.

The two men passed through the gated walls and followed the road towards the center of the ancient city. This place evoked Córdoba, only in miniature. Its markets, libraries, hospitals, schools, and public baths felt like it had been plucked up, transported south, and set down by the sea.

But Solomon and Jalal sensed that Cádiz was unlike any city they had ever before encountered, and they entered what felt like an unfamiliar world. They felt anxious, slightly uneasy.

They halted their progress at the impressive mosque with the ubiquitous minaret. The tall, domed structure loomed over a city of one-level whitewashed houses with red-tiled rooftops. The city almost felt African given its proximity to Morocco and its large Berber population. They were visible on the streets and easy to recognize with veils hiding their faces, all but the eyes.

And all eyes turned towards them as they rode slowly down the road.

Perhaps it was the horses. The beautiful geldings

couldn't help but impress with their heads held high, stately and majestic. Animals that befitted royalty. Then again, maybe it was the two riders. A swarthy, dark-eyed Jew and his blonde-haired, blue-eyed companion.

It was probably the unique combination of both elements. The mystery of life revealed. An inexplicable, but ever present reality.

"What's the plan?" asked Jalal in an attempt to ease the tension.

"We'll board the horses at the Castle of the Theater," replied Solomon. "Then I'd like to talk with the Chief Customs Official."

"You know this city?"

"Vaguely," replied the investigator. "I have a friend who shared the general layout with me."

That friend was Layla who'd danced in the city on many occasions and had guessed that the robbers would try to depart from the port if the thieves were part of a North African Muslim sect. It would take them too long to reach Tarifa. They wouldn't risk it. She told him all that she had remembered from the times spent entertaining in the city. And the investigator had been sure to ask pointed questions.

The soldier felt reassured, but only a little.

The Castle of the Theater didn't prove difficult to find. Its high walls and fortifications made it a kind of local landmark. After the Mosque and its minaret, of course. Beyond the tall, erect walls lay the ocean. Deep blue as far as the distant horizon.

They left the center of the city and guided the horses down a narrow street that opened up to a small plaza surrounded by shade trees. Along the walkways were shops: a fish market featuring the daily catch from the bay, a store selling spices and herbs, a fruit and vegetable vendor, and some shops selling clothes and accessories.

They tied the horses' reins to the limbs of a tree and because they hadn't eaten since morning they purchased peaches and nectarines brought over to Cádiz from the nearby tropical Costa del Sol. Jalal suggested that they reward the geldings with a carrot and the investigator concurred. They were limited to one each. They would be well taken care of at the stables of the fortress.

They found the fruits to be juicy with the perfect degree of ripeness.

Now here was a subtle adventure worthy of a poem. A sensuous description depicting a sweet experience. In more ways than one. All the better, he thought. Satisfying, fragrant, and sugary were words that came to mind. A gentle wind blew in from the ocean and they luxuriated in a balmy atmosphere, so different from the sun scorched summer of central Andalusia. They breathed in the salt air and it invigorated their senses. All of this and more. Yes, a poem. But it would have to wait until they returned home to Córdoba.

As he bit into a succulent nectarine, Solomon reflected on the city. There must have been a dozen or more small plazas like this one scattered throughout the city. Not exactly the same, but similar. At least that's what he surmised since this city of neighborhoods radiated off the central square where the Mosque held sway.

Solomon and Jalal didn't know the history of Cádiz, but the investigator knew how to remedy this deficiency. He opened his saddlebags and reached down to retrieve the book. He took it out and began to browse through its pages.

"What are you doing?" asked the curious soldier.

"Al-Razi has a chapter about the history of Cádiz," he replied. "He says we are now sitting in the oldest continuously inhabited city in the western world."

"Go on."

He's interested. Good. I'm not alone in wanting to know more about the world we live in.

"The city was founded by Phoenicians, in 1,100 BCE and it evolved into one of the major port cities of the ancient world when these sea faring merchants sailed west from the Mediterranean Sea, past the pillars of Hercules and through the Straits of Gibraltar, to establish a trading colony on this small island.

From here, they relied upon their superior navigational skills to sail south down the west coast of North Africa and north all the way to Europe's most westerly islands. This happened after they'd already established trading posts on the islands of Cyprus, Rhodes, Corsica, Sardinia, Sicily, and Malta.

He claims it was all about trade.

Their much sought after purple dye became the envy of kings and queens along with multi-colored woven garments, metal work, stone work, jewelry, carved ivory, and glassware. They exported timber: cedar, juniper, fir, cypress, and oaks. They also acted as middlemen, transporting incense and spices from Arabia, and they engaged in searching for raw materials.

The Carthaginians subjugated Cádiz after their First Punic War with the Romans. Hannibal lived here when Carthage began its military campaigns on the Iberian Peninsula. From here he set off to cross the Alps and invade Italy.

But the city fell to the Romans and Julius Caesar bestowed citizenship upon all if its inhabitants as the island evolved into an essential naval base and commercial center. Within the city walls, the Romans constructed an outdoor amphitheater in the 1st Century."

"The Castle of the Theater," interrupted Jalal.

"I see you've been listening to me."

"I seem to be developing a fondness for all things Roman," admitted the soldier.

The Romans were a military culture, thought the investigator. And Jalal has spent most of his life as a soldier. Easy to understand the attraction.

"Shall I continue?"

"Please . . ."

"The city's immense wealth was based on garum. This fermented fish sauce became the most popular condiment in the Roman empire. It was used to give a savory flavor to the dishes of their cuisine. It was produced in various grades and used by all social classes. The best garum brought extraordinarily high prices. The garum made in Cádiz emerged as a major export product to Rome where it was considered among the very best. Large fortunes were made in the garum trade."

"I've never heard of garum," said Jalal. "We should try it while we're here."

"You keep interrupting."

"Sorry."

"You'll like this. It's about the Romans. Al Razi says that most of the wealthy Romans lived on the mainland or on a nearby island. The luxurious lifestyle maintained on those estates led to Cádiz dancing girls becoming infamous throughout the ancient world."

"He actually mentions dancing girls," exclaimed Jalal.

The investigator didn't answer the question. Another

interruption. Guess he can't help it, thought Solomon as he smiled, closed the book, and returned it to his saddle-bags. He didn't need the historian to inform him of what took place after the Roman occupation.

"The Visigoths took over from the Romans and sub-jugated my people for hundreds of years. They were de-feated by Arab led Berber armies during the invasion of 711. The year that my people were finally able to breathe easy here in Andalusia."

Fortified for the time being, they continued on from the plaza. The narrow street led down along the southern side of the island to a sheltered harbor.

The Muslim fortress had been built atop the founda-tion of the Roman Theater destroyed by the Visigoths. What have we got? That's what we'll use. This might have been the slogan of the Umayyad Caliphate from its begin-nings, in Damascus, to its Islamic expansions from Af-ghanistan to North Africa and then on to Spain.

Always making use of existing materials. Building their mosques using marble columns and blocks of stone left by the Romans and Visigoths. It was the same process in the Middle East and Asia. The Umayyads, opportunis-tic scavengers, realized the true value of salvaged mater-ials. Enough to create an Empire.

They arrived at the Castle of the Theater, an imposing battlement with a wide view of the sea. Solomon asked Jalal to proceed on his own. He didn't want idle soldier's gossip to reveal his presence in the city.

The plan was for Jalal to gain entrance to the castle. When questioned about his presence at the fortress he would say that he had come on a secret mission. The soldiers might not believe him, but there could be little doubt that the two geldings were prime stock from the

Royal Stables in al-Zahra. It was just as obvious that the blond-haired, blue-eyed mercenary was a member of the Silent Ones. It wouldn't be difficult to arrange for their safe keeping. He could always drop the name of General Naja if one of his army counterparts needed a little extra convincing.

Solomon held back, still intent on keeping a low profile when it came to making contact with high-ranking government officials. He found it disconcerting to think that he might not be able to trust officials of the Caliphate's Army or Navy. But he was determined to follow his instincts in this matter. One mistake could bring the Kingdom crashing down around them.

The investigator retrieved his saddlebags and waited outside.

Jalal had no trouble gaining entrance to the fortress.

He returned less than an hour later carrying his own saddlebags.

"They were more than happy to assist me."

"So it went smoothly?"

"Not quite," admitted the soldier. "They wanted to know if they could take the horses down to the beach to ride them. I was polite, but firm."

"Good job," complimented Solomon.

"Now what?"

"We need to talk to the main Customs Officer."

Jalal liked the sound of the word "we." He appreciated that his companion had included him as a part of the equation. There had been times when he had felt left out. Times when Solomon questioned suspects, or spoke with dignitaries by himself while he was left outside to guard the horses.

He didn't feel bitter, but it stung his pride. He'd

worked hard to learn Arabic so that he might be considered by others as an equal. True, he wasn't yet a free man, but he felt certain that his manumission would come in time. Yes, he liked the sound of the word "we." Maybe this time would be different. Then again, perhaps that "we" was just a figure of speech. He would find out soon enough.

CHAPTER 25

They found the Customs House two short blocks away.

It made sense to locate it close to an Army facility so they could draw upon its resources if any trouble arose. Smugglers were always attempting to devise ingenious methods for trafficking illegal goods both into and out of the harbor. Some of these operations became well financed and also well-armed. Caliph Rahman III relied heavily upon his customs revenue and transgressors were dealt with rather severely. But they never tired of trying.

Solomon was good to his word. Both he and Jalal, saddlebags slung over their shoulders, walked into the reception area and approached the nearest official. The investigator explained that he was on an assignment for the Foreign Minister, and he asked to see the main Customs Official.

They followed the man down a long hallway to an office with a closed door, and he asked them to wait outside as the low-ranking bureaucrat entered the room and closed the door. Along their way down the corridor Solomon and Jalal had taken the opportunity to peek inside open doorways where they found men pouring over ledgers and stacks of documents.

A short time later, the door opened and the official left to resume his duties.

Standing inside the open door and waiting to greet

them was a tall black-skinned man dressed in an official uniform. Was Customs a part of the Navy, wondered Solomon as the man bowed politely and invited them inside. They followed him into a spacious office that dwarfed those already seen. Two wooden chairs faced a matching desk and the man gestured for them to be seated as he went around and sat down in an upholstered chair. They placed their saddlebags on the floor as they complied.

They found the desk and chairs situated in such a way as to give everyone seated a magnificent vista of the wharf and all its activities. What's a Chief Customs Official without a view of the docks, mused the investigator.

"Welcome, gentlemen," the man said with an easy smile, one unaffectedly sincere. "Nizar mentioned that you are here at the behest of the Foreign Minister."

Solomon held up his hand to display the signet ring. He watched the man's eyes study the ring before him. A smile of recognition filled his face. The Chief Customs Officer recognized the royal seal immediately. He had obviously seen the ring before at some time in the past. This indicated he had also been in Hasdai's presence at some point. The investigator lowered his hand to his lap.

"I am Nasr Abdul," he announced. "I am at your command."

Two Abdul's in one day, thought Solomon. It was a common name so he gave the coincidence no more thought.

Jalal squirmed in his chair. The soldier wasn't used to having anybody at his command. In fact, quite the opposite. He usually found himself working under somebody's else's orders. Some Slavic officer barking out instructions to him and his fellow Silent Ones, and always in their original Slavic language. This was a new experience, and he didn't find it an unpleasant one.

"We're on a rather sensitive mission," Solomon began. "I hope we can count upon your discretion."

This came delivered as a statement and not a question.

"I am here to serve the interests of the Foreign Minister."

"That's what we were hoping to hear."

"I worked for Hasdai Shaprut at the Customs House, in Córdoba. After he was appointed Foreign Minister, I became aware this position might become available. I requested a transfer and promotion so that I might work closer to my homeland and my family, in Morocco. He agreed and arranged for me to assume this office upon the retirement of my predecessor. I have served Allah and the Caliphate faithfully since that time."

Solomon understood that Nasr Abdul's loyalty to the Caliphate was beyond question. As well as his devotion to Hasdai. The investigator was certain many of the elitist Arabs had also expressed a desire for this fabulous duty station. The weather alone was reason enough, and it was likely many bribes were offered to the Foreign Minister.

Hasdai was once the Chief Customs Minister for all the Andalusian ports. This was a huge responsibility. The Caliph rewarded him with this lucrative and sought-after position in return for his loyal services as a physician. Poison had emerged as the most popular mode of revenge in mid-10th century Andalusia. Hasdai was considered an expert in antidotes. Summoned to the palace to treat the Caliph during a debilitating attack, the physician used his knowledge of herbal medicine to affect a cure. He might just as easily have poisoned the Caliph while acting as an agent for one of the ruler's numerous enemies.

He earned the young sovereign's trust and respect for his integrity and it wasn't long before Hasdai accepted a promotion to Foreign Minister. The trusted Jewish leader had emerged as one of the most powerful men in the kingdom. Hasdai was never an office seeker. His meteoric rise to prominence had materialized because he placed his intelligence and his talents, not to mention his amazing erudition, in the service of the Caliphate.

Although Rahman III approved all Chief Customs Official's appointments, oftentimes it was after considering the endorsement of his Foreign Minister, who in turn was acting upon the recommendations of other high-ranking officials.

The position in Cádiz had only become available after the previous official had relinquished his post. This newly appointed Chief Customs Officer seemed to be a man who could be trusted. And why not? He'd been assigned an important duty station on an island with mild winters. A location closer to his family, in Morocco. He'll help facilitate the search for the two thieves, Solomon told himself.

"Not that I didn't serve in good faith before that," added the Chief Customs Officer in case there be any doubt.

He's established his allegiance, thought the investigator. Now it's time to return to the matter at hand. The recovery of the sacred arm bone of the Prophet Muhammad. And the search for Blue Eyes and Giant. So the investigator shared the details of the robbery of the Great Mosque and the theft of the holy relic. Nasr Abdul looked genuinely shocked that anybody would commit such a sacrilegious act. The smile quickly vanished from his face.

There was more so Solomon laid out the details of

their journey from Córdoba and how they'd out distanced their pursuers on horseback. He told of the encounter with the Relic Master and the ingenious method by which the relic was hidden in the fingerboard of an 'ud. He spoke of the attack in Seville.

"I can assign men to protect you," offered Nasr Abdul.

"That won't be necessary."

"What would you like me to do?"

"Have your men keep their eyes peeled for a blue-eyed Arab, or perhaps Berber, traveling with a dark-skinned giant of a man. A man who will stand out in a crowd. They may attempt to gain passage on one of the ships departing from these docks so be on the lookout for the 'ud, but don't tell your people why we're looking for these men and the instrument. Just ask them to report back and take appropriate action if they encounter any suspicious activity. Especially if anybody attempts to bypass customs, or offers a bribe. They just might be desperate enough to attempt to smuggle the holy relic out of Andalusia illegally, which is the only way they could get it out."

"I will do all that I can to assist you," promised Nasr Abdul. "I will give instructions for my men to be on the lookout for these two men you described and the 'ud as well."

"We also need for you to check ships to see when they are departing," instructed Solomon. "Find out who is loading or unloading goods destined for North Africa."

"Anything else?"

"Yes, we're wondering where they might attempt to launch a private boat."

"Difficult to say," replied Nasr Abdul. "There are a number of small beaches and coves on the island. Our waters are patrolled by the Navy in an effort to reduce smuggling. They might slip through, but it's unlikely."

There ensued a long pause in the conversation as all three men reflected upon the task before them. Each man knew what was at stake. Not just the continuance of their own private lives and personal ambitions, but the future of a kingdom whose vast intellectual wealth and material prosperity led a foreign observer to deem it the "ornament of the world."

The pause continued.

Nobody spoke.

The investigator couldn't help but look out the window towards the waterfront where he discovered dock workers loading and unloading ships from all over the world: amber coming in from the Baltic region, tin imported from Britain, and Andalusian silver exported to the rest of the world. Some of these goods would make their way up the Via Augusta.

Sea gulls flew overhead, unfazed by the activity below.

Solomon looked up and found Jalal and Nasr Abdul staring at him. His reverie broken, he realized that he still needed to attend to practical matters.

"We're looking for a place to stay," he ventured to say.

"You must stay at my house as my guests," insisted Nasr Abdul.

"I appreciate your generosity," said Solomon. "However, we're attempting to keep a low profile."

"In that case I have a friend who owns an Inn down by the waterfront. He caters to sailors and their appetites."

Solomon imagined women of questionable morals carousing with long overdue sailors. Men who had been at sea for long stretches of time. This didn't seem promising although he wondered if Jalal would mind the inconvenience. He decided to answer for both of them.

"I'm not sure we'd get much sleep under those circum-stances."

"No, no," laughed the Chief Customs Officer. "I meant the sailors tend to be voracious eaters."

Relief and the laughter it generated eased the tension in the room.

"In that case, we're grateful," responded Solomon. "You've been very helpful."

"Please give my regards to the Foreign Minister when you see him again."

Solomon didn't share what he was thinking, but it weighed on his mind.

If we see him again.

CHAPTER 26

The importance of the Customs Office in Cádiz cannot be overestimated.

Although the subject didn't come up in Solomon's meeting with Nasr Abdul, the principal reason for its existence, besides regulating international trade, was its proximity to Tangier and the sub-Sahara trade route bringing a most essential element to Andalusia: gold.

The city of Tarifa, though closer geographically to North Africa, didn't have the advantage of the proximity of the Via Augusta as a direct link to al-Zahra and Córdoba.

The metal was mined in the gold fields of West Africa at Bambuk, Boure, Lobi.

Two routes from these mining areas converged at Taghaza before combining into one route continuing north to Sijilmasa, a city and trade center situated on the fringes of the Sahara Desert, extending for five miles along the Ziz River, in the Tafilatt Oasis. Sijilmassa, the northern terminus of the trans-Sahara trade route, became the most important trading center in the Maghreb.

Its rulers and merchants had been made wealthy from the precious metal mined near Timbuktu, in the Niger Valley. From Sijilmassa the gold was transported by caravans of camels more than 1,.400 miles to Fes and then on to the port city of Tangier. Loaded on ships, it made a relatively short sea journey to the docks at Cádiz where it was placed under the control of the Customs

House and protected by the joint forces of the Caliphate's Navy and Army.

The reason the gold trade came directly through Cádiz? The Via Augusta remained the fastest way to get it to al-Zahra and the Caliphal mint. Silver coins (*dirhams*) remained the mainstay of monetary system in Andalusia. Gold coins (*dinars*) were not minted on a yearly basis which only added to their value.

Solomon and Jalal found the Inn recommended to them by Nasr Abdul. They entered the premises and sought out one of the employees. They mentioned that they had been sent by the Chief Customs Officer. The Innkeeper was called out from a back room to attend to them personally, and he arranged for two spacious rooms in a quiet area of his establishment. Each room, furnished in simple decor, opened out to a lush garden patio. With the door left open, birdcalls and the sounds of the sea could be heard. Nothing had been left to chance. The two travelers even found prayer rugs on the tile floor for the devout.

Nasr Abdul exerted a powerful presence in the city and the investigator and the soldier became the beneficiaries of his influence. They had obviously been given the best rooms at the Inn. Rooms designed with people of means in mind. Ones the sailors couldn't afford. Probably reserved for those arriving late by sea, conveniently located close to the waterfront.

Solomon wondered what the sailors' accommodations looked like, but he wasn't going to pursue this curiosity. They took to calling their new home away from home the Inn of the Sailors and not the Inn by the Sea.

When it came time to eat, they entered a cavernous dining room. The hungry sailors, boisterous and loud, had Jalal feeling quite comfortable amidst the male comradery. Solomon not so much. The attentive Innkeeper led them to an area in a far corner of the room so that they might converse over the din.

They sat cross-legged on the ground with pillows at their backs and off to one side, an arrangement creating an intimate enclosure. Seating areas looked much the same throughout the dining area although some enclosed spaces accommodated six to eight men.

The menu was simple. The catch of the day served on top of a bed of rice. Hearty food. Sailors fare. Caught in fishing nets out in the bay. That night the owner served a delicious sea bream. Nothing fancy. Just the whole fish cooked and laid out over a bed of rice. No three course meals like they enjoyed in Córdoba and al-Zahra. Every table included a bowl of garum, the savory sauce so important to the Romans and now serving as the city's specialty.

The investigator and his traveling companion decided to forgo adding the condiment to their food after trying a brief sample. Jalal's fondness for all things Roman was bound to include some exceptions.

They ate with their hands, picking out small chunks of the dense, juicy white fish and enjoying its clean taste and delicate flavor. Solomon bemoaned the lack of vegetables, but he didn't openly complain. He felt hungry and the meal satisfied, being both appetizing and nourishing. They drank water because the Inn of the Sailors served no alcohol. They found this surprising since it catered to sailors. However, the owner and innkeeper, a devout Muslim, maintained a strict discipline.

The sailors may have been loud, but they remained decidedly sober.

They finished eating and Solomon took a small clove from his pocket and slipped it into his mouth to freshen his breath.

After dinner, they strolled down along the waterfront where waves washing in from ocean splashed against the pier. They walked down the street, turned around, and went back in the opposite direction. This gave them a chance to view the wharves and to get to know the basic layout of the dock area. Longshoremen still worked at the loading and unloading of seafaring vessels, but it would be busier in the morning with ships readying for departure.

Then it would be easier for Blue Eyes and Giant to lose themselves in the crowds of workers and passengers and sailors and customs officials. The two men stopped to gaze out at the Atlantic Ocean. North Africa lay to the south. They couldn't see the Dark Continent, but they knew it was out there somewhere in the distance.

Birds fished out in the Atlantic with hopes of one last meal for the day. Dining on fish just like Solomon and Jalal. Sans rice. Raw. But ever so nutritious. All competing for the abundant sea life: squawking seagulls, slender terns with their long pointed wings and forked tails, black razor bills sporting white undersides, and plunge diving gannets.

A low-lying full moon, big and fat and surrounded by pink clouds, lit up the twilight as they made their way back to their rooms. A balmy breeze blew in off the bay giving the summer night a tropical feel. The scene felt otherworldly. Africa felt so close. Its presence almost palpable. Its mystery unfathomable.

They arrived back at the Inn of the Sailors and made their way to their rooms.

They agreed to get back together at first light.

It was important to get an early start.

They said goodnight to one another and went their separate ways.

Solomon found it impossible to sleep.

He rested atop his bed and closed his eyes. He thought about Sara. How much he missed her. This mission had put their plans to find a place where they could live together on hold. Such a disappointment. For both of them. He saw her sweet face before his mind's eye for a fleeting second, but he didn't have time to dwell on his personal life. The best resolution to his problem was to recover the sacred relic as soon as possible and to return it to the Great Mosque.

His thoughts turned to the assignment, and he found his mind whirling with so many possibilities. A torrent of thoughts that he couldn't prevent from flooding in upon him. Would Blue Eyes and Giant head for the waterfront and take the first vessel they could book passage on? But that's what they'd be expected to do. Could they be smarter than that? Did they have a boat waiting in some deserted cove and where might that be? Were the Navy and Army and police also looking for them or was this a secret mission?

Knowing Hasdai and what was at stake convinced the investigator that his cousin was relying upon him and Jalal to succeed without bringing in any additional outside resources.

He wondered if he and Jalal had been followed after they left Jerez?

Solomon tried to imagine what Blue Eyes and Giant might be thinking. Were they trying to keep a low profile?

How could they accomplish that with Giant attracting attention everywhere he went? Why him? Would they attempt to pass him off as some kind of new Deity if he returned to North Africa with the arm bone of the Prophet Muhammad?

They seemed nowhere to be found. Almost like they had vanished. Perhaps they were lying low before they made their move. He'd ask around the waterfront in the morning, but maybe they'd decided to stay nearer the city center. Perhaps they had passed the relic on to others who would complete the mission for them. Maybe not.

Who were these two men and where did they come from?

Earlier that night, down at the waterfront, he had wondered if the thieves destination might be North Africa. He remembered Hasdai telling him that the ruler of Sijilmasa was considering declaring himself Caliph. The precious relic, unique throughout all Islam, would bolster his claim to legitimacy. Abd al-Rahman III would move quickly if this situation presented itself.

The Umayyad Caliphate maintained a strong presence in North Africa and had established bridgeheads on the south side of the Straits of Gibraltar. From their African outposts a watchful eye was kept on the region through a network of spies. Rahman III cultivated Berber chieftains in the area to prevent them from drifting into the orbit of the competing Fatimid Caliphate.

The Fatimids wouldn't interfere. They would let the Umayyads do their dirty work for them having no desire to see a Berber ruler set himself up as a rival Caliph representing the Islamic world.

Solomon entertained another disquieting question.

Could he really trust Nasr Abdul?

    With all these possibilities swirling around inside his mind he finally gave in to sleep.

CHAPTER 27

Solomon opened his eyes.

The room appeared much brighter than he expected. After years of getting up during the predawn hours, to work on his poetry by candlelight, he had become an early riser.

It shocked him to see so much light in the room and he knew that he had overslept. This assignment weighed heavily on him. Mentally, and most of all physically. He tried to overcome his weariness for the sake of the mission, but on this occasion he'd failed.

He dressed quickly, went to Jalal's room, and he knocked on the door.

The door opened and the soldier greeted him with a smile.

"Are you ready to go?" asked Jalal.

"Sorry," apologized the investigator. "We don't have time to eat."

"I've eaten."

Another "sorry" was all Solomon could muster in the way of an apology. He felt downhearted because he knew that he'd compromised the assignment by sleeping late, but it didn't seem that late. Jalal, too, was an early riser given the life of a soldier. He decided to take things in stride.

"It's only been light for a short time," Jalal said, consoling his companion.

They were soon back out on the street and Solomon

set a fast pace as he headed for the waterfront.

He didn't really have a plan and this too bothered him.

The wooden wharves were a hive of activity. Mostly laborers loading ships for their morning departure. Heavy lifting with no shortage of grunts. Customs agents were present in their crisp uniforms, working their checklists and matching the lists against the cargo to make sure the Caliphate received all the export duties it was entitled. This was serious business.

Solomon and Jalal held back, stopping on the corner of the waterfront's main street. The one feeding the wharves. They scanned up and down, but no sign of Blue Eyes or Giant. Such a fruitless approach. Just hoping to get lucky with no real leads. The investigator began to feel impatient. Had they slipped past while he overslept? They kept looking. Nobody stood out from the crowd. Certainly no giants.

After a frustrating hour, the investigator decided that it was time to leave. This was made easier knowing the Nasr Abdul's agents were also keeping a lookout for the two robbers.

Solomon devised a plan of sorts. They would backtrack to the Customs House, which was surely open by now, and check in with Nasr Abdul. If he had nothing of interest to share with them, they would walk up to the mosque. Ask around a little. This approach had succeeded, in Seville, when he was attempting to locate the shoemaker.

They walked a couple of blocks. Away from the waterfront. The Customs House was open for business just as the investigator had imagined it would be. They sought out the same low-ranking official who'd helped them on their first visit hoping familiarity would help them gain quick access.

They weren't disappointed.

An office door opened and their smiling guide filed back out past them as he went back to fulfilling his normal duties.

Nasr Abdul, his white teeth contrasting sharply with the ebony black face, welcomed them inside. The two visitors sat in the same two chairs as they had on their first visit. Solomon was tempted to gaze out the window to the waterfront, but he squelched this impulse. He had to remain focused.

"Anything to report?" he asked the Chief Customs Officer.

"I'm afraid not."

"You'll get word to us if anything develops?"

"Of course."

This proved disappointing, but the investigator knew they were all facing a challenging situation. Since there wasn't anything else to say, Solomon rose from his chair and offered the Chief Customs Officer a curt bow from the waist. This was reciprocated. Jalal stood and followed suit. A tension filled the air. All three men felt it. Did we think this was going to be easy? wondered Solomon. Shame on us.

They left the Customs Office and the waterfront behind.

They hurried through the narrow streets leading to the mosque.

Through the plazas until they finally arrived at the center of the thriving city. Not yet time for the noontime call to prayer, but the devout were already arriving and engaging in the ritual act of ablution, washing body parts in the fountains of the mosque courtyard before the prayer service. The spiritually devoted entered the court-yard through a pathway leading into a small grove of orange trees. From here they seemingly disappeared into the foliage.

An old beggar sat outside the mosque entrance col-lecting alms. A cane lay at his side and one of his arms was missing below the elbow. Probably the result of an ac-cident or perhaps an injury received in battle. His clothes were ragged and his long gray beard unkempt. Although Islam discouraged and even frowned upon begging it was understood that it might be a necessity for those with de-bilitating maladies or severed limbs.

This beggar presented a pitiful sight, and he appeared to be doing quite well as passersby dropped coins into a ceramic bowl laying at his feet. Eyes closed, he bowed his head every time he heard a clink. It was no surprise that his head bobbed up and down many times.

Solomon and Jalal approached a dozen or so mer-chants working in the square. They started with the per-fume and spice dealers, casually asking them questions about two men matching the description of Blue Eyes and Giant. Further back stood the fishmongers' stands, located at a distance far enough away that their smells wouldn't discourage those going to the mosque. Nobody seemed to have seen the two men.

Solomon decided to try the area on the other side of the mosque entrance.

As he was walking towards it the investigator lost his footing just as they passed the beggar. The jolt was so un-expected he almost fell down on the street, but he caught himself and regained his balance. At first, he thought he'd stumbled on a loose cobblestone. He then realized that something far more disconcerting had occurred.

"You tripped me!" exclaimed Solomon. This was followed by an accusation. "You did it on purpose."

The old man stared up into Solomon's brown eyes.

"Shhh! Not so loud," he said in a voice barely above a whisper. "You want to give away my cover?"

"Your cover," replied the dumbfounded investigator keeping his voice down. The weird scene began to make sense in his mind. So much so that he laughed to himself before stating the obvious.

"You're a spy."

"The Foreign Minister has many eyes and ears."

"So why did you trip me?"

"The Foreign Minister sent a message to Cádiz via carrier pigeon," answered the beggar. " I was supposed to be on the lookout for a Jew traveling with a blond-haired Slav. I saw you two enter the square. I observed the ring on your finger."

"And you realized that it was us?"

"I'm not blind," laughed the beggar.

"You mentioned a message," reminded Solomon. "Is there something the Foreign Minister wanted to share with me?"

"No, there's something that I need to share with you," began the beggar. "I told you Hasdai Shaprut has many eyes and ears. I was instructed to be on the lookout for anything or anyone unusual that might pass my way."

Solomon retrieved a silver *dirham* from his pocket and dropped it down into the ceramic bowl. He decided to play along with the ruse so as not to attract undue attention. The old beggar reciprocated with the obligatory bowing of his head.

"Meet me around the corner," the beggar instructed.

"It's best if we aren't seen leaving the square together."
"Understood."

CHAPTER 28

They watched as the not-so-blind beggar tapped his cane along the cobblestones.

Soon he disappeared around a corner. Solomon and Jalal followed his route, turned the same corner, and found the old man waiting for them in a doorway halfway down the deserted street.

They joined him and he motioned for them to follow him. Another five long blocks and then the narrow street entered a wide plaza where signs indicated vacancies for small lodgings. This location, although close to the city center, appeared quiet and out of the way.

The beggar looked reluctant to enter the plaza.

He ducked into another doorway and motioned for them to join him.

"I saw a giant of a man leaving the mosque yesterday after the noon prayer. His companion was waiting for him outside. This man carried a box with him. These two aroused my curiosity, so I followed them here to this plaza." The old beggar stepped out of the doorway long enough to point something out. "They entered that building. The one with the blue and white flag posted out front."

"Do you think they saw you?" asked the investigator.

"No, I'm adept at tracking suspects."

"Did you wait outside for them?"

"I returned to the mosque," replied the beggar. "It's best for me not to arouse suspicion by a prolonged absence from the mosque entrance. In fact, I should return before the midday prayer concludes."

"I think we'll stay behind."

"Cádiz is deeper than you think," uttered the beggar.

"What's that supposed to mean?"

The old beggar declined to answer the question. He gave the two men a curt bow, and then he turned and tapped his cane on the cobblestones as he walked slowly back up the street in the direction from which they had come.

Solomon decided to continue down to the plaza. He wasn't surprised by the number of vacancies given that the business of Cádiz took place down at the waterfront. The blue and white flag seemed an anomaly. The only flag in the area. He wondered if the flag and its colors held any special significance. Perhaps betraying a North African origin.

They found an eatery with outside seating in one corner of the plaza. From this vantage point they could keep an eye on the doorway on the left side of the blue and white flag. A flag connected to a wooden pole and inserted into a metal holder attached to the wall. A flag waving gently in the afternoon breeze.

After sleeping late, Solomon had skipped breakfast in an attempt to assuage a guilty conscience, and so that he might get on with the mission without further delay. He found himself quite hungry from the morning exertions, so he ordered fruit and cheese and bread for both himself and Jalal. They also wanted coffee.

"We'll have to wait here to see if we catch sight of them."

"For how long?" Jalal inquired.

"As long as it takes."

The outdoor lunch venue included a metal brazier attended by a burly cook who stood smiling as he grilled fresh caught fish over wood chips. This released aromatic smoke into the air.

The food arrived and both men began to devour their lunch between sips of coffee. They had only eaten about half of the meal when the door to the left of the blue and white flag suddenly opened. Out into the plaza stepped two men, Blue Eyes and Giant.

The investigator and the soldier couldn't believe their eyes. He really is a giant was Solomon's first thought. The tallest man he'd ever lain eyes upon.. He must be more than seven feet tall. His companion stood almost six feet tall. The contrast was stunning. The giant held a box under one arm and the two men began to walk away towards one of the four streets entering the plaza.

Solomon gave Jalal a resolute stare and nodded his head to indicate that it was time to go. The investigator took a single gold piece from his pocket and laid it down on the tabletop to pay for the food. The gold *dinar* was way too much recompense, but they didn't have time to wait for service or for change. They got up quickly and made a beeline for the street the thieves had chosen, but before they made it halfway across the plaza four armed men ducked out of a storefront and followed the two thieves.

Solomon gave Jalal a questioning look. The soldier shrugged his shoulders. Neither one of them had any idea what was going on. When the four men turned down the same street as Blue Eyes and Giant all they could do was to follow. It became obvious that the two searchers from Córdoba weren't the only ones attempting to get their hands on the sacred relic. The situation had become more complicated.

Solomon and Jalal strode across the plaza and turned at the narrow street. It seemed like it led to the waterfront, but Solomon couldn't be sure. He wasn't that familiar with the city. At least not yet.

They remained at the top of the street until they spotted the four men about a block and a half in front of them. None of them turned to look back up the street. They seemed to be focused only on what was ahead, Blue Eyes and Giant.

The street veered slightly to the left giving Solomon and Jalal the opportunity to gain ground without being seen. They ran easily for a few blocks, spotted the four men, and stopped to wait until they had another chance to proceed unseen. This stop and go pursuit continued for another quarter mile before the street led into another small plaza.

Solomon and Jalal arrived at the plaza in time to see Blue Eyes and Giant enter a shop. The front door closed behind them as they vanished from sight. They took a closer look at the four men who'd followed the thieves. They were heavily armed and had taken cover behind a couple of shade trees shielding the plaza from the summer sun. The investigator and the soldier backed their way up to the street without being seen.

All eyes were trained on the shop.

Six men waited.

They continued to wait until the shop door opened and Blue Eyes and Giant walked out of the shop. Only the robbers didn't come out alone. Three men walked out of the store. The newcomer was an Arab. Solomon remembered seeing the Arab somewhere before, but he couldn't recollect where. He racked his brain. Where was it? Where had he seen this young man before?

Then it dawned upon him. The sparsely grown beard. When he was leaving Malik's villa this young man sneered at him as he passed by on his way to visit with the Arab elitist. What is he doing here with Blue Eyes and Giant?

Giant still carried the box under his arm. As soon as the shop door closed behind them, the four armed assailants sprang into action. Emerging from behind the trees, with swords drawn, they crossed the plaza to accost the three men.

Blue Eyes and his companions were armed, but Giant had to place the box on the ground so that he could fight. Once that was done, he drew two long knives from his belt and began to fend off the attack. Blue Eyes and the Arab drew swords and the threesome fought back bravely, pushing the fight out into the middle of the plaza. Giant's incredibly long arms gave him a distinct advantage. He kept the attackers at bay with the two long knives and, try as they might, they couldn't get their thrusts close to his body.

Solomon and Jalal watched the action from their vantage point on the narrow street.

It seemed that Blue Eyes and the Arab elitist were using Giant for a shield because the man's fighting was so fierce. Then, one of the four attackers circled around behind the melee. Now the odds were three on three. The investigator kept staring at the fourth assailant, and he could hardly believe his eyes when the man reached down to grab the box off the street. At first. he thought it might be Ibn Hawqal, the Fatimid spy. He mentioned that he was lecturing in Cádiz when they had run into each other back in Seville. Solomon was mistaken. He soon realized that he was looking at a different, albeit familiar face. That of Abbas, the Relic Master.

What the hell? How did he get involved in this business? Of course. He knew about Blue Eyes and Giant. He'd talked to his good friend, the luthier. Abbas could have had the two thieves followed from Seville from the very start. Perhaps Abbas was desperate and willing to risk everything for a chance to cash in and retire from a lucrative, but dangerous business.

Abbas snatched the box from the road and ran back towards the street used to follow the thieves. All this while the six men in the center of the plaza continued their struggle. The Relic Master made a successful escape and now ran up to the street only to discover Solomon and Jalal waiting for him with swords drawn. He practically skewered himself, stopping just short of Jalal's sharp blade. Solomon took the box from him while the soldier applied pressure to his neck.

"You'll leave Andalusia sooner rather than later if you know what's good for you," came the warning. "Now go back down there and call off your men."

"I underestimated you," confessed Abbas.

He turned and walked dejectedly down to the plaza to put a stop to the attack. There was no reason to continue the conflict. His flight had failed. A lost opportunity that might come back to haunt him.

Solomon and Jalal didn't wait around to see the finale. They headed back up the street with the prized box, made a turn on a side street, and waited briefly to see if they'd been followed. Who knew how many others were searching for the coveted relic? Once satisfied they were on their own, they resumed their route. Then navigated one last turn before heading straight for the Inn of the Sailors.

It was still early when they arrived at their lodgings, so they took the box directly to Solomon's room. They put it down on the bed. Before they opened it, Jalal felt compelled to share a concern of his.

"Do you think the Relic Master and his men will come after us?"

"I doubt it," said the investigator. "He's failed once. He can't risk another failure. He's finished and he knows it. He'll return to Seville and try to get away with his relic collection before we close down his shop. My guess is that he'll take his wares to France or Italy. I don't think he'll be bothering us again while we're here in Cádiz."

The two men turned their attention back to the box with great anticipation. They opened it expecting to find the 'ud. Solomon and Jalal looked inside and discovered rags. They assumed the 'ud had been swathed in these rags so they unraveled them. There was nothing wrapped inside the cloth.

"I don't get it," admitted a perplexed Jalal.

"This was a ruse," announced Solomon. "These two are smart. Very smart. Or, maybe it was Malik's underling's idea. They knew somebody else would be after the holy relic. They staged the entire scene outside the shop. The question now is: did they leave the holy relic behind in their room? That wouldn't be smart. So where is it? Did they give it to someone else for safe keeping? Did they hide it until things settled down?"

The investigator's questions elicited no response.

Solomon replaced the rags in the box and took it from the bed. He went to one corner of the room and placed it on the floor.

"Should we go back and talk to that beggar?" asked his companion.

"You mean that spy?"

"The very same."

"No, I don't think he can be of much assistance at this point."

"What shall we do?"

"I need to think about that," said Solomon. "I suspect they'll lie low for a time before making their next move. Their ruse proved successful so they may let their guard down. Perhaps their plan is unfolding just as they imagined it would. We just need to anticipate their next move."

"That won't be easy."

"I'm going to get some rest," said Solomon. "I suggest that you do the same. We'll head back to the plaza later today."

Jalal took his cue and departed the room. Solomon climbed on his bed and closed his eyes. As much as he desired rest, he found it impossible to quiet his mind. He opened his eyes with a heavy sigh.

Solomon lay on his bed staring at the box in the corner of his room.

These guys are smart, he thought to himself.

Had he underestimated Blue Eyes and Giant just as Abbas had misjudged him? The two thieves had correctly anticipated the Relic Master's treachery. They hadn't made a false move yet.

They had probably reasoned that the robbery of the sacred relic would initiate a recovery operation. Somebody from Córdoba coming after them. The ruse was dangerous. They might have failed, but Giant had proven a formidable opponent. One thing they didn't know. They didn't know that Solomon and Jalal had pinpointed the location of their lodging.

CHAPTER 29

Solomon and Jalal returned to the plaza with the blue and white flag.

They were fortunate that the restaurant they'd eaten at earlier in the day had remained open. They ordered coffee and waited for events to unfold. It wasn't long before Blue Eyes and Giant entered the plaza and went directly into their lodgings. The Arab that the investigator saw outside of Malik's villa was no longer with them.

"What do you make of it?" asked Jalal.

"I'm not sure," replied Solomon in an honest moment.

And he wasn't. He attempted to make sense of the situation in his mind. Where was the third man? Why wasn't he with them? Most importantly where was the sacred arm bone relic of the Prophet Muhammad? How did they intend to smuggle it out of Andalusia? Would they attempt to bribe one of Nasr Abdul's customs agents? He had no answers for his questions and decided he would have to respond to events as they transpired.

The coffee arrived.

Solomon took a sip and then another.

More patrons arrived to fill the empty tables around them and everyone seemed to enjoy the balmy evening breeze. A young man walked in off the street carrying a five stringed 'ud. He went from table to table taking requests or simply playing from his considerable repertoire. Most of the songs were familiar classics. Songs written by the courtier Zirab, a century earlier after he arrived in Córdoba from Bagdad and opened a music academy.

The young musician wore the front of his hair in bangs, a style popularized by the Courtier along with numerous innovations he'd introduced to Andalusian society: the three course meal, glass stemware, toothpaste, and deodorant among others. Some of his innovations had stood the test of time, but the music had become an out-of-date style. Nobody seemed to mind and the youth smiled knowingly as he collected tips and slipped them into a waiting pocket.

Solomon might have enjoyed the music if something new hadn't occurred to him. It sent a chill up his spine. If the Arab elitists helped establish a rival Caliphate, in North Africa, one which they recognized and supported, they might be in a position to more easily overthrow Abd al-Rahman III. The Umayyads would be discredited and Malik or one of his associates could proclaim himself Emir and establish a new government.

There existed a precedence for this action. Umayyads with the title of Emir had ruled Andalusia for more than two hundred years before Rahman III took on the role of Caliph and announced his intention to reestablish the original Umayyad Caliphate of Damascus on the Iberian Peninsula. The investigator understood that this alliance between Berbers and Arabs made their mission more difficult and also more dangerous.

The wandering musician came over to the investigator's table, but Solomon waved him off.

"Something troubling you," inquired an astute Jalal.

"The old beggar said 'Cádiz is deeper than you think.'"

"And ... "

"He may be right."

"What's that supposed to mean?"

"I'm not sure," admitted Solomon. "I think it was a warning."

"A warning about what?"

"A city where treachery abounds."

Blue Eyes and Giant finally emerged from their lodgings as twilight brought on the night.

Jalal had been keeping a close eye on the front door and he was the first to witness them leave. "Pssst," he said in a low voice, wanting to get Solomon's attention without drawing attention to their own location. Solomon looked his way and then his eyes followed the soldier's nod out into the plaza where he found the two men on the move.

He reached into his pocket and withdrew a silver *dirham*. Even this was too much to pay for the numerous cups of coffee they'd ordered, but better than parting with a gold *dinar*. They didn't have time to wait for change, so they rose quietly and left their table and the convenient eatery to follow their suspects.

Solomon and Jalal walked across the plaza and turned at the top of the same narrow street they'd been led down earlier in the day. Did it lead to the waterfront, Solomon wondered for the second time that day. Perhaps this time they'd find out.

They remained at the top of the street until they spotted Blue Eyes and Giant halfway down the block in front of them. Neither of them had turned to look back up the street. They seemed to be focused only on their destination.

The street veered slightly to the left giving Solomon and Jalal an opportunity to gain more ground without being seen. They quickened their pace for a few blocks, until the two robbers came into view. Neither man carried anything with him. Where was the bone relic?

They stopped and waited until they had another chance to proceed unseen. The same route, only this time they didn't have the inconvenience of Abbas and his henchmen coming between them. The stop and go pursuit continued for another half mile before they found themselves at a familiar plaza.

Solomon and Jalal arrived at the plaza just in time to see Blue Eyes and Giant enter a shop that they recognized all too well. Would Malik's young accomplice, if he was in fact working for the Arab elitists, emerge from the shop once more? They waited at the entrance to the plaza to find out.

They waited for what felt like an eternity as the twilight deepened the sky to an intense cobalt.

The full moon had already begun to wan leaving just enough light for the robbers to find their way to the water. Is that where they're headed, wondered the investigator. Are they going to make their move tonight? He'd forgot to keep track of the tides. This information might have given him some insight. Too late now. He'd have to let events play out.

The shop door opened.

Blue Eyes and Giant came out of the shop with Giant holding something under his arm. It was too small to be an 'ud. Even Solomon could see that. Maybe they had detached the fingerboard from the body of the instrument. That makes sense if they are going to attempt to smuggle the holy relic out of Andalusia tonight, thought Solomon.

The investigator and his soldier companion kept their eyes trained on the shop.

They weren't surprised to see Malik's man walk out through the door behind the two thieves. They were astonished, however, to observe two more Arabs follow him outside. The shop door closed and the entire group walked across the plaza. They never once looked back. They made their way to a side street and turned the corner and vanished from sight.

Solomon and Jalal ran across the plaza, turned the same corner, and followed the group of men through street after narrow street. There were no more plazas and it occurred to the investigator that their route was leading them towards the water. The cobblestones soon gave out as the path turned to dirt. This led them into a grove of trees where darkness enveloped them with only the moon lighting their way.

The path through the trees ended where the beach began. Solomon and Jalal observed the scene from the cover of these trees. The waning full moon had risen high in the sky illuminating the scene below.

Down at the shoreline the five suspects were joined by a second Berber, probably the owner of the vessel. Its captain or a navigator at the very least. He was talking with Giant as they stood next to a small boat, its bow partially resting in the sand with the stern floating in the water, while ocean waves gently lapped against the sides.

Blue Eyes stood conversing with the Arabs.

Giant undid the cloth covering the object he was carrying under his huge arm. He allowed the cloth to drop into the sand, and then he held something high in the air for the second Berber to admire. Giant's body language was triumphant, but he didn't utter a sound. His intelligence hadn't deserted him. No need to bring attention to themselves as they were about to make their escape.

The fingerboard of the 'ud, wider than most, and held ten feet up in the air, glowed under the light of the waning moon. All eyes turned to witness the spectacle and all remained glued on the varnished fingerboard. It seemed to emit a luminous light as if energized from some mysterious interior source. Giant gazed up in disbelief and his lips moved without him making any audible sound. From his vantage point in the trees, some fifteen yards away, Solomon would swear he'd read the man's lips and he believed Giant had uttered a simple and sacred "Allah!"

Giant lowered the relic. He reached down and grabbed the cloth from the sand. He wrapped up the fingerboard and slipped it back under his arm. The other Berber bowed to him and gestured towards the boat. Blue Eyes bowed to the Arabs as he and the Giant prepared to depart.

Solomon knew the time to act had come.

CHAPTER 30

The investigator didn't care for the odds. Six against two. But he and Jalal had been left with no other options. They couldn't allow the sacred relic to be whisked away to North Africa for the creation of a new Caliphate.

He drew his sword and attempted to steady the heart pounding wildly in his chest. Jalal heard the weapon slide out of its sheath so he withdrew his own sword. The soldier's nerves weren't an issue. He exuded a sense of stoic determination. Death had no hold on his emotions.

"God help us," invoked the investigator.

"May Allah give us strength," whispered Jalal.

There was nothing more to say.

They emerged from the trees, but the two men quickly froze in place.

Down at the boat a fight had already begun. The three Arabs had taken the Berbers by surprise in an unexpected attack. A classic double-cross. The odds were three against three, but Solomon observed the boat captain already falling down into the sand. Stabbed in the back with a long knife. This ambush was not meant to be a fair fight.

Giant positioned himself between the Arabs and the path into the grove.

The three Arabs surrounded the powerfully built Giant, but not before he'd passed the fingerboard off to his partner. Disregarding his own safety, Giant rushed at the Arabs to give Blue Eyes a chance to escape with the sacred relic. Sweeping two knives in wide, threatening arcs allowed him to keep his assailants at arms length while his companion ran with all his might for the pathway through the woods.

Solomon and Jalal witnessed the attack from the cover of the trees and waited for the blue-eyed Berber with swords drawn. Blue Eyes stopped in his tracks and turned around to see if he might have a clear escape route along the beach. Before he could decide in which direction to continue, Jalal reached him and snatched away the fingerboard.

They heard screams from the beach.

They all turned to see the three Arabs bring Giant to his knees as they continued their attack like a pack of vicious jackals. He fought on though he was clearly defenseless.

Thrust after violent thrust. The stabs continued to penetrate deep into the body of Giant. One of the Arabs turned and looked up towards the path to find the soldier holding the fingerboard. That Arab called to his companions.

Jalal had seen and heard enough. He knew the consequences of failing to secure the holy relic, so he trusted his instincts. No time to think. They must act. And act fast.

"Let's get out of here!" ordered the soldier.

Solomon turned to Blue Eyes.

"You may want to come with us," he shouted. "Otherwise, you're probably a dead man."

Time to make their escape.

Jalal ran back through the grove of trees with Solomon following close behind.

Blue Eyes hurried after them.

They were headed for the far side of the island.

Jalal sprinted while keeping a tight grip on the holy relic safely concealed inside the fingerboard of the 'ud. He wanted to put a great distance between the Arabs and his threesome because the soldier was determined to avoid a fight if at all possible. Solomon attempted to match the swift pace while Blue Eyes fell behind. They didn't have time to help him. He'd have to take his chances.

Nobody had time to look back. They had no idea how close or far away their pursuers might be. Breathing heavily, with hearts pounding furiously in their chests, the three men continued to run with all their might. Jalal pulled away from them as the path came to an abrupt end, and he emerged on the far side of the grove of trees.

Jalal stopped, waiting for Solomon to catch up. The investigator soon arrived, but Blue Eyes was nowhere in sight. The soldier, taking in deep breaths and then slowly exhaling them, tried to gauge his companion's strength. He observed heavy, out of control breathing and suspected it might be necessary to slow the pace or also risk leaving Solomon behind.

"Are you okay," he asked with genuine concern.

"Don't worry about me," gasped Solomon. "Just need to catch my breath."

How long could they stay here until the Arabs finally caught up with them? No, this wasn't an option. They must outrun them and make it safely to the Navy docks located directly across the bottle-shaped island. The distance was half a mile at most.

"I want you to go on without me if you have to," Solomon insisted while he continued to get his breath back under control. "You must get the relic back to the Great Mosque."

"All right," lied the soldier. "Whatever you say."

"Promise me!"

Jalal considered the consequences, but he would never leave his friend behind. He was spared the indignity of making a promise he didn't intend to keep because, before he could answer, Blue Eyes arrived in their midst panting breathlessly. He looked relieved to see them as he bent over, grabbed his knees, and struggled to suck in some air.

The sound of feet pounding the earth came from inside the grove of trees.

Jalal knew that he couldn't wait much longer.

"Solomon, we've got to go!"

The investigator saved his precious breath, agreeing with a nod.

Off they ran, once again leaving Blue Eyes behind. Jalal took the lead and set a more measured pace. He reasoned their Arab pursuers would also be winded from the exertion and be forced to slow their pace as well. Solomon was able to keep up this time and soon the two men ran side by side. The investigator had gained his second wind and a renewed confidence in his ability to sustain an even stride as they continued to jog towards the galley waiting for them at the naval docks.

Jalal turned his head around to look back over his shoulder. He discovered that the Arabs had gained ground. He estimated they were forty or fifty yards behind with Blue Eyes about halfway between them. Even though the moon shone bright, it was difficult to make out the figures behind him, but his instincts had always proven themselves dependable.

He jogged alongside Solomon while appraising the investigator about the situation. Ahead of them, in the distance, the slight of two triangular sails offered hopes of them reaching a safe haven. They didn't dare take time to look behind themselves again. Every second counted.

"Try to stay with me," he shouted to Solomon as he quickened the pace.

With muscles straining, and lungs burning, the two me ran stride for stride until the hull of the galley suddenly appeared before them. It was lit by the light of dozens of torches. The captain and his crew had made ready to leave at a moment's notice. Day or night. Under orders from the Foreign Minister.

Another thirty yards to go. Jalal broke out into a sprint and made for the ship.

Solomon followed his lead, but he couldn't keep up with the well-conditioned soldier. He fell behind a yard, two yards.

Jalal held the sacred relic high overhead as he bounded onto the deck of the ship.

He turned in time to see his friend stumble and fall to the ground.

"Solomon!"

CHAPTER 31

The investigator jumped to his feet and ran for the ship. He made it to the side of the galley where Jalal extended a hand to help him onboard.

They both turned to find Blue Eyes only ten yards away. But he was walking and not running. Barely walking. When he finally arrived at the galley, Jalal and Solomon each threw out a hand to pull Blue Eyes up onto the deck of the boat where he quietly collapsed at their feet.

The Arabs, upon seeing Solomon and Jalal safely on board the Caliph's galley with the sacred relic secured, stopped their pursuit. The chase had ended and so too their prospects of pulling off a double-cross.

Then the unexpected occurred. Nasr Abdul and the local police arrived to arrest the Arabs who were taken totally by surprise. They'd let their guard down and a rear action resulted in them being taken prisoner. They'd failed on two accounts. No relic recovered. No making a clean getaway.

The Chief Customs Officer left the prisoners with the police and walked on to the side of the galley to explain what had happened. Solomon and Jalal left Blue Eyes lying in a heap as they went to the starboard side to hear the explanation. Nasr Abdul's smile revealed two rows of gleaming white teeth.

"I was concerned for your safety," he told them. "I knew how vital this mission was, so I enlisted the help of the harbor police to make sure that you weren't placed in danger."

"You had us followed," said the investigator.

"We saw you enter the grove and watched from afar," came the explanation. "You reappeared with the Arabs chasing you, so I knew that you faced grave danger. We followed in pursuit."

"Contact the Foreign Minister," instructed Solomon. "He'll provide directions on how to proceed with your prisoners."

"It will be my pleasure," Nasr Abdul assured them. "I should take my leave."

"We appreciate your concern for our well-being and the assistance you've provided us, Nasr Abdul."

The Chief Customs Officer left to rejoin the police while Solomon and Jalal turned their attention back to the center of the galley. A familiar face approached. None other than the Arab Captain who had brought them back from Galicia with two murder suspects in tow.

"We meet again," announced the bearded Captain in a commanding voice.

"We must sail at once," cried Solomon. "Time is precious."

"Of course," the Captain agreed without hesitation.

This wasn't a horse transport like the one used in Galicia. Not wanting to leave two of the Caliph's prized Arabian mares and a healthy Balearic mule behind in the Christian north was the reason that transport had been sent to bring them back to Andalusia.

This time, Solomon and Jalal left their saddlebags and the two fine geldings behind. Their personal belongings could be easily replaced. As for the geldings, the officer who oversaw the Caliph's stables in al-Zahra would have no trouble arranging for a horse transport to sail them back along the Guadalquivir River if he so desired.

This galley was called a runner. The fastest vessel in the Caliphate's formidable navy.

And time was of the essence.

"That man is our prisoner," said Solomon as he gestured towards Blue Eyes who still lay semi-conscious on the deck of the ship. "We need to tie him up, hands and feet."

"Understood."

"We don't want him getting away."

"Of course not," agreed the Captain.

The investigator, in a moment of anxiety, imaged the Berber prisoner grabbing the fingerboard and diving overboard with it. Out into the river in an attempt to make his escape. Unlikely he'd get far given that Jalal was an excellent swimmer.

Two massive triangular sails with broad, vertical red and white stripes of stitched linen, the same color scheme used for the horseshoe shaped arches inside Córdoba's Great Mosque, rose above the galley's planked and framed hull. If the winds ceased they could draw upon the physical and spiritual prowess of one hundred and twenty rowers arranged sixty on each side of the vessel, with twenty-five oarsmen beneath and thirty-five above the deck on each side.

The investigator looked around and discovered that the crew was predominantly made up of Coptic Christians, the indigenous people of Egypt and the direct descendants of the ancient Egyptians. No surprise that they provided the bulk of the crew for this Muslim galley, as they did for the entire fleet of Andalusia. No other mariners sailed the seas with such expertise.

Rahman III demanded the best and he usually got what he wanted. He certainly had no trouble paying for it since the royal coffers of Andalusia were spilling over.

The Captain gave the order and the oarsmen began a rhythmic motion, rowing the ship away from the docks and out into the gentle waters of the bay.

Navigating by the stars, they found it easy to find their way at night, From the Bay of Cádiz they sailed to the northeast, making their way out into the Atlantic Ocean before heading almost due north another thirty miles. Turning west they entered the mouth of the Guadalquivir River as it reached the sea near Sanlúcar de Barrameda.

Once the galley entered the river, the Captain gave orders for the lighting of more torches to illuminate the sides of the boat. An unusual arrangement, but this was no ordinary voyage. The Captain knew they'd be better off waiting until morning to sail because of the possibility of rocks or fallen trees close to the shore as he navigated the Great River.

This wasn't an option and the old sailor also knew that he possessed two important advantages: there'd be little or no traffic on the river at night, and he knew the Guadalquivir, with its twists and turns, intimately having worked its course for decades. He was capable of navigating its currents even on the darkest of nights.

Everybody on board knew that their success required them to sail by night. This was the only way they could possibly return the sacred relic to the Great Mosque in time for the annual procession.

They caught a strong tailwind blowing up from the Atlantic and took advantage of it to give the oarsmen the rest they'd need if the winds ever failed them.

The wind continued, and all hands breathed a sigh of

relief.

They just might make it in time.

Now that they were on their way back to Córdoba, Solomon had time for reflection.

The investigator wasn't sure if this was the same crew that had sailed with him from Galicia. He thought that he recognized a few of the rowers, but he couldn't be sure. He had no doubts about the bearded, barrel-chested Captain. This was definitely the same man. A man with a good memory. He'd remembered them from the Galician voyage.

Every time he looked at the man he also remembered the first time he'd sailed with him. It had only been a couple of months since they'd brought two suspects back from Galicia. He simply couldn't help remembering the old sea dog's warning on that journey. He told them they'd have to avoid sea monsters if they wanted to make good time on the open seas. This had unnerved Solomon because he vividly recollected his initial response. The potential danger had evoked deep emotions inside of him. He'd heard stories of monsters in the ocean as a young child.

He knew his imagination had run wild at such an impressionable age, but he'd seen some of those frightening images floating before his mind's eye as his memory dredged them up from some forgotten, buried past as they sailed south down the Atlantic Coast of Andalusia towards Lisbon, and then on to Cádiz.

Best keep this a distant memory. But somehow he couldn't. He wouldn't.

The investigator searched the main deck and found the Captain silhouetted in torchlight and gazing down along the sides of the galley runner. Since Solomon found it impossible to put the matter aside, he decided to approach him. It was time to put his mind to rest about so-called sea monsters once and for all.

"The last time I sailed with you we were told that you'd have to avoid sea monsters," Solomon began. "What did you mean by that. What are sea monsters exactly?"

The bearded face broke out into a grin.

"Don't you remember? I also said we'd need some wind in our sails and the Captain can't get drunk," came the response.

"You laughed and told us that you were joking because you never drink unless your feet are firmly planted on *terra firma*," Solomon replied. "You never elaborated about the sea monsters."

The burly captain shook his head from side to side, but the wide grin remained. He sensed the investigator's anxiety and understood that it was time to defuse the situation in order to put an important passenger's mind at ease.

"There's no such thing as sea monsters."

"I heard stories about them when I was a boy."

"Please believe me," pleaded the Captain. "Sea monsters happen to be a creation of the Phoenicians. A trick they used centuries before the birth of Abraham to dissuade other cultures from exploring the seas. A ruse those seafarers cultivated so that they could monopolize Mediterranean trade. And it worked for centuries."

A sheepish frown was all an embarrassed Solomon could manage.

"I thought you knew," said the Captain. "Your people traveled with the Phoenicians in order to trade."

"No, I had no idea."

The old seadog raised a finger and then he looked to

the sails. Their tautness slackened. The wind had died down. Not yet time to lower the sails and use the oars, but it might not be long. The smell of salt air had faded away hours ago.

"If you don't mind I have work to do."

"I'm sorry," apologized the investigator. "I didn't mean to distract you."

The Captain gave a knowing smile before turning and walking back towards the stern of the galley runner. He prayed the wind would last the night. Otherwise, they would never arrive in Córdoba in time for the annual procession.

CHAPTER 32

Hours passed but the investigator and the soldier couldn't sleep. Everybody seemed anxious. Everyone waited for the wind to strengthen. And they waited.

Jalal realized that he still held the fingerboard in his hands. He handed it over to Solomon. Even through the wood the investigator could feel a mysterious presence evoking an energy sacred and special and spiritual. An invisible force emanating numinous currents of energy and power. He rubbed the fingerboard gently, back and forth . . . back and forth.

The breeze finally picked up. It wasn't enough, so the Captain ordered the oarsmen into action. As the banks of rowers worked in unison to maintain a rhythmic tempo the sound of oars splashing water provided an auditory accompaniment to the voyage.

Solomon was amazed at the endurance of the oarsmen. He marveled at the speed the runner had attained as it sliced through the water. He guessed that they would arrive, in Seville, in a couple of hours. Maybe even less.

The torches were doused as the first light of morning reflected off the water. About the time that the investigator had begun to estimate when they might arrive back in Córdoba. Neither he nor Jalal had slept a wink. Both men felt apprehensive and they relied upon their adrenalin to keep them awake. Nobody had slept, except perhaps Blue Eyes who was kept prisoner somewhere below deck.

Solomon decided to have his prisoner brought up on deck for questioning.

Before long, they saw him shuffling along with his hands and feet still bound by rope. Two crew members brought him over to the investigator. Solomon leaned down and placed the fingerboard on the deck of the galley before untying the ropes securing Blue Eye's legs. He was taking a chance, but he felt there was little risk involved.

Jalal was at their side with his sword drawn lest their prisoner get any ideas about making a run for the side of the galley. The investigator hoped his gesture of goodwill would produce the desired results. He picked up the fingerboard and turned to Blue Eyes.

"Let's walk."

The three men walked down the port side of the galley.

"If you cooperate with me I'll put in a good word for you with the Foreign Minister."

Blue Eyes remained silent, but Solomon could see that he was considering his options. They encountered a mast, stopped, and turned to walk back in the same direction they'd come from.

They walked half-way back to their starting point, Blue Eyes looking straight ahead and giving no indication which way he might choose. Solomon and Jalal kept their eyes on the prisoner. Jalal suddenly drew ahead of the Berber and thrust the blade of his sword right up to the man's neck.

"I've had enough," he yelled in a venomous tone. "Tell my friend what he wants to know or I'll slice you from ear to ear."

Gripped by fear, the relic thief froze. He tried to stand as still as a statue, but he couldn't help but swallow hard as he turned his eyes towards Solomon. Only his eyes. The soldier, sensing a more cooperative attitude was coming, lowered the blade so that it now rested straight in line with the man's heart. He was free to talk.

"Why did you purchase a second 'ud if you didn't intend to smuggle the relic out of the harbor by ship?" asked the investigator.

Blue Eyes hesitated, looked down at the sword, and then he began:

"Knowing the importance of the holy relic, I was afraid the Caliphate's Army would set up inspection stations along the Via Augusta to search travelers. Especially entering Cádiz. I thought we could pass ourselves off as two itinerant musicians."

Traveling musicians. How clever, thought Solomon. It might even have succeeded had he and Jalal not been sent to recover the holy arm bone.

"Who sent you and Giant to steal the holy relic from the Great Mosque?" the investigator asked. He still hadn't stopped referring to Giant in a familiar way. This seemed odd to Blue Eyes, but he said nothing. He didn't want to antagonize his interrogator.

"The Emir of Sijilmassa sent us."

"But you weren't acting alone," stated Solomon. "You worked in league with a cabal of Arabs from al-Zahra and Córdoba."

"It was their idea," insisted the Berber. "High ranking Arabs came to our ruler with a plan to steal the sacred relic. They traveled to Sijilmassa and convinced our Emir that they would support his efforts to establish a new Caliphate if he, in turn, backed them in their bid to overthrow Rahman III. He agreed to the pact and we were sent to steal the relic. We had been assured that the local Arabs would aid us in our escape."

The classic double-cross, the investigator snickered to himself. Treachery knows no limits.

"Why send Giant?"

"People would be afraid of him and keep their distance from us. It was our ruler's idea. He insisted. He told us this had been prophesied. We felt in no position to argue with him. We made arrangements with those Arabs to secure a boat for our flight and for them to help us make our escape."

"Why use blood to write your message on the wall?" asked Solomon. "In fact, why leave a message at all?"

"Our Emir insisted we do this," replied Blue Eyes. " He wanted to scare the Imam. To intimidate him is how he phrased it. We had no idea why this was so. We were only following orders."

Solomon gestured to Jalal to lower his sword and the soldier quickly complied.

The three men walked on until they had reached their starting point on the deck of the galley. The ropes lay where they had left them. Solomon handed the fingerboard to Jalal and then he knelt down and reached over for the rope. He tied it back around the ankles of the Berber and called over to the two crewmen who'd brought the man up on deck. The two sailors arrived as the investigator stood tying rope around Blue Eye's wrists.

"Take him below," Solomon instructed.

"You'll speak to the Foreign Minister on my behalf?" pleaded Blue Eyes. His hands had never stopped shaking the entire time he'd been on deck. Solomon felt a twinge of compassion.

"I am a man of my word," the investigator reassured him.

A look of relief washed over the man's face as the two crew members led him shuffling away. Soon the three men disappeared back down below deck.

Jalal held the fingerboard under one arm while he slid his sword deftly into the sheath at his side with his free hand. Solomon stood nearby clapping his hands to show his appreciation for a good performance:

"You were very convincing."

"Acting is believing," laughed the soldier.

From high above them the voice of a man hollered, "Seville ... Seville ... "

"We'll soon be at the docks!" exclaimed Solomon in a jubilant voice.

"Yes," Jalal cried out. "And then on our way to Córdoba."

"We may make it in time after all."

A second galley awaited them in Seville.

The Captain informed Solomon that the two of them, along with Jalal and Blue Eyes, would be disembarking at the docks while leaving his old crew behind. The four men left the ship and hastened their way over to the other galley runner. Solomon, Jalal, the Captain, and Blue Eyes, with his legs now unbound, climbed aboard the vessel.

The experienced Captain was staying on to take command of a fresh cadre of rowers manning the new runner as they made their way from Seville to Córdoba. He must be held in high esteem to be hand-picked for these assignments, reflected the investigator.

The Captain wasted no time engaging his crew.

"Let's get underway," he shouted in a loud boisterous voice.

And they were ready to set off for Córdoba. Two

massive lanteen sails with broad, vertical red and white stripes of stitched linen, rose above this galley's planked and framed hull just like the sails on the first galley. A light breeze picked up and the investigator knew they'd be able to make good time if it continued to increase its velocity.

More wind.

The breeze gained strength as the rowers navigated the vessel away from the Seville docks and out towards the broad expanse of river before raising the oars and resting, conserving much-needed strength for the unpredictable journey that lay before them.

Once they reached the far side of the river and turned north the sails remained taut and the runner began to glide along the river, slicing its way north as the bow of the ship created waves along the sides of the vessel while leaving a wake behind them. One more full day of sailing lay before them. Who knew which way the wind would blow or if it would blow at all. They found themselves dependent upon the unfathomable rhythm of nature.

Solomon felt a knot developing down inside his stomach, and he knew that its cause was a deep and uncontrollable anxiety.

The annual procession of the sacred relic would take place that very night.

Or, would it?

CHAPTER 33

The day wore on.

By late morning they'd made good progress, but the winds began to fade. The Captain approached, but they already suspected what he was about to say. The sails would be lowered so the rowers could spring into action once again and the mighty galley could continue its journey of recovery and rescue and return of the holy relic.

"The winds are dying," the barrel-chested Arab told them. "We've made fast time so far, so I think we might make it to Córdoba in time. I'll leave the sails up for the time being, but it doesn't look hopeful."

"I hope we get lucky," said Jalal, but he couldn't hide the feelings of doubt he was experiencing.

"I'll need you to take control of our prisoner when we dock," instructed Solomon, placing his faith in the Captain and his crew. "We won't have time to deal with him until later. You can send word to the Foreign Minister and he'll arrange to take him into custody."

"Understood."

"Can you get a message to the Foreign Minister before we arrive in Córdoba?"

"Yes," replied the Captain. "We have carrier pigeons with us for that very purpose."

"Perfect," said the investigator. "I want to send a message as soon as possible."

"I'll arrange for it immediately."

The Captain left the two men and returned to the far end of the ship to consult with a couple of his crewmen. He ordered paper, ink, and a quill, along with the essential bird. They saw him talking and gesturing and watched as the crew members hurried off to go about their business.

"What have you got in mind?" Jalal wanted to know.

"When we get back we'll need to get the holy relic into the Great Mosque. It's an almost impossible task given that hundreds, if not thousands, will be using the main entrance and spilling out into the courtyard."

"How will we accomplish this impossible undertaking?"

"There's a tunnel that leads from the old Caliphal Palace into the Great Mosque. I think Hasdai can arrange for us to use it to gain entrance to the *mihrab* area. From there we'll have easy access to the treasury where a duplicate reliquary awaits us."

"You've thought this through in advance."

"There's only one thing to prevent us from succeeding."

"And that is?"

"Malik might have men waiting for us after we leave the galley."

"You're assuming he knows of our return," stated Jalal. "I'm not sure that's possible with his men in jail down in Cádiz."

"We have to be prepared for any eventuality."

Jalal's hand fell to his side and rested upon the hilt of his sword while he cradled the fingerboard under his other arm. The soldier was always ready for battle. His instincts had proved dependable and the investigator knew he'd give his life in the service of the Caliphate.

He hoped Jalal was right and they wouldn't have any

trouble at the docks, but he had to steel himself for the possibility and that meant keeping his emotions under control.

Two crewmen approached. One carried a cage with the bird. The other brought paper and ink with a quill. Solomon sauntered over to the side rail which would give him a solid surface to write upon. The others followed.

He was handed the implements needed, but he realized the movement of the galley would make things difficult.

"Would you mind holding this vial of ink for me, Jalal."

"Hold this for me," Jalal instructed one of the crewmen as he handed over the fingerboard for safe keeping.

The soldier took the vial, removed the lid, and held it steady for his companion.

Solomon dipped the quill into the vial of oak gall ink and began to write a letter on cotton paper pressed down on the wooden railing. He decided not to address the formal title of Foreign Minister or even the given name Hasdai. He opted for the more familiar "Cousin." The investigator did this knowing he was about to write what was perhaps the most important message of his life. One that might save the future existence of the kingdom of Andalusia and the world as he knew it.

Or, a letter that might be the last he ever wrote.

The feeble tailwind lasted half a day.

Then it died altogether and along with it died some of Solomon's optimism. He felt tired. Weary from lack of sleep and the accumulated stress experienced during the course of the week. He decided not to dwell upon himself.

His focus returned to the present and something

more critical. The timing of their arrival in Córdoba. Would they make it back in time for the annual procession at the Great Mosque? What if they didn't? What if they failed thereby giving Malik and his cohorts an opportunity to sow the seeds of rebellion throughout Andalusia.

How would he handle it?

He had plenty of questions, but no real answers.

He turned to Jalal: "I need to think."

The soldier nodded and handed over the fingerboard: "You should have this." He offered a sympathetic smile and sauntered off down the deck of the galley to join the Captain while Solomon went over to the side of the galley runner and turned his eyes north towards Córdoba. He cradled the fingerboard in his arms.

The rowers exerted their energies as the runner made its way through the water. Men giving their all in the service of Andalusia. Solomon took note of the lack of a breeze as the crew continued to lower the two massive triangular sails. He clutched the fingerboard tight and though he wasn't a particularly religious man he said a little prayer in hopes it might evoke the miracle they so desired. The miracle they needed in order to succeed.

And if they did succeed the poet could resume his life once more. Complete his translation of Aristotle's writings, enthusiastically explore the world and write new poems, and most importantly begin his new life with Sara. Her smiling face appeared before his mind's eye. Lips parted ever so slightly. A sparkle in her eyes. Oh, how he missed Sara.

Footsteps approaching on the wooden deck roused him from his reverie, and he turned to see the Captain and Jalal coming towards him.

"I'm sorry, but the winds have deserted us," spoke the Captain. "We'll probably have to row the rest of the way to Córdoba ."

"How long will it take us to return to Córdoba?"

"That's hard to say. We'll do our best to get you back in time for the annual procession, but we're not miracle workers."

"What a pity," sighed Solomon. "It may take a miracle."

It was late afternoon when clouds began to appear on the horizon, but still no wind.

Jalal and the Captain honored Solomon's request to be left alone once again. The investigator sat on the deck of the vessel caressing the fingerboard and staring off into space. The Imam's cross-hatched, wrinkled face suddenly appeared before his mind's eye. He wondered if he might be hallucinating.

The vision was accompanied by an auditory message: "May Allah give you the strength and courage you need to return the Prophet's arm bone home safely." It felt as if he was hearing this for the very first time. It felt so real. So necessary.

Jalal returned and sat down beside him.

"You should try to get some sleep," he advised.

"I won't sleep until this is over," said Solomon as he turned to his companion.

"I understand," said the soldier. "I feel the same way."

The investigator patted his friend on the shoulder a couple of times in a gesture of affection. The two men took measure of one another and smiled. They felt more than ready to face the future together. They'd become close in ways never imagined, and had found themselves appreciating a kind of emotional intimacy men seldom shared.

"Something troubling you?" asked Solomon.

Jalal no longer felt surprised when one or the other of them sensed a mood.

"If we're making such good time why didn't the Foreign Minister send us by galley to Seville in the first place?"

A question answered with another question.

"Think about it!"

Solomon gave his friend some time.

Jalal merely shrugged his shoulders to indicate he didn't have a clue.

"You asked me this same question in Galicia," the investigator reminded him. "Hasdai thought we had a chance to overtake them on the road."

"Slim chance."

"But a chance nonetheless."

"I'll grant you that."

"It actually turned out to our advantage," insisted Solomon. "We might never have discovered the relic was hidden inside the fingerboard of an 'ud."

"Yes, there is that."

Solomon grew tired of talking about past circumstances.

He realized time was running out. They only had four or five hours before the nighttime procession at the Great Mosque began. The faithful had already flocked into the city from the surrounding countryside along with pilgrims from all over the Islamic world. All expecting to view, and perhaps even to touch, the glass reliquary housing the arm bone of the prophet Muhammad. Disappointing them might have dire consequences because it played into the hands of the Caliphate's enemies.

The investigator reasoned that the four bloody pages of 'Uthman's Quran would be paraded around the Great Mosque as the ceremony's opening prelude. This would be an attempt to reestablish the legitimacy of the Umayyad Caliphate by acknowledging its origins in Arabia and Syria. This would buy him more time to return the holy relic before it's expected display. The Imam might even offer some opening prayers and commentary in an effort to stall if this became necessary.

He soon realized all these thoughts were mere conjecture. Empty imaginings. How many times had he envisioned a future that never came to pass? So many imaginary futures that had never taken place in the reality of his life. Still, he had to have a plan of sorts even if it never came to fruition. He decided to create a tentative plan and share it with Jalal. Then allow events to take their course, because now the situation called for mindfulness and living in the present. Trusting his instincts above all else.

His mind entered a place where thoughts became impossible as if the words needed to construct them had been thrust out into a void from which they couldn't return. A state of mind created by his deep desire to overcome any obstacle placed in his path. Solomon Levy had attained an inner confidence beyond hope and fear.

He felt prepared to die if necessary.

Jalal shook him hard to get his attention and the investigator opened his eyes and stared into his companion's with a steely determination.

"You ready?" Solomon asked the soldier.

"I'm ready."

"Here's the plan."

CHAPTER 34

T he late summer sunsets of southern Andalusia worked in their favor.

There was no daylight remaining because twilight had overtaken the day. But it wasn't quite dark yet either. The oarsman of the galley runner seemed to be making a superhuman effort and their rowing soon brought them just south of the city docks. The minaret of the Great Mosque was the first landmark coming into view.

"Córdoba . . . Córdoba . . . " came the shout from above deck.

It felt so good to be home at last, but this was no time for nostalgia.

The galley continued north, but the oars were raised once they arrived at the ancient Roman Bridge.

The vessel dropped anchor just offshore and a small rowboat was lowered over the side. Solomon and Jalal sat inside the dinghy staring with affection at the bridge and the Great Mosque. Two crew members manned the oars and began to row them over to the shore with the precious holy relic in their possession. Everything was going according to plan. At least so far.

The evening call to prayer echoed from the top of the mosque's minaret as they neared the shore. This summons to prayer, called the *Isha'*, served as a reminder to Córdoba's devout Muslims to take time to honor God's presence and to pray for guidance, mercy, and forgiveness. On this very special night the viewing of holy relics would reward the faithful for their never tiring efforts.

But only if Solomon and Jalal proved successful.

The two men hopped out of the boat near the banks and landed in the shallow waters of the Guadalquivir, not caring that they were getting soaked up to their waists. Solomon held the fingerboard of the 'ud high overhead with one hand as they splashed their way towards the shore. They found a footpath between the floodwall and one end of the bridge.

No time to waste.

Once on dry land they ran in the direction of the old Caliphal Palace, up a road guarded by Slavic mercenaries, the Silent Ones. Hasdai had placed Jalal's fellow soldiers along the road to the Palace for the twosome's protection.

This had been the plan. Solomon had anticipated, and wisely so, that huge crowds would gather inside and around the main entrances to the mosque. He realized that he and Jalal stood little chance of making their way through the throngs of worshipers.

He'd sent a message by carrier pigeon requesting that Hasdai secure their entrance to the old Caliphal Palace. He remembered the Imam telling him how the second door flanking the *mihrab* led to a passageway linking the mosque and palace.

When they reached the entryway to the palace the front door swung open, and they were greeted by the Foreign Minister and one of the mosque's assistant Imams who had been apprised of the investigator's plan. The two couldn't help but gape at the fingerboard in Solomon's hand. It showed a long cut running along its length straight down the middle.

"Follow this man," shouted Hasdai.

The young Imam led them across the marble tiled foyer. He turned down a long corridor, and then led them back outside to a covered bridge that linked the palace to the mosque. They entered the passageway and Solomon took the lead, sprinting as fast as he could. Jalal ran after him, followed by the assistant Imam.

They emerged from the passageway, walked straight across the backside of the *mihrab*, and then the three of them entered the second passageway. The one leading into the treasury. Solomon went directly to the designated table. Upon it rested the duplicate reliquary. Gold framed with glass panels. Just as he'd requested in his initial meeting with the Imam.

"Please open it," he told the assistant Imam.

The Imam did as he was instructed and then he waited.

"Help me, Jalal. I need for you to pry half of the fingerboard open while I work on the other half."

Solomon placed the fingerboard on the table next to the reliquary, and the two men placed their hands on opposite sides of the groove carved down its center. They worked carefully, applying just enough pressure to force the instrument open. The wood began to crack. Only a little at first. They continued to work each side simultaneously until the crack widened and they saw part of the arm bone resting in the cradle that had been formed around it.

The fingerboard soon opened wide enough for them to view the entire arm bone from elbow to wrist.

"It's unharmed," said Solomon.

"Praise be to Allah," evoked the young Imam.

"I need for you to take out this holy arm bone and place it into the reliquary."

"I am honored."

Solomon and Jalal held their breath as the assistant Imam gingerly grasped the sacred relic while they continued to hold open the two sides of the fingerboard.

"Make sure you have a firm hold on it."

The young Imam nodded assertively as he raised the holy arm bone and laid it down slowly until it rested on a white silk cushion fitted to the bottom of the reliquary. All three men released a collective sigh of relief. The assistant Imam closed the lid and secured it with gold latches.

Solomon reached over and gently ran his fingers over one of the glass panels. Many of those attending the annual procession would have envied him.

"I must leave you," the young Imam declared. "They are waiting for me."

"We understand."

"I'm afraid you aren't allowed to witness the procession," he told them. "I must apologize, but that is the law."

"Again, we understand," said Solomon in a sympathetic tone of voice. "We'll find our way out."

The assistant Imam smiled as he took the reliquary off the table and held it high so that the investigator and the soldier could catch a glimpse of what the faithful would soon be experiencing with their own eyes. Then he disappeared through the doorway leading out to the *mihrab* and into the open spaces of Córdoba's Great Mosque.

"What do you think's happening out there?" asked Jalal, referring to the celebration inside the mosque.

"I imagine dozens of hanging oil lamps have been lit to create a dreamlike atmosphere," Solomon began. "They'll parade the four bloody pages of Caliph 'Uthman's

Quran around the mosque, the one he was reading when he was assassinated. This will help establish the legitimacy of the Umayyad Caliphate both here and back when it was established in Arabia and Syria."

The investigator picked up the cracked fingerboard and gazed at it longingly. He rubbed the surface back and forth and appeared deep in thought. Jalal waited patiently. What else is going to happen inside the mosque, the soldier wondered. Before long his patience was rewarded as Solomon finished his rendition of events.

"After that the head Imam will lead a procession through the Mosque so that the faithful can see the holy relic for themselves. See that it remains in the possession of the Umayyads and their Great Mosque. The viewing will remain pious and orderly and the future of Andalusia will appear bright. At least for now. I'm basing all this on what the Imam has told me, but I'm just guessing."

"You've done well, Solomon."

"*We've* done well, my friend."

In a moment both spontaneous if not somewhat awkward, the two men embraced. They'd faced death together and emerged unscathed and the natural affection that they shared for one another couldn't be denied. A hug, and a few pats on the back, for a difficult mission brought to a successful conclusion. They dropped their arms and stepped back to consider one another. They couldn't help but smile.

Solomon spoke first.

"Come on, let's get out of here."

CHAPTER 35

Four individuals entered a room designed with a thirty-foot high ceiling and massive walls carved from translucent marble blocks. It's grandeur and openness offered an impressive sense of space.

Solomon laughed to himself. Every time he entered this room the same thought occurred to him. We're meant to feel dwarfed in the presence of the Caliph's hand-picked advisors, he mused for the umpteenth time.

The investigator was joined by three others: his girlfriend Sara; Jalal, and the soldier's inamorata, Bahja.

They found the Foreign Minister sitting in the center of the well-appointed room behind an oak-carved desk. He appeared to be working on some correspondence. He looked up and then put down his quill. He stood behind the desk and motioned the foursome towards chairs arranged in a semi-circle.

"Please, come in and be seated," invited Hasdai.

And they did.

Five attractive individuals, each in their own way, gathered together for a very important occasion. The Jewish poet with curly dark hair whose eyes were the color of overcooked peas. His olive-skinned Mozarabic girlfriend who could pass as a Jewess or Arab woman with her dark eyes and dark hair. The powerfully built ruddy-skinned, blond-haired soldier. Hasdai with his light sandy beard and luminous eyes.

And there in their midst sat Bahja, the soldier's girlfriend. This was the first time that Solomon and Sara and Hasdai had ever laid eyes upon her exquisite, fine-featured face with its dancing dark eyes and cinnamon colored skin. A natural beauty who presented a dramatic facial contrast when compared to her Slavic lover.

"I'm afraid this ceremony of manumission isn't going to be very elaborate, Jalal," apologized Hasdai. "Solomon asked that I make it happen sooner rather than later."

All eyes turned to Solomon who merely shrugged his shoulders nonchalantly before pointing a finger in the direction of his cousin so everybody would focus back on him as he picked up an official looking scroll.

"Please rise in honor of this occasion," Hasdai instructed them.

All four rose from their chairs in anticipation.

Hasdai unrolled the document and began to read from it.

"This decree of manumission is based upon the following grounds which include service to the Umayyad Caliphate upon more than one occasion. Let it be known, the recipient undertook an arduous journey to the far northern region of Galicia, at the risk of his own life, which led to the successful completion of a mission to return a missing murder suspect to the Kingdom of Andalusia, thereby helping to insure the continued security of the Caliphate. Let it be known, this individual also proved his worth on a dangerous assignment calling for the rescue and recovery of the kingdom's most holy relic. Again, putting his own life at risk. Both of the above cited missions provide evidence of grounds for this individual's manumission. The recommendations of General Naja, Supreme Commander of the Caliphate's armed forces, and Hasdai Shaprut, Foreign Minister of the Kingdom of Andalusia, reinforce the grounds for manumission. I, Caliph

Abd al-Rahman III, decree that Jalal the Slav is now and evermore a free man with all the rights thereof."

Hasdai rolled the scroll up and placed it upon the surface of his desk. He took a cube of red wax and a candle, lit for this occasion, and he burned the wax into the crease of the scroll. He then used his signet ring to stamp the melted wax with the official seal.

The room remained silent.

"I'd like for you to come up to receive the official document," beamed Hasdai. "A copy will be deposited in the Caliphal administrative files in perpetuity. I thought you might like to possess the original."

Jalal stood and approached the Foreign Minister's desk. Solomon looked over at Sara and Bahja and found they had tears in their eyes. As for himself, he felt a calmness that surprised him. As if he had already known somewhere inside of himself that this day would surely arrive bringing his friend his much deserved freedom.

Jalal stood in front of the Foreign Minister's desk.

"We have one final piece of business before I give you this precious proclamation," Hasdai said in a voice loud enough for all to hear.

Hasdai came out from around the desk and placed his hands upon Jalal's shoulders. The Foreign Minister turned the soldier around and around and around in circles. He finally halted his progress so that the soldier stood facing his friends. Then, as he held Jalal by the shoulders, he suddenly pushed him forward releasing him from his grip.

"You are now a free man!" exclaimed Hasdai.

The moment had arrived. The hopes and dreams of a lifetime now realized. Freedom. The most precious gift in the world, especially if it's one that you've never experienced. All the struggles of the past seemed worthwhile if not a distant memory. Jalal spread his arms out wide like they were wings and he was about to take flight.

"Wait!' called Hasdai. "You might need this."

Jalal turned back to the Foreign Minister.

Hasdai held out the scroll and the soldier reached for it with a trembling hand. Once he had a firm grasp on the precious document, he turned back to face his friends. He was beaming from ear to ear as he raised the precious scroll high overhead.

"This concludes our little ceremony," Hasdai told the assembled. "Solomon, please remain behind so that I might speak with you."

Another surprise on an occasion full of surprises.

"Please wait for me outside and I'll join you as soon as I can," Solomon said to his friends as he remembered the bottle of special liqueur he'd brought back with him all the way from Jerez. "We have some celebrating to do."

"Yes, we do," agreed Jalal.

Solomon turned to Sara. Their eyes met. They'd been holding hands since the time of the reading of the manumission proclamation. Sara knew how much Solomon had used his influence to bring about this wonderful ceremony. She gave his hand a gentle squeeze before releasing it.

"We'll be waiting for you, Solomon," said a smiling Sara.

Jalal and the women filed out of the office leaving Solomon alone with his cousin.

"Sit with me for a moment," implored Hasdai. "I thought you might appreciate some closure."

Solomon sat quietly and waited for his cousin to take the lead.

"I was told Malik's face turned ashen when he saw

the reliquary holding the holy relic held high during the annual procession at the Great Mosque," said Hasdai. "The Chief of Police was waiting for him personally when he came out of the mosque. He shocked everybody by swallowing a vial of poison right there on the spot. He probably suspected the alternative would be far worse."

This time Solomon wasn't surprised. He'd always suspected a coward lurked behind the mask of false bravado. His double-cross had failed. That proved to be a good thing. Had the two thieves been captured at the Great Mosque, he had little doubt the Arab elitists could have wiggled their way out of suspicion.

"We found the original reliquary at Malik's villa," said Hasdai. "It provided all the evidence we needed to convict him of a capital offense."

"Rather careless of him."

"I suspect his plan was to place the holy relic back inside the reliquary at some future time," guessed Hasdai. "He could then say that Allah had told him in a vision where to find it, establishing him as a favorite of the Prophet and strengthening his claim to be the legitimate ruler of Andalusia."

"What about Blue Eyes," he asked. "Will he be hanged or decapitated or will his life be spared?"

"I believe the Caliph has special plans for the Berber," Hasdai asserted. "He'll be allowed to return to Sijamassa to deliver a warning to the Emir of that kingdom. The Caliphate will move reinforcements into the Maghreb region. Enough to deter any thoughts of future actions against our sovereignty."

"He's lucky," Solomon asserted. "Somehow, don't ask me why, I'm glad for him."

"There's something more you should know," said Hasdai with a mysterious glint in his eye.

What's he hinting at, wondered Solomon.

"I informed the Caliph that I would prefer not to entertain requests for you services ever again. You've given far more of yourself than we should expect, even for a loyal servant of the Caliphate."

"What was the Caliph's response?"

"He agreed and told me that he understood the sentiment behind my feeling."

"So that's it for me?"

Hasdai stood and walked around the desk to where Solomon sat waiting for his response.

The grateful cousin placed a hand on his shoulder in a gesture of affection.

"You almost sound disappointed."

"I'm not disappointed cousin," Solomon insisted. "I just find this hard to believe."

"I will never request your services again," promised Hasdai. "You have my word."

Solomon knew his cousin's word was his bond.

A smile spread across his face as he thought about having more time to spend with Sara and his friends and time for writing new poems and completing his translation of the Greek philosopher Aristotle's work. A whole new life now awaited Solomon Levy, and he felt more than ready to enjoy the future and the blessings it might bring his way.

ACKNOWLEDGMENTS

I owe a debt of gratitude to María Rosa Menocal who introduced me to the world of Islamic Spain in her stimulating book *The Ornament of the World: How Muslims, Jews, and Christians created a Culture of Tolerance in 10th Century Spain.* It was in the pages of this fascinating account that I first encountered the amazing Hasdai ibn Shaprut. I warmly recommend the book to readers who would like to learn more about a society that embraced religious tolerance.

I'm grateful to Visnja Murgic who reviewed early drafts of the manuscript and provided helpful comments as well as editorial assistance.

In Mexico, I'm indebted to editors Alejandro Grattan-Dominguez and Judy King for an opportunity to pursue and succeed at a lifelong dream. Judy published a dozen and a half articles in her e-zine, *Living at Lake Chapala.* Alex published seven cover stories in *El Ojo del Lago*, Mexico's most widely read English-language magazine (print and online editions.).

INVITATION TO READERS

Thank you for reading this novel. If you enjoyed the story, please consider leaving a review on your favorite book seller's website. This is the most generous act you can make to help an author find new readers.

Reviews are hard to come and give credibility to the book. They are greatly appreciated. If you aren't interested in posting a review, please consider leaving a rating. Thank you, again.

William Mesusan

THE ANDALUSIAN TRILOGY

The Andalusian Trilogy brings to life the exotic world of 10th century Islamic Spain during a little known time in history when Muslims, Jews, and Christians created a harmonious society based upon religious tolerance and enlightened self-interest.

The Galician Woman

Translator Solomon Levy's deepest desire is to write poetry fulltime. He's forced to put his dreams on hold when the unexpected murder of the Caliph's nephew, Umar abd-Rahman, threatens the future of Andalusia and the Umayyad Caliphate. His knowledge of Latin, make him the perfect choice for a mission to far-away Galicia in search of a missing suspect. The reluctant investigator faces dangers, both real and imagined, in his quest to discover the identity of the murderer while tracking down Lia, a mysterious entertainer thought to be the last person to see the victim alive.

The Missing Vizier (In Progress)